HENRY'S SALVATION

A CRIMSON AND SHADOWS NOVEL

V.I. DAVIS

OLIVERHEBERBOOKS

Cover art by Dar Albert at Wicked Smart Designs

Published by Oliver-Heber Books

0 9 8 7 6 5 4 3 2 1

To my readers,
Thank you for taking a chance on me.

For those whose world rages around them,
May you find a moment of peace.

BONUS CONTENT

Want more of Sophie and Henry? Upload proof of purchase on my website (www.vidavisauthor.com) to get a spicy novella, *Henry's Refuge*, delivered to your email for free!

Henry's Refuge is part of the Crimson and Shadows series and covers the period between the end of book two and the beginning of book three. It's a short, sweet, and spicy novella that captures our heroes in the brief moment of peace between their trials. No major plot points are revealed in that installment, so reading it is not necessary for you to enjoy the series to the fullest. The novella does contain spoilers for *Josephine's Tear* and *Sophie's Ruin,* so it is recommended that you read it after the first two books.

CRIMSON AND SHADOWS READING ORDER

Josephine's Tear
Sophie's Ruin
Henry's Refuge (free novella available on the author's website)
Henry's Salvation

PROLOGUE

CELESTE

The black metal box that was confining me had expanded, but I knew better than to take that as a good sign. The demon who was holding me hostage was becoming more confident. He was letting me closer to the surface of my mind because he knew I couldn't do anything but be a prisoner in my own body. It was the strangest sensation. I was aware of everything that was happening around me, *to* me, but I was not in control. At that moment, my legs were carrying me through the dark Black Forest, my destination unknown.

"Where are we going?" I asked Damien. No sound came out of my mouth, as my voice was only in my head.

"You'll see," the demon hissed back.

I loathed having him in my head, in my body. I swore black ooze was coursing through my veins instead of blood. Even if I somehow won back control, my soul would forever be tainted. Because of how foolish I had been. I should have asked for help.

At that point, no one could have heard my cries of despair. They would have heard only the words Damien put in my mouth. I had tried fighting him. I had given it my all but to no avail. It seemed once the darkness had dug its claws into me, there was no reversing the agonizing decay of my soul. The darkness had been gnawing at the light inside me, devouring anything pure and good bit by bit, leaving me weak and depleted. Despondent and without hope.

At least, the Black Forest was healing, I noted as my body walked deeper into the heart of the woods. The dark shadows that had been hovering over the area had lifted after the Dark Witches had been defeated. The heartbeat of the forest that had stopped over a century earlier had returned. It was faint but there. The woods breathed easier, no longer continuously poisoned by black magic. Breathing also became easier for me as hope flickered in my chest. I might have been a lost cause, but the woods were reviving. If only I could have found a way to tell the other White Witches about what had happened to me. They could have killed me before the demon inside me could have undone what Sophie had accomplished.

Damien laughed, the sound like talons raking through my mind. Because he knew what I was thinking. There was no hiding from him. When he had taken over, he'd gained access to my thoughts and memories, to the most intimate parts of me.

"It's only a matter of time before the darkness reclaims these woods. And we are going to help it," the demon's eerie voice rang out in my head.

"What do you mean?" I whispered, the hope in my chest sputtering.

"You and I have a mission. My sole purpose for existing is to help Xanthus prey on innocent souls."

My body halted and looked around. I was in a clearing, standing before a rock formation.

"And to do that," Damien continued, "we are going to use the healing state of the woods to our advantage."

The heartbeat of the forest stopped at his words, and my heart seemed to stop with it as my gaze dropped to the ground. The spark of hope in my chest dimmed and died out, plunging my soul into never-ending darkness.

1

 e arrived at Santoria in the late afternoon. I couldn't wait to show Sophie the house I had picked out for our new life together. Anticipation buzzed in my veins, but I also felt nervous as the carriage jerked to a stop before the modest white cottage.

What if she didn't approve of my selection? She was perfect, and she deserved the perfect life, but what if I wasn't able to provide that for her?

My chest constricted with pressure as I heard the driver disembark the coach.

"Are you alright?" Sophie asked from where she was tucked against my right side. "You look a bit pale."

I almost laughed at the statement. As a vampire, I always looked pale. Except not anymore. It was amazing how quickly my pallid complexion had turned golden after only a few hours in the sun.

"I'm okay, just excited to show you the house," I said as I pressed her hand I was holding.

My brows pinched slightly as I brushed my thumb over the wedding band on her finger. I wished I hadn't butchered the proposal. I'd never thought about marriage. Not until that day in my bedroom when I'd felt the strongest urge to make her mine in every definition of the word. The emotion had overpowered me, and the question had spilled from my lips before I could stop it. I didn't regret it, of course. But I did regret not making the moment more special. That was my chance to make up for it. The sound of the driver's footsteps approaching the carriage door pulled me from my thoughts.

"Ready?" I looked at Sophie.

Her stunning hazel eyes were bright as she nodded. When the driver opened the door, her gaze stretched past me to the cottage I knew she could see outside. A rough exhale of relief almost left me when her face lit up. *That's a good sign.*

I jumped out of the carriage first and turned around to offer Sophie my hand even though she didn't need my help. Placing her hand in mine, she clutched the skirts of her long floral dress with the other hand so the fabric didn't snag under her feet as she climbed out of the cabin. The top half of her golden-brown hair was pulled up away from her face, while the bottom half was left to flow around her shoulders and down her back. The sea breeze played in the wavy locks as we took a few steps away from the carriage.

When she stopped in front of the house, I halted beside her, holding my breath as I watched her gaze sweep over the white-washed wooden facade. The teal-painted windows and door added a splash of color, while the potted purple-pink flowers scattered on the wraparound porch gave it a whimsical touch. The cottage sat a bit elevated off the ground since it was so close to the water.

"Henry, it's beautiful," Sophie breathed, her eyes misting over with tears.

Pride swelled in my chest at her words, but I didn't want to celebrate success prematurely.

"Let me show you the inside," I said, leading her up the steps to the front door.

The house was bathed in natural light when we walked in, and as I closed the door behind us, serenity washed over me. It felt as though I'd left the world behind, sealing us away. When I turned from the door, Sophie was standing in the middle of the cozy living room. Slowly, she spun in a circle before facing me again.

"What do you think?" I asked her, my tone cautious.

She doesn't have to like it. We can find another place, I tried to tell myself as I waited for her answer.

"I think it's home," she said simply. I chuckled as all the tension left my shoulders. "But then again, anywhere is home as long as I'm with you."

She closed the distance between us and threw her arms around my neck.

"Want to see the rest of the house?" I asked her enthusiastically when she rose on her tiptoes and puckered her lips.

Her expression turned into a pout as she lowered back down. A second later, a sly smile pulled at her lips. "Sure," she purred. "Show me the bedroom?"

I smirked. "I'll show you the kitchen first. It's small, but I figured we don't need much."

She rolled her eyes in mock annoyance but let me pull her in the direction of the kitchen. After a brief stop there, I did take her to the bedroom, and she plonked on the bed as soon as we entered.

"Should we test it out?" She beckoned me to her.

"Oh, we will. But first, come look at this view."

I grabbed her hand and led her to the door hidden behind the lightweight white curtains. It opened onto the back porch, and when we walked out, the Starling Sea whispered its greeting, the waves rolling onto the shore only a short distance away from the cottage.

"Breathtaking," Sophie whispered as she placed her hands on top of the porch railing.

She stared out at the shimmering blue waters for a few seconds before she closed her eyes and inhaled deeply, a look of utter bliss on her exquisite face. I suddenly wished I could paint because I wanted to capture that moment somehow. I wanted to preserve it for eternity. Sadly, I couldn't, but I hoped I didn't need to because we would have many more moments like that one.

"There is one more room I want to show you," I rasped as my nervousness returned.

When Sophie opened her eyes and nodded, I took her to the one room that I was the most excited about. A space just for her. My present to her.

"The library," I said as I opened the door.

Sophie loved books and had read a lot before her mother, Eloise, passed. When her quest for Josephine's Tear—the amulet with the power to destroy the supernatural forces—had led her to the Duval Estate, she and Rory, the young servant girl I'd taken in as an orphan, had also bonded over books. Both Eloise and Rory had died at the hands of Everett Stern, whom Sophie had later killed, getting her revenge. I had dedicated that space in the house for the library in hope that Sophie would find joy in reading again and feel close to those we had lost too soon.

I heard her breath hitch when we stepped inside the medium-sized room. White floor-to-ceiling bookshelves lined the four walls, interrupted only by the door we'd walked through and the one that led onto the porch. A tufted chaise lounge occupied one corner, with an end table beside it. A regular armchair and a bar cart sat close by for the days when I wanted to join her in there. With her eyes wide and her lips parted, Sophie looked awestruck as she slowly walked to one of the shelves and ran her fingertips down the row of books. I followed, stopping right behind her.

"I have purchased a few titles that I thought you might like, but, as you can see, most of the shelves are still empty. You can build your collection over time," I told her.

"Henry, I…I don't know what to say," she whispered, still with her back to me.

"I hope you will say 'yes'…again."

"What?" She turned around to face me.

I pulled a small black box out of my pocket and opened it to reveal the key to the house.

"You already have the one to my heart," I told her, one side of my mouth turning up. "Until I met you, my immortality seemed like a burden, but now it feels like the most precious gift because I get to spend my eternity with you. We can make this place our refuge, our safe haven, for years to come. What do you say?"

"Yes," she breathed as she fisted her hand in my shirt and hauled me to her.

I crushed my lips to hers, and our tongues began a wild dance as I caged her in against the bookshelf. After I'd slipped the key back into my pocket for safekeeping, I let my hands roam over her lithe body, gathering up her skirts to dive underneath. Grabbing her thigh, I brought her leg over my hip as I ground into her.

"Sophie," I panted, breaking the kiss. "Do you truly like the house?"

I pulled away slightly to look at her. She stared up at me, her cheeks flushed and her eyes nearly black with desire.

"I love it. And I love you, my husband." She uttered the last two words almost reverently and with a coy smile.

My heart skipped a beat at the title.

"I will never grow tired of hearing you call me that," I said as I leaned in. "My wife," I murmured against her lips before I kissed her again.

2

———

TWO WEEKS LATER

SOPHIE

The Starling Sea was glistening in the early morning light, painted in orange and pink hues where the rising sun was reflecting off the rippling blue surface. The sparkling waters were calm like my heart, like my soul, as I stood on the porch that overlooked the sea. The waves' soothing whisper matched Henry's soft breathing in the bedroom behind me. With a coffee cup in my hands and a serene smile on my face, I thought about those he and I held dear. I wondered how my father was doing—and Ezra, Rory's younger brother, whom we'd left in his care. I thought about Isabelle and Wren, who had promised to eventually join us in the Southern region, and Waylon and Amelie, whose blossoming romance warmed my heart. I hoped everyone was doing well while Henry and I were enjoying our honeymoon at our coastal cottage.

A sigh of contentment escaped as I brought the coffee cup to my lips and took a sip, savoring the bold, rich flavor. Coffee grew there, and I'd acquired quite a taste for it in the past two weeks. I'd also acquired a taste for that life—for the sea that greeted me every morning and lulled me to sleep every night, for the leisurely rhythm of the coastal town of Santoria, and for the daylight that I hadn't even realized I'd missed in the short time since I'd turned.

Lowering the cup back down, I closed my eyes and lifted my face up to meet the rising sun. I breathed in the salty sea air as it washed over me, the slight breeze stirring my unbound hair and lifting the hem of Henry's tunic I was wearing. His fresh and woodsy scent had seeped into the fabric, enveloping me in its embrace, making me instantly long for him. I opened my eyes and turned around, parting the sheer white curtains draped over the glass door to step inside the bedroom. Cradling the coffee cup in my hands, I leaned against the doorframe and took in the sight before me.

The view was no less beautiful than the majestic sea behind me. Henry was lying on his stomach on the bed, with half of his face buried in the pillows. The light top sheet was covering very little of his naked body, and I let my gaze roam over every glorious inch of him—from his sculpted arms to his muscled back and lower, to his powerful legs, all the way down to his feet, which were peeking through the bunched-up bedcovers. He looked relaxed—as if every last drop of tension had left his magnificent body. I'd gotten used to many things in the past two weeks, but seeing him like that was still strange. No less strange was seeing the golden tone of his skin creating a striking contrast against the white sheets and bedcovers.

We'd spent nearly every day of our time there playing in the waves under the sun. And our nights... It was a good thing vampires couldn't procreate because there wasn't an inch of me Henry had left unexplored. He'd made love to me every night, sometimes slowly and thoroughly, as if we had all the time in the world, sometimes fast and desperately, as if he feared it was our last night together. Whether fast or slow, each time had been powerful and overwhelming in the best possible way, leaving my body and my mind scattered into a million dazzling pieces. Henry had always been there to put me back together, holding me until I'd caught enough breath to beg for more. And I always did.

I smirked into my cup as I once again brought it to my lips. If anyone had suggested a few months earlier that I would be completely and utterly at his mercy, I would have laughed in their face. At that time, there wasn't a part of me that didn't belong to him. There wasn't a part of me I wanted to hide from him, and it was hard to remember my life from before I'd met him. Before that all-consuming love and total acceptance.

Lowering the cup from my lips, I let my gaze travel back to Henry's face half-obscured by the pillows. Long, dark lashes cast shadows on his cheek, and his raven locks were tousled, spilling across his forehead. I wanted to sink my fingers in his hair, pulling on the silky strands. I wanted...I *wanted*. There wasn't a moment when I didn't crave him. As if my piercing stare had pulled him from his slumber, those thick lashes lifted, and Henry opened his right eye. His blue gaze immediately locked on me, and my breath snagged as the short distance between us became charged.

"Good morning," he drawled, lifting his head off the pillows. His lips stretched in a lazy smile, his fangs starkly white against his tan skin.

"Good morning," I replied as he appraised me.

He took his time drinking me in, and it felt as though I were wearing nothing. His intense perusal was like a physical touch caressing my skin, making it flushed and sensitive.

"What are you doing?" he asked, dragging his gaze back up to my face.

His eyes had turned darker, and my pulse quickened in anticipation.

"Enjoying my coffee before I enjoy you," I replied, my voice husky and lush with promise.

"I like that plan," he said, his own voice deeper than before. "Perhaps I can motivate you to finish your coffee faster."

His smile turned daring a second before he rolled onto his back, unabashedly displaying the hardness between his legs. My throat dried as my gaze darted to it before returning to his face. His smile had faded, and desire, raw and uninhibited, had settled into his features. Staring back at me, he reached and stroked his proud length. Breathing became difficult as I watched him pleasure himself, his hooded gaze on me the entire time. Desire flooded me, and I had to squeeze my thighs at the pulse of arousal between them. I wanted to be the one touching him. I *needed* to be.

My mind made up, I stepped to place my cup on the bedside table, but before I could reach it, a bloodcurdling scream stopped me in my tracks. The sound sliced through my head as my vision blurred and dimmed. Images flashed in my mind, one after another—razor-sharp claws, glistening teeth tearing flesh, mahogany hair, brown eyes with upswept corners...

My knees buckled, and I felt Henry at my side in an instant, his hands on my arms to hold me up when I started crumpling down, shocked and disoriented. The vision dissipated as suddenly as it had appeared, and when my eyes refocused, I was staring at the ground—at the fragments of my shattered cup and coffee splattered on the floor.

"Sophie, are you hurt?" Henry asked urgently, snapping my attention to him.

"No," I replied, meeting his worried gaze. Thankfully, the images I'd seen hadn't manifested in physical sensation. "I just... I saw something..."

"Through the threads?" he asked.

I nodded in confirmation. Henry knew about the threads that carried information about the world—I'd told him about them a while back. The voices had been quiet for the past two weeks, and I thought it was because Celeste had defeated Damien—the demon sent by Xanthus to torment souls in our realm. Henry and I had been prepared to help her fight him, but when we'd shown up at her cottage on the night following our wedding, the witch had informed us that it had already been done—she'd banished Damien out of our world, back to the realm he'd crawled out of. So Henry and I had left New Haven and gone there—to the quaint little cottage on the coast of the Starling Sea. Right then, it seemed our honeymoon would be cut short.

Mahogany hair...brown eyes with upswept corners...same as Rory's...

"It's Ezra," I said past the knot in my throat. "He was attacked… I think… I saw… I don't know what I saw."

All color drained from Henry's face. He cared greatly about Ezra, just like he'd cared about his sister, Rory, before she'd been killed.

"It's okay. We will figure it out," he finally said.

"Is it over?" I asked in a hushed tone.

A gust of wind billowed the curtains over the door that led onto the porch, and I cut a glance outside, at the sea that was churning as if it were matching my volatile emotions. I'd always known that day would come—that the moment of peace wouldn't last long. I'd just hoped we'd get more time before our next trial. The look on Henry's face told me he'd hoped for the same thing. His brows knitted in a frown at my question.

"Over? No, darling, it's not over. We will be back here soon. We own this place, remember?" He'd bought the cottage for us, making the former owners an offer they couldn't refuse. A forced smile accompanied his words to put me at ease, but it swiftly faded as he added, "Let's go check on Ezra. Once we are sure he is okay, we will return here."

All I could do was nod as he gently kissed my forehead. After making sure I was steady on my feet, he quickly cleaned up the fragments of my broken cup and the spilled coffee before walking to the bathing chamber to get ready. I knew I needed to follow him, but I was frozen in place as a dark feeling invaded my chest. The strange, thorny sensation pricked my heart, making it ache. For some reason, I knew we wouldn't return soon…if ever.

"Glimmering would be faster," I told Henry after we'd showered and gotten dressed in practical clothing. He pressed his lips in a thin line as his eyes turned stormy, nearly matching the deep-blue hue of his shirt. His reaction wasn't entirely surprising, given that I hadn't practiced my magic in the past two weeks. "Or we can ride horseback until nightfall and then cross the remaining distance with supernatural speed," I suggested as I smoothed out my purple tunic. "I just don't think we should risk doing that in broad daylight." Since the vampires had gone into hiding, it was crucial for us not to attract attention to ourselves.

"No, it's okay. You can glimmer us to New Haven," Henry said after another beat of hesitation.

"Are you sure?" I asked, my gaze flicking over his drawn features.

"I'm sure. It's just…you know your magic makes me uneasy," he admitted as he reached up and tucked the Tear and the locket with my mother's picture under the collar of my tunic.

The truth was my powers made me uneasy as well. I hadn't practiced my magic in the past two weeks, not only because

Henry had kept me thoroughly occupied but also because I'd been nervous to do so. What if I had accidentally unlocked the darkness I'd buried a few weeks before?

My gaze dropped to Henry's chest at the thought—to the spot where I'd inflicted the wound that had almost cost him his life. Tears threatened as I swallowed the lump that had formed in my throat. When I forced my gaze back up to Henry's, he was watching me as if he knew exactly what I was thinking. He always did.

Wrapping one arm around my waist, he hauled me to his chest and kissed me deeply, stealing my breath away. Each stroke of his tongue melted away some of my anxiety, but the thorny feeling didn't disappear completely. I wondered whether it ever would. If I was being honest with myself, dread had been my constant companion even over the past two weeks of pure happiness. It had been muted, barely there, but present nonetheless. At that moment, it was back in full force. The sweeps of Henry's tongue over mine became less fierce as they slowed and eventually stopped when he broke the kiss.

"I love you," he whispered against my lips before he pulled away.

"I love you too. More than anything."

A shuddering breath left me as I placed my hand on his chest, over his strong and steady heartbeat. The wound might have healed, but I could still see it in my mind as it had appeared on the night I'd hurt him—gruesome and bleeding.

"I know," he said, covering my hand with his.

My gaze snagged on the wedding band on his finger. He'd bound himself to me even after I'd almost killed him. Instead of leaving me, he'd asked me to be his forever. He'd given me a second chance, and I wasn't going to take that for granted. I would spend the rest of my life proving to him he'd made the right choice.

"The sooner we get it over with, the better," he said, pulling me from my thoughts.

With my hand still on his chest, I summoned my magic. My powers flared to life, rushing to the surface of my skin until they simmered just below it. I was surprised by how quickly they'd answered the call, but I knew better than to get overly confident. Glimmering was tricky, as I could always launch Henry and myself into the void, where we would be stranded in the empty nothingness forever.

You know what to do. Magic runs in your blood; it is a part of you, I tried to reassure myself as I inhaled deeply and closed my eyes.

I pictured New Haven with its narrow streets and cobbled roads. Stone mansions of noblemen living in the city center flashed through my mind, as did Rosewood and Mayfair Parks in the Garden District. Concentrating, I quickly traveled through the familiar streets in my mind's eye until I ended up in front of my childhood home, which was huddled next to other small wooden houses in the humbler part of the city. I could picture it clearly, as if I were standing before my father's front door. Just as clearly, I could picture people rushing by all around me on their way to carry out their daily tasks.

My brows knitted. Glimmering to the spot right in front of my father's home would be unwise if Henry and I wanted to stay undetected. The people of New Haven knew that the White Witches still existed, but flaunting my magic would attract attention we didn't need. So I moved away from my childhood home in my imagination to the alleyway closest to the house. Once I could picture it clearly, I concentrated on the magic lighting up my veins.

Henry tensed next to me, and I didn't blame him—the process of glimmering was strange, albeit swift and painless. My skin began to hum and tingle as I imagined a beam of light connecting the spot where I was standing to the alleyway hundreds of miles away. My power poured out of my pores, enveloping Henry and me a second before we were sucked into the beam of light that would take us to New Haven. My breath caught at the same time I heard Henry's sharp inhale. I felt weightless for a moment, floating in the void, before my feet touched solid ground again. When I exhaled and opened my eyes, Henry and I were standing in the alleyway I'd pictured.

"I don't think I will ever get used to that," he said with a rough exhale. He looked a bit pale, but the color was quickly returning to his face. Glancing to his left, he let go of my hand and gestured toward where the alleyway opened onto the street. "Lead the way."

I found I couldn't move. I wasn't sure what I'd seen in the vision back at the cottage, and I suddenly wished I didn't have to find out. A feeling of foreboding slithered down my spine, but I pushed past it as I willed myself to take a step. Henry followed me out of the alleyway onto the street, where people were rushing to and fro, going about their days just as I'd imagined they would be. A few cut us curious glances when we emerged from the narrow passage between the houses, but most didn't pay us any attention as we made our way to my childhood home.

My anxiety rose higher the closer we got to the house, reaching its peak when we found ourselves before the weathered front door. Holding my breath, I lifted my hand and knocked. A few seconds passed, then a few more. When no one answered, Henry stepped closer to the door, his features pinched in concentration.

"The house appears empty," he said after a moment.

I also stepped closer to the door, straining my vampire ears as I listened for any movement inside the dwelling. When all that greeted me was silence, I let out the breath I'd been holding and opened up my other senses.

"Do you smell it?" I asked Henry, my nostrils flaring.

"Yes…blood," he confirmed as he sniffed the air. "Ezra's," he added as his face crumpled.

I swallowed. "What do you think this means?"

He schooled his features. "There is only one way to find out. We can track the scent of Ezra's blood."

"I think I know where it leads." I turned away from the door and looked to the east, in the direction of the city center.

"Waylon?" Henry ventured a guess.

I nodded in confirmation. "We can walk. His place is not far from here."

Henry grabbed my hand, and together, we began walking down the street, farther away from the outskirts and deeper into the heart of the city. It was a clear and sunny morning, so many people were out and about. Some walked past us without saying a word, others nodded in greeting, and a few even exchanged friendly pleasantries with us. I could almost pretend that Henry and I were like any other couple out for a morning stroll…if only I could have pretended to forget the reason why we had returned. The reason that was constricting my chest with unbearable pressure, making it difficult to breathe. My unease must have been palpable because Henry squeezed my hand in a gesture of comfort.

"Have I told you how much I love the gift of sunlight that you bestowed on me?" he asked under his breath so as not to be overheard by the passersby. It seemed he was pushing his worries about Ezra aside until he knew they were warranted.

A corner of my lips turned up despite my anxious state. "You have. Many times."

"I don't think it will ever cease to amaze me," he murmured, lifting his free hand slightly in front of him and flexing his fingers. The wedding band that carried the magic that granted us the ability to walk in daylight without bursting into flames gleamed in the sun. "*You* will never cease to amaze me," he added, lowering his hand and glancing at me with a smile that could always brighten my world, even in the darkest hour.

"Celeste helped me forge the rings," I reminded him. "We need to check in with her while we're here. To make sure Xanthus hasn't sent another demon to prowl the Black Forest, seeking the ruin of souls."

Henry nodded. "We will also check in with Isabelle. To see if she and Wren are ready to join us in the Southern region."

If we ever return there... The thought popped into my mind, and I shook my head to clear it.

"I didn't think we'd be back here so soon," I said with a heavy sigh.

"I didn't either," Henry admitted low.

"In a way, it's a relief," I added, as if to myself.

"A relief?" He gave me a questioning look.

"Yes. I was waiting for the next trial to rise. I just hoped we'd have more time, but now that it's here, at least I no longer have to hold my breath, waiting for something to happen."

Something *had* already happened; I just didn't know what it was.

We were about to find out.

"We're here," I said, tugging on Henry's hand to stop him in his tracks.

4

We were standing in front of Waylon's place. As I'd suspected, the scent of Ezra's blood led there, like a red thread connecting my father's house to that one.

The dwelling before us was bigger and newer than my childhood home. Waylon didn't live in the best part of the city—that area was reserved for the nobles—but he was able to afford more stately accommodations than most with his border guard salary. Even with the Dark Witches no longer a threat, the Governess, Madam St. Clair, hadn't disbanded the Border Guard. She still wanted the stone wall that separated New Haven from the Black Forest to be warded in case other dangers that were lurking in the woods decided to encroach on the city.

"You were right about bringing us here," Henry said, sniffing the air and undoubtedly picking up on the scent of Ezra's blood.

He pulled on my hand to lead me up the three low porch steps, but I felt rooted in place again, scared to see what we would find inside the house.

"Sophie?" he asked gently. His gaze was empathetic when I looked at him. "We need to find out what we are dealing with so we can resolve it and return to our honeymoon," he offered quietly but firmly.

Deciding there was no point in delaying the inevitable, I quickly climbed the steps to the front door. The sun was at my back, and while I felt its warmth, my insides were as cold as ice with trepidation. Suppressing a shiver, I watched Henry reach up and knock on the door.

Waylon opened it a few moments later. "Sophie? Henry?" His fair brows climbed his forehead. "What are you two doing here?"

"I had a vision about Ezra," I said, cutting straight to the point.

Waylon's forest-green eyes widened before his expression turned grim. "You weren't the only one," he said. "He's here. Come in."

When he opened the door wider to let us in, the smell of Ezra's blood intensified. I also picked up on two other familiar scents—my father's and Amelie's. After Henry and I had walked in, Waylon shut the front door behind us before leading us deeper into the house.

"Amelie also had a vision. Well, not exactly. She sensed that something was wrong and urged me to go check on your father and Ezra," Waylon explained as the three of us reached his bedroom.

I halted abruptly right on the other side of the open bedroom door. I knew I needed to step inside, but I couldn't force myself to do it. Henry stopped next to me, placing his hand on my lower back. He didn't say anything, but his touch grounded me, giving me the courage I needed. Taking a steadying breath, I walked into the dimly lit room.

The curtains on the single window were closed, nearly blocking the daylight reigning outside as a small lamp on the bedside table filled the space with a muted yellow glow. My attention immediately zeroed in on Ezra. He was lying unmoving on the bed, with his face turned away from the lamplight that was casting shadows onto his profile. Fear that he might have been dead spiked, but I quickly tamped it down, using my heightened senses to pick up on his shallow breathing and the faint beating of his heart. He wasn't dead, just unconscious or in a deep sleep. Whatever state he was in, it wasn't peaceful. His limbs twitched almost imperceptibly as sweat slicked his brow and plastered his dark hair to his forehead. He was shirtless under the bedcovers that came up to his chest, and I could see the bandages that were covering his left shoulder.

I dragged my gaze away from Ezra and looked around the room. My father was sitting by the right side of the bed. With his shoulders slumped and his head hung, he looked dejected.

"What happened?" Henry asked, his deep voice amplified in the tense silence.

My father bristled at hearing Henry's voice, as if realizing for the first time that we were there.

"Sophie," he said weakly, rising to his feet.

Amelie, who was standing behind him, moved out of the way as he stepped toward me. With her hands clasped demurely in front of her and her lips in a thin line, the young witch gave a small nod in greeting when our gazes met.

"I'm not going to ask what you're doing here," my father said as he approached and pulled me into a quick embrace. "I'm just glad you're here," he continued, letting go of me. "I failed him," he said low, his voice gravelly with emotion.

He'd taken Ezra in before Henry and I had left New Haven. He'd given him a place to live, and I didn't doubt he'd treated him like a son.

"What happened?" I asked, looking into my father's blue-gray eyes.

I took his trembling hands and pressed them lightly to let him know that I was there for him and he could lean on me.

"He was out with some friends last night—the other boys who used to work for the Duvals." He nodded at Henry before he continued, "I'd just gone to bed when I heard a scream right outside the house." He paused, tears filling his eyes, before he cleared his throat and forged on, "I found him a few feet away from the front door. He was badly injured. I was going to carry him to the infirmary, but that was when Waylon showed up."

My thoughts began to race, tumbling over each other. The attack had happened so close to the house, to where my father had been sleeping. He, too, could have been injured...or worse.

But he wasn't, I told myself to subdue the rising panic.

He's okay. I quickly scanned him from head to toe, only then noticing that his clothes were stained with Ezra's blood.

"You didn't fail him," I said vehemently. "I don't know what happened, but I know that part without a doubt. We'll get to the bottom of this."

"How is he?" Henry asked as he left my side and walked closer to the bed. He stopped right by it, his gaze flicking over Ezra, assessing his condition.

"He's alive," Waylon replied from where he was standing by Amelie on the other side of the bed. "His shoulder was shredded. He lost a lot of blood. I knew it was no ordinary wound, so I didn't take him to the infirmary. I brought him here instead, and Amelie helped me clean him up and made a salve for his shoulder."

That explains the herbal scent mixed in with Ezra's sweat and blood.

My gaze shot to the girl. "Waylon said you had a vision about Ezra. Did you see what happened to him?"

Amelie shook her head. "I didn't see anything, only felt it. Pain and suffering. Coming from Thomas's house. I'm sorry."

"You have nothing to apologize for. Thank you for your help," Henry told her in a strained voice, his gaze never leaving Ezra.

His nostrils flared for a second before his brows pulled into a scowl. I wondered whether he felt responsible. He'd taken the siblings in when they'd had no one else left. Rory had died at Stern's hands, and last night, Ezra had almost lost his life.

"Was he able to tell you what happened?" I asked, refocusing on my father, who shook his head no.

"He was in agony and incoherent," Waylon chimed in, drawing my attention back to him. "Amelie made a concoction to put him in a deep sleep so he wouldn't suffer."

"I wanted to alleviate his suffering. I figured he can sleep until the worst of it passes," the witch explained.

Her green eyes, usually bright and sparkling, were dull with worry. Even her flaming-red hair seemed less vibrant in light of the situation.

Henry's chest heaved on a rough exhale at her words as he lifted his hand and bared his fangs. He bit into his wrist, drawing blood, before pressing it to Ezra's mouth. I watched the boy's throat bob as he instinctively swallowed. Henry didn't linger, quickly removing his wrist from Ezra's bloodstained lips. The boy remained asleep, but his breathing evened out, and some color instantly returned to his ashen face. I knew that under the bandages on his shoulder, torn tissue and flesh were stitching back together.

"He is no longer suffering," Henry said, wiping his wrist on his shirt.

"Do you want to wake him and see if he can tell us what happened?" I asked Henry as I left my father's side and walked to him.

When I approached, I reached for his hand, and he immediately threaded his fingers through mine.

"I'm afraid you can't," Amelie interjected. "The concoction I gave him will keep him in a deep sleep for a few more hours."

"It's okay," Henry assured her. "He needs it. My blood has healed the wound, but the shock of what happened still remains. We will let him rest."

He and I stood in silence for a moment.

"Do you smell anything?" he suddenly asked under his breath.

Frowning, I sniffed the air. I detected many scents—that of

Ezra's blood being the most predominant one. Realization hit me then. I knew what Henry was asking. If I could smell Ezra's blood, then I should have been able to also smell the one who'd made him bleed. I should have been able to pick up on the scent of the attacker, whether it was a person or an animal. I closed my eyes in concentration and sniffed the air again. Nothing. Not even a faint trace of the something or someone who'd hurt him.

When I opened my eyes again, I found Henry watching me. Silently, I shook my head.

"What is it?" Waylon prompted.

"Have you been patrolling the streets at night?" I asked him instead of replying.

Before Henry and I had left for Santoria, Waylon had told us he was going to bring back the Order of Light to keep the vampire clans in check.

"We have, but there hadn't been any attacks that I know of. Until Ezra, that is… His shoulder did look like he was mauled by a wild animal…" Waylon paled slightly. "Do you think someone's making Ravagers again? Or could it be one of the clan vampires not adhering to the terms of the Blood Pact?"

Henry and I exchanged a glance.

"We should be able to pick up on the scent of the attacker, but we don't smell anything," I explained, looking back at Waylon.

"What does that mean?" he asked, perplexed.

I turned to Henry for any possible explanation, but he just shook his head. "I don't know what it means," he said with a heavy sigh. "I don't know how to explain it. We should be able to pick up on something—anything—but there is no trace."

Waylon scowled. "I will check with Lucas and Jules. They patrolled last night. Perhaps they saw or heard something," he finally offered.

"And we will check with Celeste," I said, thinking it over. "If it is one of the clan leaders stepping out of line, the contract that they signed in their blood will reveal them to us."

"What if it's not one of the leaders?" Waylon asked. "It could be anyone from any of the clans."

"It could," Henry agreed. "But Sophie's right. Checking the contract is the next logical step. If it reveals nothing, we will figure out where to go from there."

"I will stay with Ezra," my father said, returning to his seat by the right side of the bed.

"So will I," Amelie added softly.

"Thank you," I told the witch, hoping my voice conveyed how appreciative I was of her. "Ready?" I reached for Henry, preparing to glimmer us to Celeste's cottage in the Black Forest.

"Not really," he grumbled but took my hands.

With one last glance at Ezra, I called upon my magic, anxious to begin searching for answers to the questions that had brought us back to New Haven.

5

J'd been to the Black Forest only ever at night. The woods looked different during the day—less menacing and hungry. Or perhaps the forest had simply become a less dark place. Celeste had told me before that with the Dark Witches gone, the woods would eventually restore to their former glory and become beautiful and thriving again. She had made it sound like the process would take a while, but perhaps it was happening faster than she'd thought it would.

"I have never seen the forest in daylight," Henry said, echoing my thoughts when we appeared in the clearing where Celeste's cottage was located.

He let go of my hands and slowly spun in a circle, taking in our surroundings. A look of wonder washed over his features before he closed his eyes and lifted his face up to the sky, enjoying the sunshine. My heart swelled with emotion as I watched him. I lived for moments like that one. Henry had said the gift of sunlight I'd given him would never cease to amaze him, but the truth was, every time I got to witness him like that, bathed in the sun, was a gift in and of itself. It stole my breath and warmed my heart.

The moment of serenity ended far too quickly as Henry lowered his chin and opened his eyes, unease settling into his expression. I wasn't ready to let go of it yet. Reaching up, I cupped his cheeks and pressed my lips to his. He made a noise deep in his throat, bringing me flush with his body. The kiss was fleeting and not enough—it was never enough—before Henry pulled away and rested his forehead against mine. He didn't say anything, and I supposed there wasn't much to say because there we were again, staring in the face of uncertainty, never quite knowing whether the kiss we'd just shared would be our last. With a rough exhale, Henry lifted his head and took my hand in his, turning us toward Celeste's cottage, which appeared even more rustic than usual in the daylight.

"I have been expecting you," the witch said when she opened the door as I was reaching up to knock.

"Why am I not surprised?" I smiled at her. Celeste's connection to the world was strong, which meant she often knew things before they transpired.

The witch didn't smile back before she turned and walked away from the door, expecting us to follow. We were one step behind her all the way to the small kitchen, where she began rummaging around, making her customary herbal tea.

"Have you been practicing your magic?" she asked with her back to me as she placed the kettle on the hearth.

I grimaced at the question and, for a split second, considered telling her I had—Celeste was my mentor, and I didn't want to disappoint her. I quickly dismissed the idea, deciding she would see right through my lie. "I haven't," I admitted.

The witch whirled around and gave me a scathing look. "Without practice, you can't grow stronger. You are wasting your potential," she said sternly, cutting Henry a sharp look, as if he were to blame.

"It's nice to see you too, Celeste." He only smirked at her. If her glower was bothering him, he wasn't showing it.

It was bothering *me*, but I decided to brush that aside. The witch had always been rough around the edges, so her behavior was nothing new. Besides, there was a larger issue at hand.

"Do you know what happened to Ezra?" I asked.

Her shrewd cerulean eyes met mine. "I got bits and pieces through the threads. I don't know who attacked him if that's what you are asking."

"I'm not." I frowned. "I know that's not how the threads work."

A witch could get only glimpses of information from the world around her, and they were muddled at best, even for Celeste. We had been extremely lucky she'd been able to warn us about the imminent attack of the Dark Witches, but that had been the exception, not the rule, to how the threads usually worked.

"We're here because we want to check the Blood Pact to see if the clan leaders have been upholding their end of the bargain." I used the last word loosely, but I supposed it was a bargain nonetheless—the clans had agreed to stop killing for blood, and in exchange, we'd let them live.

"Very well," Celeste said. "I will fetch the contract. Take a seat at the table."

As the witch left the kitchen, Henry pulled out a chair for me. I went to sit down but froze, my skin prickling with a strange sense of awareness. The tiny hairs on the back of my neck lifted as my gaze shot to the small kitchen window—I felt like I was being watched. I sped to the window and peered out. The forest stared back at me. I scanned the tree line several feet away from the house, but all was still in the tangled branches and thick foliage.

"Is everything okay?" Henry asked.

"Yes," I replied, turning away from the window. "I thought I felt something...like I was being watched," I told him, stepping back to the table.

His dark brows pulled together. "The witch has a protective barrier around the cottage. No forest creatures should be able to cross it, right?" he pointed out.

"Right," I agreed as I sat down.

Henry took a seat next to me just as Celeste returned to the kitchen. In her hand, she was carrying a rolled-up parchment I recognized as the contract we'd signed a little over two weeks earlier.

"Would you like some tea?" the witch asked, her tone warmer than before.

"No, thank you," I replied as politely as possible, my gaze glued to the scroll in her hand. I doubted I would be able to force any tea down as my stomach churned with unease.

"I will take a cup, please," Henry said with a small smile, and I wondered whether that was his way of trying to put their earlier interaction behind them.

Celeste deposited the parchment on the table before she took the kettle off the hearth and poured two cups of tea. She placed one in front of Henry and took a seat opposite us at the table, cradling her own cup in her hands.

The silence stretched as she took a sip of her drink. Henry did the same next to me. My knee began to bounce under the table as my anxiety climbed, my patience wearing thin. Just when I was about to say something to hurry the conversation along, Henry put his hand on my knee, pressing it lightly. I stopped bouncing it and took a breath, buying myself a few more minutes of patience. Celeste took a couple more sips of her tea, eyeing me over the rim of her cup as if challenging me to say something before she set it down and moved it to the side. A breath of relief almost left me when she reached for the scroll. Henry also moved his cup to give the witch more room as she unfolded the contract on the table before her.

My gaze dropped to the parchment. The words on it were

seared in my mind. They were the rules of the new world—the one where the vampire clans were no longer the ruling class.

"The spell I placed on the contract should tell us if a clan leader breaks any of the rules, but I don't see anything amiss," Celeste said, studying the parchment.

"What are you looking for, exactly?" I asked as nonchalantly as I could. I didn't want her to think I was doubting her.

"If any of the clan leaders violate the terms of the contract, their blood will turn blue," the witch said, pointing to the dried splotches of blood on the contract. They were all still dark red.

"Are you sure the spell is still in effect?" I asked, wincing inwardly. Celeste was a powerful witch, and I trusted in her ability, but I still had to cover my bases.

"Yes, I am sure," she said through her teeth, clearly unhappy about me questioning her. "Only the leaders signed the contract in blood, not the rest of their clans. It wouldn't show if any of *them* broke the rules."

She was right, of course. Having everyone in the clans sign the contract would have been ideal, but Henry had insisted against it.

"You don't want to be a dictator," he'd reasoned with me back then. *"We should only require the clan leaders to sign it to let them feel like they still have a sliver of control and to show that we trust them to keep their families in line."*

I had agreed with him then, but at that moment, a part of me wished I hadn't.

"What do we do now?" I turned to Henry, unable to hide the exasperation in my voice.

"Now we proceed with the next logical step," he said calmly. "If we think Ezra was attacked by a Ravager, it makes sense to start by questioning Yvonne."

Yvonne Durand, the leader of the clan that had ruled over one of the Midland regions, had created Ravagers to help her fight against me. Four of them had remained, and instead of killing them, Henry had left them in her care, ordering her to bring them out of bloodlust and make them full-functioning members of her clan. Perhaps that hadn't gone according to plan and one of the Ravagers was on the loose.

I nodded in agreement and turned back to Celeste. "Will you help me find her?" I asked the witch.

After each of the five clan leaders had left a drop of their blood on the contract, I'd smeared my own blood across theirs to bind their wills to mine. Having done so allowed me to track them as well as summon them to me. Provided the binding spell worked.

"Give me your hand," Celeste said. When I did as she'd instructed, she placed my palm on the parchment. "Repeat the incantation after me, and while you are doing it, think about the one you want to find."

The instruction sounded similar to the one Damien had given me when I'd set out on my quest for revenge, hunting for the clan leaders who'd hurt Henry. Back then, I'd used dark magic, imagining black tendrils of my power crawling over the world, searching for my victims. The magic I intended to use that time was light, but the concept was the same.

"I'm ready," I told Celeste, bringing forth my powers.

When I felt them traveling through my veins in tiny sparks of light, I closed my eyes in concentration. Celeste began chanting, the words beautiful but foreign. I tried to repeat them as best I could while I pictured Yvonne's tall and slim figure in my head. Her angular face with high cheekbones and a dusky complexion appeared in my mind. It was set with amber eyes and framed by thickly curled chestnut-brown hair.

Where are you, Yvonne? I thought, still chanting the words of the spell.

The parchment seemed to heat under my hand, making my palm tingle at the contact.

I stared at Yvonne's face, which I'd conjured up in my mind, until the image began to waver and distort. A few seconds later, it had mottled into something new. I was still staring at Yvonne, but she looked different from what I'd pictured. Her eyes were closed, her sharp features relaxed in the semidarkness. She was asleep, I realized, her hair spilling around her on the pillow. It felt like I was in the room with her but also far away. The sensation reminded me of the time I'd projected myself into Stern's lair in my dream when the clan leaders had been holding Henry captive.

Hovering like an apparition above Yvonne's sleeping form, I pushed up and away from her to take in my surroundings. We were in a medium-sized bedroom, modestly decorated in rich hues of scarlet and gold. The heavy red velvet curtains draped over the window were closed tightly to prevent daylight from slipping inside. Yvonne was lying in the middle of the wide bed, alone. I'd been able to locate her, but I still didn't know exactly where she was. I let myself float up higher, pushing farther away from her. A moment later, I was hovering above the house where she was sleeping. I kept rising higher until I was looking down at the neighborhood, then the city. Rising higher still, I realized she was in the Western region.

"I know where she is," I declared, opening my eyes.

Celeste stopped chanting, and the parchment, which had been simmering under my touch, instantly cooled. I lifted my hand from it and flexed my fingers, trying not to dwell on the level of satisfaction I was feeling about being able to track Yvonne. The Blood Pact also allowed me to summon the clan leaders if I so wished. I truly held their lives in my hands, and the rush of power that came with that knowledge was intoxicating. I suspected it fed off the darkness within me that was subdued at the moment but never entirely gone. Perhaps that was why Henry had been so against binding all of the vampires to my will. He'd known that so much power and control would have fed my dark side and wanted to prevent me from succumbing to it.

When I turned to him, I found him watching me with a strange expression.

"She's in the West," I told him, even though he hadn't asked. "It seems she heeded our advice and didn't remain in her home region." We'd strongly encouraged all of the clan leaders to leave the regions they had ruled over, hoping that their moving to other areas would make it easier for them to stay hidden. Given that the humans no longer needed the vampire clans for protection from the Dark Witches, there were some who would want to seek revenge for the century of oppression.

"That's several days of travel away," Henry pointed out. "I don't want to leave before Ezra comes to."

"I could just glimmer to collect Yvonne and bring her here," I suggested.

"Not here," Celeste interjected as she rolled up the parchment. "Remember, those who come here can later find their way back, even through the protection barrier. I don't want to invite another vampire into my home."

"You're right," I told the witch. "Can you meet us at Isabelle's place? We might need your help with tracking down Yvonne's Ravager if there is one on the loose."

I wasn't sure where the words had come from, but I suddenly felt that we would need Celeste. Perhaps the world had whispered it to me.

"Why would you need my help?" the witch asked, frowning. "Shouldn't you be able to track the Ravager by scent? In fact, why didn't you do that in the first place?" She arched one white brow.

"Because we couldn't detect the attacker's scent on Ezra," Henry explained. "Do you know of a possible explanation? Could it be a masking spell of some sort?"

I glanced at him, chiding myself for not having thought of that.

"It's possible." Celeste shrugged. "Though I think Sophie would have still felt some residual magic if that was the case.

Besides, don't you think it was a Ravager who attacked Ezra? Where would one have gotten a hex bag with a masking spell?"

The three of us sat in silence for a few minutes. Seeking Celeste's help had resulted in more questions than answers.

"Alright." The witch nodded. "Tell me the address of Isabelle's place. I will glimmer there in an hour."

"Thank you," I said, rising from my seat.

I quickly told her where Isabelle was staying while Henry stood up as well, tucking his chair back under the table. He looked displeased when I faced him and reached for his hands, making me wonder whether he would have rather walked or run back to New Haven. Still, he let me take his hands in mine and glimmer us out of the witch's cottage.

CELESTE

Sophie had been right there in my cottage. She had been so close, yet I hadn't been able to reach her. I had sensed her arrival before she'd shown up, but so had Damien. He'd been prepared when I had flung myself against the wall of the black metal box that was confining me. While Sophie and Henry had visited with him, I had thrashed against the walls of my prison until my legs had given out and I'd slid to the ground, bruised and weak. They'd had no idea about the fight I had tried to put up inside my own body. The fight against the nefarious intruder who controlled me.

Damien had been apprehensive about the visit but also delighted to see Sophie. He still harbored hope that one day she would succumb to the darkness. He had been disappointed to learn she hadn't been practicing her magic because the more she used her powers, the higher the chance she might get enthralled by the darkness again. Even if she did, Henry still posed a problem for the demon. A devoted mate, he would always help her find her light. I had sensed Damien's unease climbing in the vampire's presence. He felt threatened by Henry and hadn't tried to hide his loathing toward the male, throwing him a blistering look using my face. Hope that Sophie might notice that something was off about me had sparked but fizzled out quickly. She hadn't suspected anything about my condition, and I couldn't blame her. My cold demeanor was nothing new as I had always been mercurial and taciturn by nature.

After I had grown too weak to push against the walls, I had tried crying out for help from where I was slumped on the ground in my cell. I had tried until my throat had grown raw, but the sound had never left my mouth. My body had carried on, manipulated by Damien. It had retrieved the Blood Pact to confirm that no clan leaders had stepped out of line and even performed the spell to help Sophie track Yvonne. When Sophie and Henry had prepared to leave, despair had surged. They had been right in front of me, yet I had been able to do nothing. I had tamped down the feeling of distress when Sophie had asked for more help.

"Alright. Tell me the address of Isabelle's place. I will glimmer there in an hour." Damien had forced the words out of my mouth as he'd nodded my head.

In an hour, I would get another chance and another respite from being alone with the demon. Though I wasn't sure what was worse—being alone with him or being surrounded by those who could save me but had no idea that I needed saving.

6

Isabelle's place was, in reality, Wren's place—a small house near the city center he'd bought with his sign-on bonus when he'd first moved to New Haven and joined the Border Guard. Henry and I had helped Isabelle move there before we'd left for the Southern region. The plan had been for her and Wren to follow us to Santoria after we'd enjoyed a few weeks alone. We'd even found a place for them not far from our cottage.

My heart squeezed at the thought as I looked around Wren's house after I'd glimmered Henry and myself there. We were standing in the dark kitchen, and Henry released my hands, rolling his shoulders to shake the remnants of my magic off his body.

"We could have gotten here on foot," he said, his tone almost accusatory.

"Glimmering is faster." I shrugged. "Time is of the essence. We need to find the one who attacked Ezra before there are any more victims."

"I just wish you weren't so eager to rely on your magic." He frowned.

I stared at him in disbelief. Were we really having that conversation?

"You don't have a problem with my magic when it's granting you the freedom to walk in sunlight," I pointed out as my gaze dropped to his hand—to the wedding band on his finger.

"That's different. I saw the look of triumph on your face when you were tracking Yvonne. You relish having so much control over the clan leaders."

So that's what it's about.

"Perhaps I do. I wish I had even more control. We should have made all clan members sign the contract. It would be easier if we could track each and every one of them." The words escaped before I could stop them, but I didn't wish I could take them back.

Henry gave me a look of indignation. "Are you even hearing yourself?" he asked harshly.

"Are *you* hearing yourself?" I countered. "You can't enjoy the benefits of my magic one moment and then accuse me of resorting to it too fast the next."

His eyes widened as his anger visibly deflated. "You're right, I'm sorry," he said, looking apologetic. He reached up to gently cup my face. "It's just...I almost lost you because of your powers... They frighten me."

My own anger faded away. He felt he'd almost lost me, but the truth was I'd almost lost him because I hadn't been in control. I wouldn't let that happen again. I couldn't.

"I know," I told him as I wrapped my hands around his wrists. "But I am in control of my powers. I won't let the darkness creep back in," I vowed, trying to convince not only him but also myself.

My words seemed to placate Henry. Some of the tension left his taut features a second before he leaned in and brushed his lips over mine. I melted into the kiss, into him, enjoying the quiet moment we were stealing for ourselves. The spell was broken when I heard Isabelle clear her throat. Slowly, Henry pulled away from me and looked at his sister. I turned to face her as well.

"I don't want to say I'm not happy to see you two—I am—but I know you wouldn't cut your honeymoon short without a damn good reason. So, what happened? Why are you here?" Isabelle asked, looking between Henry and me.

She'd obviously just gotten out of bed. Her thick black curls fell haphazardly around her heart-shaped face as she clutched the lapels of the thin lilac robe she was wearing to her chest.

"It's Ezra," I said. Isabelle's brows pulled together at my words. "He was attacked last night. We think it was a Ravager."

"Is he okay?" she demanded, her face pinched in concern. After I'd assured her that he was, her features smoothed out, and she smirked. "I was wondering how long it would be before someone broke the rules. It didn't take long at all."

"We don't know anything for certain," Henry interjected. "Have you heard from the other clans or their leaders?"

Isabelle shook her head. "We are not exactly on speaking terms after you forced the new way of life on them—on us." She swallowed thickly.

"And how are you adjusting to this new way of life?" I asked as I quickly appraised her.

Despite her disheveled appearance, she still looked regal, like most vampires did, carrying an air of superiority everywhere she went. Standing there, in Wren's simple small kitchen, she looked out of place. She belonged in lavish settings, surrounded by expensive, elegant things that matched her beauty and class.

"I'm managing," she said quietly, shifting from foot to foot. "Of course, this place doesn't compare to the Duval Estate."

"It's no longer the Duval Estate, remember? Madam St. Clair resides there now," Henry said gently, as if he didn't want to upset her.

"I know. I just wish we didn't have to give it up…among other things…" Isabelle trailed off, looking down and to the side.

Blood. She wished we didn't have to give up the blood, but she was in a better position than most. While we'd left a small supply of blood with her, she also had Wren—her own personal human to provide her with fresh sustenance. Eventually, Henry and I would deplete the blood reserve we'd brought with us to Santoria. I didn't like to think about what we would have to do when we ran out. Henry had promised to show me the way that didn't involve hurting anyone, but I still felt uneasy about having to feed on humans.

"It was the right thing to do," Henry told Isabelle. They were the same words he'd spoken to her many times before. "Besides, you have Wren to provide you with fresh blood."

"I know," she said exasperatedly.

I wondered whether it wasn't just about the blood for her. It was about control—she'd loved holding power over the humans, much like I relished having power over the clan leaders.

"Speaking of Wren, where is he?" I decided to change the subject to alleviate some of the tension in the room.

"Sleeping," Isabelle replied. "He has been adhering to the same sleep schedule as me so we can spend our nights together. When he is not patrolling the border, that is."

My brows shot up. "Patrolling the border?"

Isabelle nodded. "He rejoined the Border Guard forces."

Learning that was a pleasant surprise. Wren had betrayed everyone's trust once by working for the Dark Witches, but it seemed he was on the path of redemption. He'd told me before that he strived to be a better man, and I was glad to learn he was following through on his intentions.

Henry seemed troubled by the news though.

"Do the other border guards know you're staying here?" he asked, frowning.

Understanding dawned on me then. Desperate to retain their power over the humans, the former clan leaders had gone on a killing spree, targeting the border guards who'd witnessed me defeat the Dark Witches. They'd hunted most of them down, but a few had remained. Waylon had warned us before that the survivors might seek retribution for what had transpired. Henry was worried about his sister's safety.

"I have been keeping a low profile," Isabelle said. "Besides, most of the guards who were on the border that night retired and moved away, eager to put what happened behind them."

Henry relaxed a fraction next to me, but the tension didn't leave his body completely.

"Still, you and Wren need to leave the region sooner rather than later. When we have solved the mystery of what happened to Ezra, you two should follow us to Santoria," he implored.

"We will." Isabelle nodded. "How do you plan to find Ezra's attacker?"

"We have already checked with Celeste," Henry told her. "The Blood Pact didn't reveal that any of the clan leaders have gone astray."

"Which doesn't mean that any of the other clan members haven't," Isabelle remarked.

"Exactly," I chimed in. "That's why we're here. You should probably wake Wren. Celeste will be here soon."

"Celeste?" Isabelle's brows lifted.

"Yes, and Yvonne. I'm going to glimmer to her place and bring her here."

"To interrogate her about her Ravagers," Isabelle said, as if to herself.

I could see on her face that she was thinking everything through.

"'Interrogate' is a strong word," Henry said, wincing. "We will *talk* to her about the Ravagers we left in her care. We are starting with the most obvious suspect first. If our conversation with Yvonne does not shed light on what happened, we'll move on to the other clan members."

Isabelle gave a nod of understanding. "I will go wake Wren."

She went to leave the kitchen but stopped with her back half turned to us, her big brown eyes flicking between Henry and me. "You two look well," she said with a small smile.

It took me a moment to realize she must have meant our sun-kissed skin. A strange look settled into her beautiful features. It wasn't one of envy but longing. She'd worn the same look when Henry and I had told her what our wedding bands could do—the freedom they gave us. She hadn't asked me to forge a similar ring for her, but I'd still vowed that one day I would. I just had to get stronger first. Creating an enchanted object like that required potent magic. I'd fed some of my powers into the rings under Celeste's guidance, but it had been mostly her magic that had fueled them.

Isabelle erased the look of yearning from her face a moment before she left the kitchen.

"I still want to make her a daylight ring one day," I mused, staring at the empty space where Isabelle had stood.

"And one day you will," Henry said as he flipped on the lamp on the kitchen table.

One day… I momentarily got lost in thought as yellow light filled the kitchen. Great power churned inside me—I could feel it —but it was locked away behind a vast obsidian door. I'd forced it there after I'd almost killed Henry. I'd locked it away but hadn't thrown away the key. If only I could have tapped into it without the risk of darkness bleeding through. But I knew it was there, crouched in the shadows, waiting for me to show any sign of weakness. I knew it was there, and I was afraid, so I held back. Still, I couldn't help but wonder what I could have accomplished if only I could have found a way to channel that great power without the fear of succumbing to the darkness.

"Sophie? What are you thinking about?" Henry asked, pulling me from my thoughts.

I wanted to tell him—we never hid anything from each other —but I knew he was already on edge about my magic.

"Nothing," I lied, rallying my powers. "I'm going to get Yvonne."

"You should take me with you," he said, stepping closer to me.

I shook my head. "If I take you with me, I'm not sure I will be able to bring both you and Yvonne back." When he scowled, clearly displeased by my answer, I reached up and cupped his cheek. "It'll be okay. I'll be back shortly. Hopefully with Yvonne in tow."

The scowl on Henry's face remained, but his eyes softened as he lifted his hand and placed it on top of mine. "Be careful," he said in a strained voice.

With a nod, I slipped my hand from his face and gave in to the tingling sensation of my magic.

HENRY

Glimmering. I hated it, though I had to admit it was a convenient way to travel when you needed to get from one place to the next, faster even than vampire speed allowed. Still, my chest constricted with unease when Sophie disappeared. With a heavy sigh, I dragged a hand down my face, bracing myself for the miserable wait until she returned.

"Are you okay?" Isabelle asked as she strolled back into the kitchen.

She had dressed in a simple cream gown, and her hair had been brushed to fall in voluminous waves around her face.

"Oh, you know, just...magic." I gestured at the spot where Sophie had just stood.

Isabelle's gaze slid to it before returning to my face. "Well, she is a witch," she pointed out unnecessarily.

"I know, I know," I grumbled with a small shake of my head.

"I overheard you two arguing earlier. You need to trust her."

"I do trust her." I frowned.

"I mean, trust she can take care of herself." Isabelle folded her hands over her chest.

"I almost lost her," I said as if that was explanation enough.

"But you didn't. Her feisty spirit is one of the reasons you fell for her, no? Don't try to stifle it now."

"I just want to protect what's mine." My words came out as a growl. "I didn't even realize I'd been looking for her until I found her. Nothing had ever felt so right. I want to ensure that nothing and no one takes her away from me."

Isabelle's eyes widened at my outburst, and she didn't say anything for a long time as her gaze roamed over my features. "This…overprotectiveness may push her away," she finally said in a warning tone.

I gritted my teeth and looked away for I knew she was right, but I wasn't willing to admit it.

Thankfully, Wren walked into the kitchen, interrupting our conversation.

"Henry," he said in greeting. "Long time no see."

"Not long enough," I bit out, turning my attention to him.

"Be nice," Isabelle snapped at me as Wren joined her side. "It's not his fault you had to cut your honeymoon short. Don't take it out on him."

"It's alright," Wren told her under his breath before turning back to me. "Isabelle told me what happened. Is Ezra okay?"

"He is. I gave him my blood to heal the wound," I replied, trying to keep my voice even.

Isabelle was right—I'd snapped at Wren for no reason. It wasn't like me to lose my temper, but worrying about Sophie brought out the side of me I usually liked to keep contained. Overprotectiveness, Isabelle called it. Perhaps "obsession" was a more accurate term for it. Ultimately, I knew that my sister was right—Sophie wouldn't like me imposing restrictions on her.

Threatening her freedom was the last thing I wanted to do; I just hated that she took so many risks.

"I hope you find the one who did it," Wren said, pulling me from my thoughts. "What can we do to help?"

"Nothing at the moment. Celeste will be here soon, and hopefully, Sophie will return any minute, bringing Yvonne with her."

And if she doesn't return soon, I will go after her, and gods help Yvonne if she hurts her.

SOPHIE

As soon as I appeared in the dark bedroom, I was shoved against the wall with such force that the back of my skull embedded in the stone. Yvonne's clawed hand squeezed my windpipe as she held me by the neck, her face mere inches from mine. Her eyes black and her fangs bared, she let out a menacing hiss. I bared my fangs as well and hissed back as my hand flew up to wrap around her wrist.

"Let go," I growled, low and guttural.

Yvonne's eyes widened with recognition. She hid her fangs and sheathed her claws as she swiftly let go of me and backed away.

"Sophie? What are you doing here?" she asked, her chest rising and falling heavily.

The smell of adrenaline, which had been pumping through her veins when I'd first arrived, was quickly replaced by one of fear. A small part of me rejoiced at such a reaction, and a gleeful smile tugged at my lips, but I suppressed it.

"We need to talk," I said simply, stepping away from the wall.

Fragments of it crumbled to the ground when I did. As I brushed the pieces off my shoulder, the skin on the back of my head that was torn from the impact stitched back together.

"I'm sorry I attacked. I didn't realize it was you," Yvonne began speaking, her voice trembling slightly. "I awoke from a dead sleep because I knew there was a vampire in my room."

I didn't respond for a few moments, folding my arms over my chest and taking a look around the bedroom. Yvonne fidgeted where she stood as the smell of her fear grew stronger. I couldn't fight a small smile that time—I was enjoying myself, prolonging her state of dreadful unease. When I realized what I was doing, my smile faded, and I shook my head to clear my thoughts.

"There's been an attack," I said, meeting Yvonne's wary gaze.

She swallowed audibly before she said, her tone measured, "I had nothing to do with it."

What about the rest of your clan? The words were on the tip of my tongue, but I forced them down. Henry and I had agreed to question her together. I could have taken matters into my own hands, but I wasn't sure I wanted to. Yvonne was clearly afraid of me, but if I pressed too hard and she decided to lash out, I wasn't sure I would prevail. After all, she was older and stronger than I. I had my magic, but it was the kind that was still developing and weak. Once again, I found myself wishing I could have wielded the dark magic without consequences.

"Get dressed," I barked the order. Yvonne bristled. "I'll take you to New Haven, to where Henry is. The three of us can talk."

"I just told you I had nothing to do with it," she said through her teeth, balling her hands into fists at her sides.

I unfolded my arms from over my chest. "That wasn't a request," I said as I brought some of my power to the surface of my skin. It sparked as short bursts of white lightning, reflecting in Yvonne's dark eyes, which grew big again.

"Alright!" She raised her hands halfway, turning her palms toward me in a placating gesture. "I will get dressed."

In a flash, she was gone, and my ears picked up on her rummaging around in the adjacent clothing chamber. A few minutes later, she walked out of it, dressed in dark-brown leather pants and a forest-green tunic.

"Do I need to pack for travel?" she asked begrudgingly.

"No, I'll take us back using my magic." Moving in the blink of an eye, I crossed the distance between us, stopping before her.

"I was afraid you'd say that," she said with a heavy sigh. "What does it feel like?"

"You're about to find out." I lifted my hands to get a hold of her.

"I want to be prepared."

"It feels like being yanked from one place before being spat out in the next," I told her the truth as I felt my power rise to the surface again.

"Lovely…" Yvonne seethed but didn't resist when I clasped her arms above the elbows.

"Do me a favor and don't vomit," I said a second before my magic enveloped us and everything went black.

Shortly after, I was back in Wren's kitchen, still clutching Yvonne's arms, which was a good thing, too, because the female would have crumpled to the ground had I not been holding her up.

"Breathe," I told her. "Focus on one spot to keep the nausea at bay."

Curling her hands around my forearms for support, Yvonne did as I'd instructed, taking a few deep breaths, her gaze fixed on a spot on the floor. Once she was steady on her feet, she let go of me and looked around the kitchen. I knew when her gaze fell on Henry because she swallowed and took a step back to put more distance between them. A futile move since Henry stepped closer to me and therefore her.

"Why do I smell your blood?" he asked, scanning me for injuries. "Did she make you bleed?" His eyes flashed as he glanced at Yvonne.

The female stilled, all color draining from her face.

"No. Well, yes, but it was unintentional," I assured him. "I'm okay."

His features became taut as he stared at me. I wondered if he was trying to decide whether to make Yvonne pay for hurting me. He must have decided against it because he turned toward the female and nodded in greeting.

"Yvonne," he said, placing his hand on my lower back.

"Henry," she answered meekly before her entire demeanor changed. "You look…different," she said in a shocked voice. "You both do." She looked between Henry and me with wide eyes.

Shit. Of course she would have noticed the new golden tone of our skin.

"How is it possible?" she asked, reaching up with one hand as if to touch us. When she realized what she was doing, she curled her fingers into a fist and lowered it to her side.

"It just is," Henry replied, his tone final.

I half expected Yvonne to press for answers, but she didn't. Instead, she just stared at us, all disbelief.

"Thank you for coming here," Henry said, changing the subject. "We just want to talk."

Yvonne glanced at Isabelle and Wren before returning her attention to Henry. "Sophie told me there has been an attack."

"Yes. A Ravager by the looks of it."

Yvonne's face fell at his words—she knew something. Quickly smoothing out her expression, she attempted to lie, "I had nothing to do with it."

Henry stared at her for a few seconds in silence. Yvonne stared back, but her posture became less rigid and defiant the longer the stare-down lasted. She seemed to grow smaller in size under Henry's heavy gaze.

"Do you want to try that again?" he asked with quiet menace. His hand on my lower back flexed as if he was barely containing his anger.

"The Ravagers we left in your care," I interjected, trying a different approach. "Have you been able to bring them out of bloodlust?"

"Yes," Yvonne replied quickly.

Too quickly. I narrowed my eyes at her.

"All of them?" Henry asked in a tone that suggested he already knew what she would say.

Yvonne chewed on her cheek, shifting from foot to foot. It seemed she didn't know what to do with her hands, balling them into fists one moment and relaxing them the next. "All but one," she finally admitted.

Henry and I exchanged a glance.

"What happened to that one?" I asked.

"She escaped," Yvonne confessed after a beat of silence, her voice dropping to a whisper.

"When?" Henry bit out.

We hadn't planned for Yvonne's visit to be an interrogation, but it had inadvertently turned into one as we had to drag the information out of her.

Her golden eyes seemed to lose their luster, and her expression turned resigned as she said, "Four nights ago. By the time I realized she had escaped, she was miles away. I began tracking her scent, but I knew I wouldn't catch up to her before sunrise, so I abandoned my search and returned home."

She suddenly looked defeated, as if she thought that by telling us the truth, she had just signed her death sentence. And perhaps she wasn't that far from the truth. Henry became a wall of coiled muscle beside me, making me wonder whether he was doing everything in his power not to lash out at the female. A tense silence ensued as different thoughts swarmed in my head.

Have we really gotten to the bottom of it? Can it really be this easy?

One thought, more than the others, niggled in the back of my mind because of something Yvonne had said. "You were able to track the Ravager's scent?" I asked, angling my head.

Yvonne's perfectly trimmed brows pulled together in confusion. "Of course."

"Why didn't you resume your search the following night?" Henry asked her.

He had a soft spot for Ravagers because they were turned against their will and forsaken to bloodlust by the one who'd sired them. They were victims, much like the humans they tore to shreds in their frenzied state.

"I…" Yvonne's heart sped up in her chest as sweat beaded her forehead. She was terrified because she didn't have a good answer.

"Because she wanted the Ravager to stay on the loose," Isabelle spoke up for the first time since I'd returned. "Isn't that right? You don't like this new world order, so you want it to fail."

"Can you blame me?!" Yvonne snarled at Isabelle.

Isabelle snarled back as Henry removed his hand from my lower back and shifted his weight forward. His nails elongated into claws as he ducked his chin and bared his fangs, preparing to protect his sister.

"Let's not lose our heads," I said in a raised voice, my gaze darting between the three vampires.

When I glanced at Wren, his face was full of sheer terror, but he hadn't moved from his spot at Isabelle's side. His loyalty was admirable for he surely knew that he wouldn't be able to do much if a fight broke out. Thankfully, it didn't come to that because a knock sounded on the front door.

"Celeste is here," I announced, looking at Henry and then Yvonne.

The former regained his composure first, hiding his fangs. A moment later, Yvonne let her upper lip slide over her fangs as well.

"What is the witch doing here?" she asked, not taking her eyes off Henry, as if she didn't trust him not to go for her throat.

"You turned the Ravagers we left in your care," I told her,

giving Wren a small nod. He nodded back and reluctantly left Isabelle's side to let Celeste in. "Perhaps we can use your blood to track the one that escaped."

The plan hadn't formed in my head until a split second before, but it had suddenly become clear to me that was the reason I'd asked Celeste to come.

8

The witch walked into the kitchen a moment later, garbed in her usual blue cloak. Her sharp gaze immediately locked on Yvonne before sliding to me. "What did you find out?" she asked without further ado.

"One of her Ravagers escaped. We need your help tracking her down," I explained.

"The Blood Pact will only allow us to track the ones who signed the contract," Celeste said, matter-of-fact.

"I know, but Yvonne sired that Ravager. It's her blood flowing through that vampire's veins. Perhaps we can track the Ravager using their connection?"

It was a long shot, but if embracing my witch side had taught me anything, it was that with magic, many once-impossible things were within reach.

Celeste seemed to think it over. "There is a spell I can try," she finally said. "I need a map of the Empire."

When I looked at Wren, he nodded. "Let me fetch it for you."

"What will happen if you find her?" Yvonne asked while we waited for him to return.

I didn't for a second think that she was worried about the Ravager. No, she wanted to know what would happen to *her*.

I glanced at Henry, but he didn't meet my gaze. He was staring at Yvonne, a muscle flexing in his jaw.

"We will figure it out when we find her," I responded.

Henry and I would need to make that decision together. I didn't doubt he'd want to try to help the Ravager and bring her out of bloodlust, but when it came to Yvonne, her future was uncertain. Part of me thought that she deserved to die for all of her transgressions. It wasn't just about her letting the Ravager escape and hiding it from us; she'd also been involved in capturing Henry when Camilla had tried to retain control over the Empire. Aside from finally making her pay for hurting Henry, killing Yvonne would send a message to the others—a message that the price for any sort of disobedience would be death. The wild, vicious part of me rejoiced at the possibility of ending Yvonne, but another part of me wanted to spare her life because I refused to be a monster. So I couldn't be the only one to decide Yvonne's fate, nor should I be. Henry was my partner in everything, so we would decide together.

"Here's the map." Wren walked back into the kitchen, snapping me out of my thoughts.

He offered the parchment to Celeste, who accepted it with a curt nod before walking to the kitchen table. Unrolling the map on the flat wooden surface, she glanced at Yvonne. "I need a few drops of your blood."

"A few drops? Last time, you only needed one drop," Yvonne pointed out, looking apprehensive.

"Last time was different," Celeste said simply.

After a few seconds, during which she just stared at Yvonne, it became clear the witch wasn't going to offer more of an explanation.

"Let's get it over with." I motioned for Yvonne to step closer to the table.

After another beat of silence, she did, stopping on one side of the square piece of furniture, to Celeste's right. Henry and I also approached, flanking the witch on either side, while Isabelle and Wren came to stand opposite us, with curiosity written on their faces.

"When you are ready, drip some blood on the map"—Celeste looked at Yvonne—"and I will do the rest."

The vampire rolled her eyes and shook her head in displeasure but extended her forearm over the parchment. The nail on her index finger elongated into a sharp claw, and she used it to slice open her wrist. Her blood welled before dripping down on the map. As soon as the first drop landed with a splat, Celeste began chanting a spell, leaning over the table. The witch's power saturated the air around us as Yvonne brought her wrist up to her mouth and licked the blood off the already-healing cut. Everyone who was huddling around the table leaned in, intently watching the map. My brows lifted as the blood on the parchment became a living thing. It looked like a pool of spilled ink, but the edges were ebbing and flowing. Suddenly, a line shot out from the pulsing splotch, creating a trail.

"It's working," I said under my breath as I watched the blood, wondering where it would lead.

"The Midlands," Henry said a moment later. "Emeric's old domain."

Out of the corner of my eye, I saw him glance at me over Celeste's head. I didn't look back. My gaze was fastened on the blood trail, which I hoped would move past the region Emeric used to rule. Because if it didn't...

A few more seconds passed, but the crimson line was still pointing to the same spot on the map—to the small town close to the Maivayan Mountains, where I'd killed Emeric and buried the rest of his clan alive.

"How accurate is the spell?" I asked Celeste once she'd stopped chanting and straightened from the table.

"It's accurate," she assured me.

I didn't doubt it was, but I was looking for a way out. As if sensing my unease, Henry walked around Celeste to stand by my side.

"You know what we have to do," he said so low that only I would hear.

He meant what *I* had to do, which was face the consequences of the heinous acts I'd committed when the darkness had almost prevailed over me.

"I don't understand," Isabelle spoke up, drawing my attention to her. "You said the attack on Ezra happened last night." She was looking at Henry and me. "How did the Ravager make it all the way to that region of the Midlands?"

"She didn't," Yvonne interjected. "That would be impossible, which means she isn't responsible for the attack."

"I'm not responsible" is what I read in her eyes when she locked her gaze on Henry and me, defiantly lifting her chin.

"You're right," Henry agreed. "Your Ravager couldn't have made it that far if she was here last night to attack Ezra."

My heart sank at his words because they meant there was another predator on the loose.

"But you still failed to carry out the task we left you with," Henry continued. "You failed that Ravager and were going to hide the truth."

The longer Henry talked, the louder his voice grew. Yvonne paled and curled into herself more with each word.

"Then let me make it right," she said, her voice shaking. "Now that I know where to find her, let me try again—"

"No," Henry cut her off. "Sophie and I will take matters into our own hands."

I swallowed, wishing that taking matters into our own hands didn't mean returning to the Maivayan Mountains.

"What about me?" Yvonne asked and then seemed to hold her breath.

Henry looked at me expectantly, clearly leaving her fate up to me. I wished we had some time to discuss what should be done about her, but we didn't, so I decided to listen to the part of me that refused to be a monster.

"You're free to go. For now." I made sure to infuse the last two words with chilling warning. I hoped that my tone promised cruel punishment should Yvonne step out of line again.

A harsh exhale left her as she visibly relaxed, her features softening in the yellow glow of the lamp on the kitchen table. "Can you take me back now?" she asked me.

My brows wrinkled before I realized she couldn't return to her place on her own because it was daylight outside. Since I wasn't susceptible to sunlight anymore, it was easy to forget the other vampires' limitations.

"I'll be right back," I told Henry, stepping closer to Yvonne.

He tensed but gave a small nod. Yvonne gritted her teeth when I grabbed her forearm and summoned my magic. A moment later, we were sucked into the void, and my stomach hollowed out with the weightless feeling before my feet hit the floor in Yvonne's bedroom.

When I let go of her, the female braced her hand on the nearby wall, breathing in through her nose and exhaling slowly through her mouth, to subdue the nausea caused by glimmering. I cast a glance around the bedroom as a thought occurred to me.

"Do you have anything we can use to track the Ravager?" I looked back at Yvonne.

Celeste's spell had shown us the region and the town, but Henry and I would still have to search for the feral vampire once we were there.

Yvonne didn't respond at first, catching her breath. After a few seconds, she straightened from the wall and nodded. "Follow me," she said, heading for the bedroom door.

We stepped out of the room and walked down the long, dark hallway to the other end of the house. When Yvonne stopped before another door and walked in, I followed. The room was much smaller than her bedroom and reeked of blood and other things I decided not to dwell on. I almost gagged before I tamped down my keen sense of smell. My lip curled in disgust as I quickly took in the dingy four walls, the bare stone floor, and the filthy cage with iron bars tucked in the corner. It didn't take me long to put two and two together.

"You kept her in a cage like a fucking animal?!" I snarled at Yvonne, outraged by her cruelty.

The female only shrugged. "She is lost in the frenzy of blood-lust. For all intents and purposes, she *is* an animal."

I had to fight the urge to shove Yvonne into the cage to see how she would like being treated like a rabid dog.

With her back to me, the female didn't see my face mottle with rage as she opened the cage and reached inside. She retrieved a tattered cloth and turned around. When our gazes met, what she saw in my eyes made her stagger backward, rattling the cage.

"I wanted to kill them, remember?" she challenged, but her voice shook. "Where else was I supposed to keep them?"

My temper rose a few more notches as I struggled to breathe through my turbulent emotions. "What is that?" I demanded, jerking my chin at the rag in Yvonne's hand.

She swallowed audibly before she said, "It's…her blanket."

When she held the cloth out to me, I ripped it out of her hand. The scrap of fabric was hardly large enough to cover a small child. Yvonne was lucky Henry couldn't have come with us. If he had seen the conditions she had kept the Ravagers in, I doubted Yvonne would have lived to see another night.

She must have known it, too, because she breathed, "Thank you."

"For letting me go" was what I read in her eyes.

Her words of thanks took me aback, but I didn't show it. "Don't forget my mercy," I bit out instead. "Any of it."

I knew I didn't need to elaborate when Yvonne's face turned ashen. That wasn't the first time I'd spared her life, but it might have been the last. Or so I wanted her to believe. She didn't say anything else before I glimmered out.

When I appeared back in Wren's kitchen, he, Isabelle, and Henry were sitting around the table, the bloodied map still covering its surface. Celeste wasn't there or anywhere in the house, I realized, quickly perking my ears for any sound outside the kitchen. She must have left while I'd been gone.

Henry twisted in his chair to beckon me to join them at the table. His nostrils flared as his gaze dropped to the rag in my hand.

"Something to track the Ravager with," I explained before he had the chance to ask.

"Good thinking," he said as I took the seat next to him. "I'm glad you decided to let Yvonne go," he added low, relief flickering across his face. The emotion was there one moment and gone the next as he schooled his features.

Would he still have been glad if I had told him in which conditions Yvonne had kept her Ravagers?

"You didn't think I would let her go?" I turned to him. Then a thought occurred to me and instantly raised my hackles. "When you left the decision about Yvonne's fate to me…were you testing me?!" I asked in a challenging tone. I already suspected the answer but wanted to hear it from him.

Henry clenched his jaw as his eyes searched mine. "It was a test in a way… I wanted to see what you would do."

"You wanted to see if I would let the darkness inside me guide my decision," I finished for him, shaking my head in disappointment.

I wasn't sure whether I was disappointed in him or myself. After all, he had a reason to doubt me only because of what I had done before. But he'd told me the past was in the past. Why was he doubting me right then? Did he not believe me? *In* me?

I wanted to ask Henry all the questions crowding my head, but then and there didn't seem like the time or the place, so I forced myself to look away and face Isabelle and Wren sitting across the table.

I found Wren looking uncomfortable, his gaze cast down to the map. Isabelle's gaze was on Henry and me, but she thankfully chose not to comment on the little argument we'd just had, if one could even call it that.

Instead, she said, "So, it appears Yvonne's Ravager didn't attack Ezra."

"It appears so," Henry concurred. "Someone else is responsible for the attack."

"That would explain why we didn't detect a scent," I said, glancing at him.

He nodded in agreement.

"What do you mean?" Isabelle tilted her head to the side.

"Whoever attacked Ezra… Henry and I couldn't pick up on the attacker's scent," I explained.

"No scent?" She frowned. "But how is that possible? You should have been able to smell something."

"I don't know how that's possible," Henry told her. "I'm sure we will find out, but first we need to find Yvonne's Ravager and bring her out of bloodlust. She might not be the one who attached Ezra, but she is still a danger to others and herself."

"What if there is another attack while we're searching for her?" I asked him. "We could divide our efforts. I could stay here while you search for the Ravager," I suggested.

I didn't want to be away from him, but my plan made sense.

"No," Henry said without hesitation. "We are not going to be apart from each other."

"Why? Because you don't trust me?" I blurted out before I could stop myself.

Henry's eyes widened slightly, and he glanced at Isabelle before looking back at me. "Of course I trust you. It's others I don't trust."

He was scared of losing me. I understood his fear. After all, it was my fear of losing him that had driven me to embark on my quest for revenge. The darkness had exploited my feelings for him, making me believe I had to eradicate our enemies. But just because I understood his fear, that didn't mean I wanted to let it rule over our lives or prevent us from doing the right thing.

"I don't want to leave New Haven unprotected," I said softly, hoping he'd understand.

"It will not be unprotected," Isabelle chimed in. "I will help Waylon and his people patrol the streets at night."

"I will help too," Wren added from beside her.

I gritted my teeth—it seemed I wasn't going to convince Henry to let me stay behind. "Alright," I gave in, trying to hide my frustration. "What's our plan?"

Looking relieved that he was getting his way, Henry replied, "We will leave for the Midlands after we check on Ezra." With a nod, I rose from the table. "Let's just walk back over to Waylon's place," Henry said as he stood up as well, towering over me. "You should save your magic for when we need to glimmer to the Maivayan Mountains."

I nodded again, knowing full well that I didn't need to "save" my magic. Henry just didn't want me using it more than was absolutely necessary. I wasn't sure why I was so annoyed. I'd just gone two weeks without using it, but since he was trying to impose limitations, the desire to feel the lightning of my magic in my veins was growing stronger.

"Is that okay?" Henry asked, stepping closer to me. His tone was gentler then—he must have realized how demanding his previous words had sounded and was trying to soften the blow.

"Yes, it's fine," I told him, tamping down my frustration.

A small smile graced his lips before he wrapped his hand around mine.

"Good luck," Isabelle said, standing from the table. Wren scrambled to his feet as well.

"You too," I told her before Henry and I walked out.

CELESTE

"Excellent," Damien drawled in my mind after my body had left Wren's place. "I didn't even need to manipulate the blood trail. It led straight to the Maivayan Mountains. Oh, how I wish I could follow Sophie there. Her defenses will be weakened once she sees the destruction her black magic has caused. I wish I could be there to whisper in her ear...to convince her the darkness is the way. Alas, I have to remain here, but while her focus lies elsewhere, we can proceed with our plan."

After another unsuccessful attempt to break through the walls of my box and ask for help, I had slid all the way down to the ground. I was lying on my side with my head resting on the cool black surface. My eyes were open but unseeing as I stared into the space before me. Tears spilled, pooling under my cheek, and I found myself wondering whether the puddle would get deep enough for me to drown in them. At least then I would finally be free.

9

HENRY

"Do you think they're still alive?" Sophie asked as we began our trek back to Waylon's place.

"I hope so. We should have dug them up weeks ago."

Before we had left for our honeymoon, Sophie had asked Isabelle to excavate the rest of Emeric's clan, but my sister had denied her request.

"It is your mess to clean up, not mine," she had told her.

Sophie had been taken aback by her response, but I had to admit that Isabelle was right—my wife needed to face the consequences of what she had done when the darkness had nearly consumed her. I hadn't wanted to push her before we had left for Santoria, but at that point, it seemed we had no choice.

She was apprehensive about going to the Maivayan Mountains. I had seen it on her face when the map had revealed that we would find the Ravager there. Her features had become taut as she'd paled slightly. I couldn't blame her for her reluctance, but we had to see whether Emeric's wife and daughters were still alive.

"There isn't a part of you that wants them dead?" Sophie asked, pulling me out of my thoughts. The words were spoken in a hushed whisper, as if she were ashamed to utter them.

"There is," I confessed. "But I have spent over a hundred years trying to subdue that part."

I refused to feed the ruthless part of me that craved vengeance. Besides, the clan vampires didn't need to pay for what their leaders had done to me. The ones who were truly responsible were already dead at Sophie's hand. All except Yvonne. My blood instantly boiled when I thought about the female as my gaze darted to the rag Sophie was carrying in her hand. It reeked of blood and other bodily fluids, and I suspected the conditions Yvonne had kept her Ravagers in had been horrible. That would have explained why Sophie had looked so ashen when she had returned from glimmering Yvonne back to her place. The expression on her face had been a mix of disgust and outrage. I had chosen not to ask her to confirm what I suspected lest I changed my mind about Yvonne's fate and ended her miserable existence.

Dragging my gaze away from the rag, I focused it straight ahead as I took a deep breath to get my emotions under control.

"Control." The word had been my mantra ever since I'd turned. Control your thirst, the monster inside, your temper, and your urges. And right then, I was trying to control Sophie.

When the thought stopped me in my tracks, she halted next to me. "What's wrong?" she asked, her forehead creasing with concern.

Facing her, I hauled her to my chest. "I'm sorry," I whispered against her temple.

She tensed in my arms for a split second before relaxing into my hold. "It's okay," she said softly. "You're afraid of losing me; I understand."

Of course I didn't need to explain what I was apologizing for.

"If I'm being honest," she continued, "part of the reason why I wanted to remain behind was so I could avoid going to the Maivayan Mountains—to the place where I did such horrendous things." Her voice dropped to a near whisper again.

"I will be with you every step of the way," I assured her as I pulled away slightly to peer at her face.

"I know." She looked up at me before lifting on her tiptoes to press her lips to mine. I wanted to deepen the kiss like I always did, but she didn't linger, lowering back down. "What's our plan once we get to the mountains?" she asked as we resumed our walk.

"I think we should dig up Emeric's clan first," I told her, "because if we are able to locate the Ravager, she will require all of our attention."

Dejection rolled off Sophie in waves at my suggestion, but she didn't protest. I wished I could have alleviated the state of unease she was in. I hated seeing her like that and wished I could have shouldered the burden of her not-so-distant past, but I couldn't. All I could do was be by her side as she tackled the aftereffects of her villainy.

The rest of our walk was spent in oppressive silence, as we were both lost in our thoughts. The mood lifted slightly when we arrived at Waylon's place and saw that Ezra was up and moving around. He, Waylon, and Amelie were in the kitchen, having tea. Sophie's face lit up with relief when she saw Ezra, and the pressure on my chest lessened just a bit.

"Sophie, Master Henry," the boy said, rising from the kitchen table.

"We have talked about this before. Please, call me Henry," I implored him good-naturedly, clasping his shoulder.

He looked at me and said, "Waylon and Amelie told me about what you did. Thank you...Henry."

"No need to thank me. I'm just glad you're okay."

"Do you remember anything about the attack?" Sophie asked from where she was standing next to me.

"I don't." Ezra shook his head. "I remember walking home from the tavern…" His gaze grew distant. "I was close to the house. I could see it a few feet ahead of me…" He paused and swallowed. "Only a few more steps and I'd have been home," he rasped, unblinking. "But something barreled into me…" His breathing picked up, and I could hear his heart rate spike. He refocused on Sophie. "Everything went black… I don't remember anything after that. Nothing until I opened my eyes and found myself at Waylon's place."

"It's okay," Sophie assured him with a soft smile.

I squeezed his shoulder in quiet support before I let go.

"Did you find out anything that can help us find the attacker?" Waylon asked, rising from his seat at the table.

Sophie glanced at me before she said, "There is a Ravager on the loose."

Ezra flinched at her words.

"Here, sit down and finish your tea," Amelie, who was still sitting at the table, beckoned Ezra to her side.

I was grateful for the witch's soothing and caring nature. It seemed to instantly put the boy at ease. His tense shoulders relaxed as he joined her at the table.

Sophie must have noticed Ezra's agitated reaction to her words because she didn't say anything else. Instead, she jerked her chin toward the kitchen entrance, indicating her desire to take the conversation elsewhere. With a nod, Waylon followed her and me out into the living room.

"Where is my father?" Sophie asked him when the three of us stopped by the unlit fireplace.

"We convinced him to go home and get some rest," Waylon replied. "Amelie wanted to keep Ezra here a little while longer to make sure he was fully healed."

He *was* fully healed. At least, his body was. The emotional damage was something my vampire blood couldn't fix. The boy would have to work on overcoming it with time.

"So it was a Ravager?" Waylon prompted.

Sophie exhaled roughly, preparing for a difficult conversation. "One of the clan leaders, Yvonne, made a few Ravagers to help her fight me when I went to seek my revenge for what they'd done to Henry," she started. It seemed the words were difficult for her to get out. "I killed most of them, but four remained. We asked Yvonne to bring them out of bloodlust and make them members of her clan… One of them escaped."

"You let Ravagers go?!" Waylon asked, raising his voice. "And you didn't think to tell me?! I could have been better prepared—"

"What's done is done," I cut him off. "We were able to pinpoint the Ravager's location in the Maivayan Mountains. We are going to find her."

Waylon dragged his hand through his short light-brown hair with a noise of exasperation. "Wait, did you say 'the Maivayan Mountains'?" he asked, realization washing over his face.

"Yes," Sophie told him. "The Ravager on the loose could not have been the one who attacked Ezra."

Waylon's shoulders sagged with disappointment. "Then who was it?"

"We don't know," I chimed in. "But we will resume our investigation after we find the rampant vampire."

"We?" Waylon looked between Sophie and me. "You are both going to the mountains? Ezra's attacker is still on the loose. Can't one of you stay and help look for him?"

Sophie tensed next to me, fixing her gaze on the ground. I gritted my teeth at the question.

"Yes, we are both going," I bit out. "Isabelle and Wren will help you patrol."

Thankfully, Waylon seemed satisfied with my answer. "What's that?" he asked, jerking his chin toward the rag in Sophie's hand.

She lifted her gaze from the floor and looked at it. "Something we can use to track the Ravager," she said a moment before she ripped a small piece off and shoved it in her pants pocket. She tossed the rest of the cloth into the fireplace to be burned later.

"When are you leaving?" Waylon asked.

"Now," I told him. "We need to make preparations before we head to the mountains." When Sophie gave me a questioning look, I explained, "We need to figure out where we will bring the Ravager once we find her. Depending on her state, she might need to be restrained. And we will need to have some blood on hand for her."

"What are you thinking?" she asked.

"Let's head home first. For the sake of time, will you glimmer us there?" I asked low.

She nodded and reached for my hands.

"Be careful," Waylon said, looking at us.

"You too," Sophie told him. "We'll be back to check on New Haven as soon as we can."

With those parting words, she called forth her magic. An unpleasant tingling sensation erupted all over my body, as it always did when she glimmered us. It felt as though I were being ripped apart into a thousand pieces. The feeling was fleeting as the world turned black for a moment before colors returned and all the tiny fragments of me reassembled. An involuntary shudder rolled through me when my feet touched solid ground again, and I blinked as my eyes adjusted to the brightness of the living room in our cottage on the Starling Sea.

"Are you okay?" Sophie asked when I let go of her hands.

"Yes," I told her, flexing my fingers to rid myself of the remaining tingles.

"So, what's our plan? I figured we would wait until sundown to glimmer to the mountains to dig Emeric's clan up." Her tone was resigned, but she was right—we wouldn't want to start digging during the day and risk exposing those vampires to sunlight.

"We have a few hours until then. We need to figure out where we will keep the Ravager once we find her."

"I don't want to bring her here," she stated.

I didn't blame her. I didn't want to bring the Ravager to our home either. The cottage was our safe haven. Happiness lived there. Bringing a frenzied vampire there would interrupt the peace of that place.

"You said she might need to be restrained," Sophie said, thinking it over. "There is a place that is already set up for that..." she trailed off, her hazel eyes fastening on me.

I had feared she would suggest it. "Stern's lair," I said with a rough exhale.

I had gone back there once before to retrieve Sophie's locket, but I imagined that no matter how many times I returned to that place, the feeling of dread associated with it would never dissipate.

"We can try to find a different place—" Sophie started.

"No," I interrupted. "We don't have time to find somewhere else. The cave already has the chains"—my breath snagged, and I swallowed to force down the lump that had formed in my throat —"and Stern's estate is not far from here. We have time to hire a carriage and take a crate of blood there."

"Are you sure?" Sophie asked gently as she stepped into me and reached up to cup my face.

Her touch helped to soothe some of the trepidation, but it didn't stop the horrible memories from rushing in, flooding my mind. In an instant, I was back in that cave with Moreau hovering over me, his face splattered with my blood. I was lying on the hard ground, in the pool of my blood, drowning in the never-ending pain. My heart rate spiked, and I broke out in a cold sweat, which was my body's involuntary reaction to the horrible memories of what it had endured.

"Don't go there," Sophie's voice penetrated the haze in my mind.

Suddenly, I was desperate for her. Desperate for proof that I had escaped that place and the torture. Clasping the back of her neck, I crushed my lips against hers. When a startled gasp left her, I took advantage, deepening the kiss. I wrapped my arm around her waist, bringing her flush with me, and ground my hips into her to show her what I needed. With a throaty moan, she kissed me back, weaving her tongue with mine.

Her tunic hit the floor first. Then I pulled off her boots, pants, and undergarments. I pulled my shirt up and over my head, casting it aside, while she freed me from my pants. Nipping at my neck, she wrapped her fingers around my hardness, and a growl escaped me as my hips instinctively flexed into her touch. I captured her mouth again as my hand glided down her throat to her chest. I cupped her breast and dragged my thumb over the hardened nipple before pinching it slightly. She whimpered against my lips, all the while sliding her hand up and down my rigid length. Releasing her nipple, I trailed my fingers down her stomach to her navel and lower still, to the point between her legs where I knew slick heat awaited me.

Then it was my turn to whimper as I dragged my fingers through her wetness. I couldn't wait to be inside her. She couldn't wait either, it seemed, because she hooked her leg around my hip, trying to guide me to her entrance. Swiftly wrapping my arm around her waist, I lifted her up in one smooth motion before sheathing myself inside her in one glorious slide. We both groaned as I filled her, instantly enveloping myself in her silky tightness. She wrapped both of her legs around my hips and clutched my shoulders as I helped her move on me, bringing her down harder with each plunge. She felt divine, but I wanted more, so I lowered her to the floor so that I could drive into her with more force. Gasping with pleasure, she met each powerful thrust with the tilt of her hips.

"Fuck," I growled in her ear, feeling the building release tingling down my spine.

"Not yet," she rasped as she hooked her feet behind my knees and flipped us.

The new position buried me even deeper inside her, and I was gone, lost in the immense pleasure as Sophie rode me. Her eyes drifted closed, and she threw her head back, chasing her own release. Before long, her delicate inner muscles began to quiver around my throbbing length. Clasping her hips, I thrust up and into her, bringing her to the edge and then over it. She cried out, clamping down on me, and a harsh groan left me as I came, my entire body tensing. A moment later, all my muscles relaxed, and I seemed to melt into the floor. Sophie draped herself over me, resting her cheek on my chest.

"I love you," I told her, trailing my fingertips up and down her back.

"I wish we could just stay like this forever" was on the tip of my tongue, but I didn't say the words out loud. There was no point in uttering them because we couldn't stay like that. We had to get up and get ready.

IO

"*I* love you too," I told Henry after I'd given him what he'd so desperately needed.

The truth was I'd needed it too but for a different reason. He'd wanted to feel my body on his to chase away the horrors of the past, while I'd wanted to feel him inside me because I didn't know what the future would bring. Both of us were about to face the ghosts that haunted our nightmares. Henry was about to return to the place where terrible things had been done to him, while I was about to return to the place where I'd done terrible things to others.

"Sophie," Henry said gently, stroking my hair. "We need to get ready."

I lifted my head from his chest and eased off him. We quickly showered and changed, opting for all-black clothing that time to blend in with the night after it had descended.

When we were ready, Henry hired a coachman to take a crate of blood to Stern's lair. Thankfully, the bags looked like regular wineskins, so the driver shouldn't have suspected their contents if he decided to peek under the wooden lid.

"What's our plan when we get there?" I asked after we'd loaded into the carriage.

"The Governess of the Southern region and her family moved into the estate after the Stern clan moved out. I will compel them to leave, to go on an extended vacation," Henry said as he settled on the cushioned bench next to me.

He pulled me close, and I curled into his embrace, leaning my head on his shoulder.

"Will you teach me how to compel? Is it something that can be learned?" I asked, staring out the window at the scenery of Santoria rushing by.

I felt him tense at my question.

"You know I don't like resorting to compulsion," he said. "But sometimes, it has to be done," he added with a heavy sigh. "It is a skill that can be learned, and the older a vampire is, the better they are at it."

"Why is that?" I asked, curious.

"No one really knows, but my theory is that the older you are, the more control you have over…well, everything. Over your thirst, your vampire side… Perhaps, it also gives you more control over others."

"Only humans are susceptible, right? A vampire can't compel another vampire?"

"Right, we can only compel humans."

"How do you do it? I know you need to make eye contact." I'd gathered that much from the time Henry had tried to compel me when I was still human.

"Yes, it's mainly through eye contact, but I believe our voices also carry some of the compulsion."

"So I just look into someone's eyes and tell them what I want them to do?"

"It's not that simple. You have to make them believe they want to do it. What helps me is imagining them performing the action I want them to do." Henry paused and seemed to think it over. "I think it's similar to the gift of premonition the White Witches have. Except instead of seeing what's going to happen, you're making it happen, if that makes sense."

"It does."

The rest of the drive was spent in comfortable silence, though Henry's muscles coiled tighter and tighter the closer we got to the Stern Estate. He was visibly on edge by the time the carriage pulled up in front of the mansion.

"The Governess lives here now," our coachman said as we climbed out of the cabin. "Is she expecting you?" He eyed Henry and me with suspicion.

"That's none of your concern," Henry replied smoothly, stepping closer to him and peering into his face. "Go back home and forget that you brought us here."

My skin prickled at the tone of his voice, which was even deeper than usual. The coachman blinked a few times before he slowly turned around and hoisted himself up onto his seat at the front of the carriage. He departed shortly after Henry had unloaded the crate of blood from the back.

"Wait here," he said, leaving the blood with me.

I watched him as he strode to the wrought iron front door of the mansion, which opened before he had the chance to knock. An older man with cold eyes stared at him from inside the house. He appraised Henry with a stern expression. When he opened his mouth to speak, Henry spoke first, meeting and holding his gaze. The man's eyes turned glassy a second before he stepped to the side to let Henry in.

After the door had closed behind them, I watched it like a hawk, hoping that everything was going according to plan inside the mansion. Henry had to compel the entire household, which was a hefty task. I wished I could help him, but since I couldn't compel, all I could do was wait. Finally, a few minutes later, he emerged from the house, beckoning me to join him by the front door.

"They're packing for a vacation on the coast," he said when I approached with the crate in my hands.

Henry took it from me, and I followed him inside the quiet, brightly lit house. We immediately headed to the study, where the secret passage to Stern's lair lay hidden behind the bookshelves.

"What if they've found the cave?" I asked Henry as we walked in. "What if they've repurposed it?"

"Only one way to find out." He inclined his head toward the bookshelves that lined the wall.

With a nod, I stepped closer to them and lifted my hand to the shelf at my chest level. I ran my index finger down the row of books, stopping at one of the titles bound in a black-and-gold cover. When I tilted it toward me, a faint click sounded, and the middle section of the bookshelf separated from the wall and slid to the side, revealing a shadowy entrance behind it. I went to step toward it but stopped when I noticed Henry wasn't moving. He was standing frozen in place, staring past me into the murky depths of the passage. His gaze was unseeing, and I knew he wasn't right there with me in that room. Instead, he was already in the cave below our feet, reliving his worst nightmares.

"Henry," I said, looking into his eyes. "Darling?" I lifted my hand to his cheek. "I will be with you every step of the way," I echoed the words he'd spoken to me earlier.

The hard lines of his face softened as he closed his eyes and turned his face into my palm. When he reopened his eyes a moment later, his gaze was clearer and more focused. "I'm ready." He gave a small nod.

I slipped my hand from his cheek and entered the passage. He followed after me, and we began our descent down the narrow stone steps. The part of the bookshelf hiding the entrance slid back into place behind us, but I didn't panic. I knew there was a small indentation in the rough wall on our side that, if pressed, would grant us access back to the study. I'd discovered it when I'd been desperately trying to flee that place on the night we'd found Josephine's Tear.

Henry and I worked our way down in silence. His pulse quickened more and more the lower we went, and by the time we'd reached Stern's lair, it sounded like his heart could have beat right out of his chest. My heart rate also picked up when I suddenly realized Henry wasn't the only one who had ghosts in that place. I'd been so focused on what I had done in the Maivayan Mountains, I'd forgotten that Stern's lair also held remnants of my terrible past. The realization stopped me in my tracks as soon as we entered the dark, cool cave. My gaze darted to the far wall—I'd painted it red with Beatrice Stern's blood the last time I was there. My pulse pounding, I looked at the opposite wall, where I'd held Camilla as I'd driven a stake through her heart. Breathing became difficult as my throat closed up. It barely registered that Henry had set the crate down and reached for me. I turned around in his embrace and buried my face against his chest. He held me tightly as I fought back sudden tears.

"Breathe with me," he whispered as his own heartbeat began to slow down.

I did as he'd instructed, drawing the air into my lungs before releasing it slowly.

"Better?" he asked after a moment.

"Yes," I told him as I pulled away slightly and looked up.

He quickly pressed his lips to mine before he released me and set to work. Moving at vampire speed, he swept through the cave, lighting the fat waxy candles scattered throughout the place. While he did that, my gaze shot to the wall that held the chains Stern had used to restrain his Ravagers. The clan leaders had used the same chains to bind Henry when they'd held him captive. I hated the fucking things, but I knew that he hated them more, so I decided to check them for him. He'd just held me in his arms, helping me not to fall apart, even though it was difficult for him to be in that place, even more so than me. Checking on the chains was the least I could do. My mind made up, I walked to the wall and dropped to my haunches. The rusted metal groaned when I pulled on the links to make sure they were still securely embedded in the cave wall.

"The chains are intact," I said, looking over my shoulder at Henry, who was standing a few feet away, looking on from afar, as if he was afraid to come closer.

His throat bobbed as he swallowed and gave a slight nod. "Are you ready to go?" was all he said in a strained voice. He was no doubt as eager to leave that place as I was.

"Yes, let's get out of here." I rose to my feet and walked over to him.

When I reached for his hands, he wrapped his fingers around mine, holding on tighter than usual. We held on to each other as I summoned my powers and glimmered us out.

11

A shuddering breath whooshed out of Henry when we appeared in the Maivayan Mountains, but I didn't feel the same relief. If anything, the pressure that was constricting my chest intensified. When Henry went to let go of my hands, my hold on him tightened, my gaze fastening on his face. I was afraid to look away. Because I knew if I did, I would have found the mountain I'd demolished to my right. The same mountain I'd pinned Emeric to so he would burn in the rising sun and then brought down on his family, burying them underneath.

Henry stared back at me in silence as the setting sun cast a red-and-orange glow on his taut features. Emotions swirled in his deep-blue gaze, but two shone brighter than the rest—love and total acceptance.

"Whatever happens…whatever we find will not change anything between us," he said vehemently. "You are not a monster. I love you…forever," he added, running his thumb over the wedding band on my ring finger.

With his words, the sun disappeared below the horizon, plunging the world around us into darkness. The temperature seemed to drop, but I knew it was just my imagination because, as a vampire, I was impervious to cold. Still, I shivered as an icy feeling invaded my body. The thorny sensation was back, pricking my heart, and I had the urge to run my hand over my chest, where a dull ache had started.

"Let's get this over with," Henry said low, pressing my hands once more before he let go.

I curled my fingers into fists at my sides and turned to the right. My lungs felt crushed. I couldn't take a full breath in as I stared at what remained of that part of the mountain. Before me was a terrifying sight. It was a reminder of how destructive my dark magic truly was.

Destructive—yes—but also beautiful and powerful, a small part of me whispered.

I glanced at Henry, wondering whether he could see the intrusive thought written on my face. He wasn't looking at me though. With his eyes wide and his mouth open slightly, he stared straight ahead as he took in the devastation before him, seeing it for the very first time. My heart dropped. Would he take back the words he'd just spoken about me not being a monster? He closed his mouth and pressed his lips in a thin line. A muscle flexed along his jaw as he regained his composure.

"Ready?" he asked, glancing at me.

I wondered whether he was finding it difficult to look me in the eye.

A nod was my only response before I began walking forward, toward the debris of the once-formidable mountain. Henry was with me every step of the way, just like he'd promised. My limbs grew heavier and heavier the closer we got to the ruins, but I pushed through until we stopped right before them.

"Is it just me, or does the site look like it has been disturbed?" I asked Henry as my gaze traveled over the rubble.

"It definitely does," he confirmed next to me.

"Could they have…climbed out?" I asked low.

Conflicting emotions unfurled in my chest. I knew I should

have felt relief that Emeric's clan had survived, but a small part of me—the same part that was just admiring the devastating beauty of my dark magic—felt apprehension and…disappointment.

"I don't think they climbed out," Henry said, stepping away from me. "It looks like someone dug them out," he added as he inspected the pile of rocks before him.

"Who?" My brows furrowed in confusion.

Each vampire clan had always been out only for themselves. It was hard to imagine any of them would care enough to excavate Emeric's wife and daughters.

"I don't know," Henry said under his breath, probably thinking the same thing I was. "We need to make sure they are not still in there."

He lifted one of the large rocks as if it weighed nothing and tossed it to the side. I also picked up a rock, moving it out of the way to clear the spot where I thought my victims were buried. Henry and I worked at supernatural speed, but it still took a couple of hours for us to clear the debris.

"They are not here," he finally declared, wiping the sweat from his brow.

But they *had* been there—we'd found evidence of the crime I'd committed. Fragments of bone and tissue were scattered all over the place. Could they have perished under the rubble with no blood to help heal their broken bodies? Even if they'd survived, they must have been in a terrible condition when someone had dug them out.

Nausea churned as I looked down at the large rock I was holding. My victims' blood had seeped into the stone, coloring it dark red. It was also smeared with my blood—from the countless nicks and scratches I'd incurred while digging barehanded.

"We are done here," Henry said, coming to stand before me. As gently as he could, he pried the rock from my hands and cast it aside. "Are you okay?" he asked low as he used his tunic to wipe away the blood from my hands.

"I don't know," I confessed, my voice hollow.

"Come here." He pulled me to his chest.

I melted into him, turning my face to rest my cheek over his beating heart. The steady rhythm brought me instant comfort, but I knew I couldn't relax—not yet—because our task wasn't over.

"What do we do now?" I asked, looking up.

He thought about it for a moment. "It's a long shot, but I think we should check the Laurent Estate, or whatever it's called now after the human governor took it over."

I frowned. "Do you think they went back there?"

"They would have required blood and lots of it to help them heal once they were free..." *Because of what I did to them*, I thought, curling more into Henry's embrace, as if he could protect me from my past. But he couldn't. Nothing could shelter me from what I'd done. "It makes sense they would have gone to their estate to feed on the blood from the cellar."

"I'll glimmer us there," I rasped, my throat tight with emotion.

I wanted to feel the tingle of my magic on my skin, if only to distract myself from the sting caused by the whiplash of the terrible memories. Besides, running there, even at supernatural speed, would only have prolonged my state of uncertainty and dread.

Henry must have understood what I was feeling because he didn't protest. Pulling away from him, I took his hands and glimmered us out, wishing I could have left the past in the ruins behind me.

Their smell hit my nostrils as soon as we appeared in front of the Laurent Estate. Emeric's clan was here; there was no doubt about it. All five of them. It was strange how I instantly knew their scent—as if it had seeped into my subconscious. I was momentarily thrust into the past in my mind—to the moment when I'd stood in the middle of the cave with Emeric's wife and daughters shaking in fear behind him.

"*Mercy*," his youngest, Julia, had begged me then.

I hadn't shown them mercy. Would they show *me* mercy now? Or would they try to rip out my throat, seeking revenge for what I'd done?

"They're here." Henry's words brought me back to the present. "They must be inside the house." He looked at the mansion to his right.

"They're not alone," I stated, letting go of his hands. "There are other smells here…" My brows wrinkled as one of the scents seemed familiar.

"The human governor, perhaps," Henry said, looking at me. "I hope they didn't hurt him."

My frown deepened as I reached inside my pants pocket. "I think it smells like…" I pulled out the piece of cloth I'd gotten from Yvonne.

"The Ravager," Henry said under his breath, his nostrils flaring.

"What is she doing here?" I mused just as a whooshing sound pierced the night.

Henry opened his mouth to reply, but no words came out. Instead, blood spilled from his lips as his eyes widened in shock. My gaze dropped to his chest, and time screeched to a halt when I saw a thick metal bolt protruding from it.

"Henry!" I shouted, reaching for him.

Before I could touch him, fiery pain exploded in my chest. It felt like I was being ripped apart. I didn't need to confirm what I already knew as blood, *my* blood, climbed up my throat. Slowly, I looked down—at the metal bolt jutting out from above my breasts.

"Sophie…" I heard Henry's labored breath before everything went dark.

floated in the nothingness for a while as the jagged edges of the hole in my chest slowly pulled toward each other. Blood would have sped up the healing process, but I was too weak to open my eyes and search for what I so desperately needed. I became more aware of my surroundings the more the wound healed. Still, I couldn't pry my lashes apart for a long time. My limbs felt laden, and searing pain was eating up my chest where the hole was closing. I drifted in and out of consciousness, never quite breaking the surface to fully come to. My wrists and ankles were burning for some reason, and I could feel my life draining out of me, leaving my veins dry and brittle.

At least I wasn't alone. I could sense Henry by my side. Even with my eyes closed, I knew he was right beside me. It wasn't just his scent that told me he was there; it was as if my body always knew when he was near. Henry had given me his heart, so perhaps I'd been right before when I'd mused that it was one heart beating in both of us, like two halves of a whole. My heartbeat was slow at that moment, struggling to pump what blood I had left in my system to the center of my chest to close the wound. Something was preventing me from healing completely.

Straining my vampire ears, I listened for Henry's heartbeat. When I heard it, it sounded as sluggish as mine. Suddenly, I had to make sure he was okay. The urgency drove me to finally open my eyes.

My eyelids felt heavy as I slowly blinked, waiting for my vision to adjust. Once it had, I found myself staring at a rough stone ceiling in a low-lit room. Henry was to my left, and I tried to turn my head to look at him, but my body wouldn't obey. I could hear his labored breathing and smell his blood. His blood? My brows pinched, the muscles of my face difficult to manipulate. It wasn't just Henry's blood I was smelling... I was also smelling my blood and the blood of others. There were other vampires in the room. I smelled Emeric's clan and Yvonne's Ravager. Where were we? What were we all doing here?

Gritting my teeth, I willed myself to move, trying to lift off the flat surface I was lying on. As soon as I did, metal bit into my wrists and ankles, digging in deep, cutting to the bone. With a hiss of pain, I stopped trying to get up. Instead, I lifted my head and craned my neck to look down my body. I was lying on a wooden table. Thick metal bands embedded into the wood were binding my wrists and ankles, pinning me down. The metal cut into my flesh even when I lay flat. Blood was flowing freely from the severed veins, running down the sides of the table. The contraption must have been made on purpose, I realized with a sinking heart as I heard my blood drip to the hard ground underneath. It was built to continuously drain me of my essence so I wouldn't heal and escape. My pulse quickened at the thought as I looked down at my chest, at the ragged wound I could see through the tear in my tunic. I also caught a glimpse of the amulet and my locket. They had slid off and to the side, but at least I hadn't lost them and they hadn't been taken from me. The relief I felt was fleeting as I inspected my chest. Judging by the way it looked, the thick metal bolt that had pierced it had been yanked out rather carelessly, tearing out chunks of skin and tissue.

"Fuck," I gasped as I let my head drop to the table.

Bile rose in my throat. I'd never been injured like that before. I knew that my vampire body could withstand a lot, but knowing it and experiencing it were two totally different things. The sight of my mutilated chest made me feel lightheaded. Sweat beaded my forehead as I struggled to breathe through the nausea. It wasn't just the sight of it that made me feel like I was about to pass out again. Though I was difficult to kill, didn't mean I experienced any less pain. No, the pain was still there, excruciating and intense. I tried to breathe through it, but with every inhale and exhale, the air scorched my raw insides. Tears threatened as panic surged and swelled. Before I could succumb to it completely, a muffled groan snapped my attention to my left.

Henry was lying on the wooden table next to me, and a strangled sound escaped me as I took in his condition. He was bound to the table like I was, but he was also gagged and blindfolded. *What the fuck?*

Henry's head was turned toward me, and the tendons in his neck stood out as he strained off the table as if trying to get to me. Rivulets of blood were flowing down to the floor from where the metal bands were cutting into his wrists and ankles. More blood seeped from his ravaged chest as he struggled against the bindings. Another muffled groan tore from his throat past the gag in his mouth, and it sounded like my name.

"I'm okay," I rasped in between taking shallow breaths. "You need to relax; you're bleeding out."

At my words, Henry stopped thrashing and let his large body relax onto the table. To my relief, the bleeding from his chest, wrists, and ankles slowed. Fighting back tears, I swallowed the knot in my throat and lifted my head again to look around. We were in a large rectangular room with unfinished stone walls and no windows. Two oil lamps that were sitting on the floor by the only door were bathing the place in a faint yellow light.

I wondered whether we were still on the Laurent Estate, in the cellar where the clan used to keep their supplies of blood. The markings on the walls and the ground that looked like they were from the storage shelves confirmed my suspicion. The blood must have been moved to convert the space into a holding cell.

A holding cell or a torture chamber, I thought as a shudder rolled through me.

There were four more tables in the room. My heart pounded as I surveyed them in silence. One table was sitting to Henry's right, and a young girl I didn't recognize was lying on top of it.

Must be the Ravager, I thought, quickly scanning her from head to toe.

It was hard to judge her age because her face was covered in blood. Whether it was her blood or the blood of her victims, there was truly no telling. Her curly blonde hair was matted with it, sticking to her cheeks and neck. The tattered rags she was wearing were also covered in red, and her feet were bare like Henry's and mine to allow for the metal cuffs that were binding her to the table. Her wrists were bound to the table as well, and the gashes in them and her ankles were deep and jagged. She must have made them worse by thrashing against the bindings in the frenzied state so common for Ravagers. At the moment, she was lying unmoving because she was unconscious. A metal bolt was protruding from her chest as if someone had driven it into her body to pin her down. My eyes widened when I noticed it, and my stomach roiled with another wave of nausea.

Dragging my gaze away from the Ravager, I looked at the other three tables on the opposite side of the room. Those vampires I recognized. With hair and eyes of different shades of brown, they could have been related to each other by blood, though they weren't. Emeric's wife, Nova, was lying on the middle table with two of their daughters flanking her on each side. The oldest, Monique, was lying to her right, while the youngest, Julia, to her left. The other two daughters, Tess and Madeline, were nowhere to be seen. Was there another holding cell, or had they been able to escape?

They're dead, the world whispered to me, the hushed words prickling my skin.

I quickly squashed the thought, refusing to give in to panic. I needed to have a clear head so I could assess the situation and devise a plan to get us out of it. Stretching my neck even more, I looked at the three females to see what condition they were in. Their bodies were bloody and battered, and I winced as I took them in. Their injuries were clearly the aftermath of my burying them under the mountain. Pinned to the tables, they were also being drained of their blood, which was preventing the torn, savage wounds from healing. All three vampires were blindfolded and gagged like Henry was. My gaze darted back to the Ravager—she and I were the only ones who weren't.

"Why?" I whispered in confusion. Henry whipped his head in my direction, his eyebrows raised in question above the blindfold. I realized it must have been driving him crazy not being able to see what was going on. "We're in a cellar. Probably on the Laurent Estate," I said low. "The Ravager is here," I told him what he undoubtedly already knew from the scent. "So are Emeric's wife and two of his daughters. They are blindfolded and gagged like you are. The Ravager and I are not."

Henry's brows pulled together in a look of confusion that I knew matched my own. His muscles coiled as he strained against the bindings again, causing them to dig deeper into his flesh.

"Please, stop," I whispered. I hated seeing him hurt. "I'll get us out of here."

My neck muscles gave out at that moment, and my head dropped to the table with a thud. Gritting my teeth, I pushed through the pain and lifted my head again to look around, trying to find anything that could help us escape. All I found was another wooden table to my right that housed an array of torture instruments. I was suddenly relieved that Henry was blindfolded because seeing the display would have surely flung him back into the past—to the torture he'd endured at Stern's lair. The blades of different shapes and sizes were covered in blood, old and new. I looked back at Nova and her daughters. Deep cuts and lacerations covered their bodies. They were different from the wounds I could tell they'd suffered when the mountain had collapsed on them.

What depraved monsters were our captors? I was about to find out, I realized when I heard footsteps approaching the cellar. Everyone in the room tensed, and my breath snagged in my throat as the heavy wooden door opened, revealing a familiar face on the other side.

13

*R*ough-hewn features; short, dark hair; and hard gray eyes.

"Jared?!" I exclaimed as the man stepped into the cellar.

He was one of the guards who'd witnessed me defeat the Dark Witches on the border. Isabelle had said they'd all retired and moved away. What was he doing at the Laurent Estate?

Jared halted by the foot of my table and quickly scanned everyone else in the room before his heavy gaze returned to me. "I see you're awake," he said in a gravelly voice.

It didn't go unnoticed that he hadn't called me by my name. We'd known each other for years, but he was looking at me differently then. His eyes burned with loathing as his face contorted in disgust. A feeling of dread slithered down my spine. Waylon had warned that the guards from the border might seek retribution for what the clans had done.

"What is the meaning of this?" I demanded, infusing my voice with bravado I didn't feel.

"Oh, this?" Jared made a sweeping gesture with his arm. The black leathers he was wearing gleamed in the light of the lamps.

They were splattered with the blood of everyone in the room, judging by the smell. "This is us, humans, taking back our world."

"You already have your world back. Thanks to me," I said through my teeth.

"Ah, yes, because you eliminated the Dark Witches. Waylon never revealed how you did it exactly. He only said you're part witch yourself."

"I am. I used my magic to kill the clan leaders who hunted you—"

"But not before they killed most of us!" Jared raised his voice, glaring at me.

"And for that, I'm sorry!" I raised my voice as well. Or tried to. It came out raspy and strained as the anguish from the pain I was in bled through every word. "I did the best I could! I helped usher in a new world order—"

"You don't get it, do you?!" Jared was shouting then, spitting the words at me, his eyes blazing. "There can't be a new world order until all the vampires are dead!"

The words ricocheted off the stone walls before a stunned silence settled over the room.

I lowered my head back down, staring up at the rough ceiling to keep the tears at bay. My thoughts were racing. I couldn't help but feel like nothing I did could ever be enough. I'd become a vampire to help humans, but at that moment, I was being punished for it. I'd almost lost myself to the darkness when I'd eradicated the clan leaders, but I was being accused of acting too late. I supposed it was true I could have done more—I could have used the Tear to erase the vampires from the world, killing Henry and myself in the process. I'd refused to make that sacrifice, and it seemed the humans were taking matters into their own hands.

"What is this place?" I asked, my gaze still glued to the ceiling. I couldn't bear to look at Jared.

"We're on the Laurent Estate. The Governor lets us use this cellar and provides the weapons and resources we need to carry out our mission." I didn't need to ask what the mission was, though I was a little shocked to learn the Governor was in on it. "It was thanks to Waylon that I knew where to start," Jared continued. "He told me what you'd done to Emeric and his clan."

"Waylon? Does he know about this?" I forced the words out. I wasn't sure what I would do if my childhood friend took part in that operation.

"No," Jared said, and I exhaled with relief. "I figured he wouldn't approve of our…methods. He still has a soft spot for you, even though you're a monster now."

I closed my eyes and swallowed, trying to keep my composure.

A monster—that's all he sees me as, I thought.

I couldn't blame him. I'd thought all vampires were monsters until Henry had proven to me that wasn't the case. Until I'd become one of them but still kept my humanity. Could I prove to Jared that Henry and I were different? Would it even matter if I tried?

"You call me a monster," I said, opening my eyes. "But if you go through with your mission, you will turn into one yourself." I looked at Jared to drive my point home.

"That's different," he countered. "Just look at her." He jerked his chin toward the Ravager. "She's unhinged! I had to pin her to the table with a metal bolt to keep her in place."

"How did you catch her?" I asked. I figured Nova and her daughters had been too injured and weak to put up a fight when Jared and his men had dug them up. But I wasn't sure how the Ravager had ended up in the cellar.

"It was sheer luck, really. Just like with you and him." He jerked his chin toward Henry. "We'd planned on hunting you down, but you two brought yourselves to us. Tell me it wasn't a sign that we're doing the right thing by carrying out our mission?" He smirked.

"Your mission?!" I seethed. "It's about more than just your

mission, isn't it? You say you want to kill all vampires... Then why are we here being tortured?! You could have killed us on the spot!" I didn't want to give him any ideas; what I *did* want was for him to realize that he was becoming much like the creatures he was trying to eradicate.

Jared huffed out a baleful laugh. "Why?! I'll tell you why! The vampires oppressed us for a century. Just killing you would be too easy. You have to suffer! Just like we suffered! And the torture you mentioned?" A bone-chilling smile broke across his face. "The torture has not yet begun." He looked toward the open cellar door. "The others usually like to join in," he said before he turned back to me. "But I'm done waiting on them." He shot a glance at Henry. "I think I'll start with him. He looks like he can handle a lot. And I want to drag this out. Don't want to kill you all too quickly like the other two."

My blood froze in my veins—so he *had* killed Tess and Madeline. We had to get the fuck out of there.

Henry's heartbeat ratcheted up at Jared's words as he paled and broke out in a sweat—his body remembered all too well the last time he'd had to endure torture. A sharp smell of fear permeated the air, but Henry quickly reined it in. He didn't need to worry anyway because I wasn't going to let him suffer.

"No!" I said loudly as Jared stepped closer to the table with the blades. "You will start with me."

A strangled sound left Henry as he violently shook his head. He began thrashing against the bindings again.

Jared's eyes widened, darting between us. "He's very protective of you," he observed. "Waylon said as much. How quickly you have forsaken your people and fallen for the creature you tried to destroy." The look of disgust had returned to his face.

"I fell for him because he's not like the others. *I'm* not like the others—"

"Lies!" Jared shouted. "You're just like the rest of them! I've always wondered why it was so easy for you to make the decision to turn. Perhaps you'd always wanted to be one of them!"

"Easy?! Nothing about that decision was easy! I did it for you! For my people—"

"Enough!" Jared cut me off again. I clamped my mouth shut as he took a deep breath. "You want me to start with you?" he asked, calmer then. It was the sort of calm that coated my insides with ice. "Then I will." He thought about it for a moment. "I wish I could make him watch, but Waylon said that older vampires can compel, so I better keep the blindfold on," he added, as if to himself.

So that was why everyone besides me and the Ravager were blindfolded.

"He didn't know how it works exactly…" Jared continued as he began going through the blades on the table before him. He looked almost nonchalant, like he was sorting through silverware and not instruments of torture. "Only that a vampire can impose their will on you by talking to you. He wasn't sure if it's their voice or eye contact, so I figured it was better to blindfold *and* gag them. Better safe than sorry."

With a loud grunt, Henry bucked against the table, and it creaked, making the metal bindings groan with strain.

Jared glanced at him, and a look of fear flickered across his features before he quickly erased it from his face. "Easy there, big guy," he warned, reaching for the thick metal bolt mixed in with the other weapons on the table. He was going to drive it through Henry's chest to pin him down like he'd done with the Ravager.

"Henry, please," I implored him, barely above a whisper. "Trust me," I added so low that only he would hear.

It took a few seconds for my words to sink in, but when they did, Henry stopped thrashing.

"Stop!" I shouted to get Jared's attention. He halted on his way to Henry's table, the blood-covered bolt in one hand. "Please—

he'll behave," I rasped, my nerves stretched so tight I thought they might snap.

Jared glanced at me, then back at Henry. My heart pounded in the silence as I held my breath, waiting to see what he would do. To my relief, he returned to the table with the torture instruments and set the bolt down.

"Now, what do we want to start with?" he muttered under his breath as he resumed his selection.

I swore I could feel the tension rolling off Henry in waves next to me. He was lying silently, though, placing his trust in me as I'd asked. Nova and her daughters were silent too, probably grateful for the opportunity to delay their own torture. I looked frantically around the cellar as Jared hummed under his breath, sorting through the blades. I briefly wondered whether he'd always been that unhinged and we'd all just missed the signs somehow. A second later, he picked up a serrated knife and looked at me. Panic took over, robbing me of breath when our gazes locked. His gray eyes had gotten darker, as if the evil had bled into them like black ink. He wasn't a demon, but he almost looked like one at that moment.

Sinister energy emanated from him. It promised suffering and bloodshed. I could smell his excitement, and a part of me wanted to weep that I'd sacrificed so much for people like him. For years, I'd been so focused on the vampires and the Dark Witches that I'd forgotten that not all monsters looked like monsters. Some looked human, hiding in plain sight. A part of me wanted to weep, but the bigger part wanted to fight. With that thought, I let my panicked gaze sweep over the room again just as Jared stepped closer to my table.

"To fight monsters like you, I have to become a monster myself," I'd told Emeric before I'd killed him. But what if I didn't have to become a monster? What if I could use my black magic without succumbing to the darkness?

"How long do you think you'll last once I begin carving out

your organs?" Jared asked, the serrated blade in his hand hovering over me.

The darkness inside me stirred, but I was afraid to set it free.

I might not have a choice, I realized with a heavy heart.

"You don't want to do this," I bit out, my gaze fastened on Jared's.

He froze for a second before he blinked and shook his head. "I do," he said, his voice rough. "The truth is I've wanted to do it for a long time. Ever since they sent my little sister to the Selection."

My brows pinched—I hadn't known he had a sister. As it turned out, there was a lot I hadn't known about him. I *did* know that he wasn't from the Eastern region, so his sister hadn't been sent to the Duvals for the Selection. I recalled he was from the West, so his sister must have been…Moreau's vassal. Benjamin Moreau had been the clan leader of the Western region and a depraved psychopath who'd considered humans nothing more than pets. He'd often killed his vassals instead of returning them to their homes upon completion of their service.

"She never came back," I whispered as tears gathered in my eyes.

14

"*D*oing this won't bring her back," I said, my voice shaking. I knew from experience—killing Stern and avenging my mother and Rory hadn't made me grieve them any less.

"I know," Jared replied. "But at least no other little girl will be snatched in the middle of the night and fed on." He looked down at the blade in his hand and smirked. "You want to usher in a new world order? You can help by doing your part...by *dying*," he said as he lowered the blade to my abdomen.

When he made the cut to open me up, something opened up *inside* me. My shadows snaked out, wrapping around him. They encircled his wrists and slithered up his body to secure around his neck like a torc. A strangled noise left him, and his eyes bulged as the black tendrils of my magic began to squeeze the life out of him.

"Wait! I don't want to kill him," I told the shadows as if they were a sentient thing. Sentient or not, they obeyed, lessening the pressure around Jared's neck. "I just want him to let us go."

A thought occurred to me then. I *wanted* him to let us go.

"You have to make them believe they want to do it. What helps me is

imagining them performing the action I want them to do," Henry had said when he'd explained compulsion to me.

What if I could compel Jared to let us go? I didn't want to kill him. Not anymore. Not after I'd learned the reason behind his actions.

You can't let him live, the darkness whispered in my mind. It seemed when my shadows had darted out, they'd brought it with them. Disappointment washed over me—I wished I could have wielded my black magic without having to wrestle with the darkness again. I wished I'd had more control.

But I am in control, I told myself. *I'm in control, and I don't want to kill Jared, so I won't!*

Gritting my teeth, I imagined myself squelching the darkness that had escaped, forcing it back into the cracks in the vast obsidian door that usually kept it contained. I wasn't sure how long I would be able to suppress it, so I focused on the task at hand. My veins felt aglow with raw power, tiny shocks hitting every part of my body. The sensation was much more intense than what I experienced when using my light magic. It was nearly euphoric, but it still did little to mask what state I was in.

Wincing through the pain that was radiating from the hole in my chest and the cut in my torso, I willed my shadows to bring Jared closer to me. They complied, moving him like a rag doll until he was hovering over me, his face close to mine.

What's happening? What are you doing to me? Am I going to die? I read in his terror-filled eyes. He tried to open his mouth to ask the questions out loud, but my shadows were preventing him from speaking.

Good. I will be the only one speaking now. I just hoped that my words would have the desired effect and get us out of that situation.

"I'm going to break the bindings and free myself and the others," I began, my voice so deep I barely recognized it. Goosebumps broke out over my skin at the sound. "You will stand by and do *nothing* as we flee. You will not alert the others or try to stop us. You will not come after us. You need to put the past behind you." My voice dropped to a whisper as I uttered the last part. Could I compel him to give up on his mission of hunting down the vampires? Or would his will eventually override my command? We would have to wait and see.

I stared into Jared's eyes, trying to gauge whether my attempt at compulsion had worked. I'd witnessed Henry compel before, and those under his spell had looked dazed, their gaze unseeing. Jared wasn't wearing the same expression.

It's not working, I thought with a sinking heart.

See, you only have one choice, the darkness hissed faintly through the door of my inner vault.

No, I'm going to try again.

As I opened my mouth to speak, I imagined Jared relaxing in my magic's hold. I imagined him standing by, unmoving, even after my shadows had released him. He would watch me with glassy eyes as I freed all the vampires in that room from their bindings. He would do nothing as I gathered everyone up and glimmered us to Stern's lair—to the crate of blood Henry and I had stored there.

Please work, I chanted in my head as I repeated the exact same instructions I'd given to him earlier.

After I'd spoken the words, I held my breath and waited. That time was different. Jared's taut features smoothed out, and that hazy, unseeing look I'd hoped for invaded his gaze. A soft exhale left him as his coiled muscles relaxed. I willed my shadows to release him, and after they had, he straightened from where he'd been bent over me. He stood unmoving, his gaze distant, while my shadows pried the metal cuffs that bound me out of the table.

With my wrists and ankles free, I slowly turned on my left side, barely stifling a whimper of pain. When I braced my hand on the table and pushed up to a seated position, the Tear and my locket slid down, brushing the wound on my chest. Another whimper escaped me before I reached up and took them off from around my neck. I shoved them in my pants pocket and swung my legs off the table, trying to catch my breath while my shadows released Henry. Unlike me, he seemed impervious to the pain, quickly ripping the blindfold and the gag off. Moving in a flash, he stopped right in front of me, where I was slumped sitting up, gripping the edges of the table for support.

"Are you okay?" he asked urgently as he cupped my face. When I nodded, his wild gaze dropped to my chest and then lower, to the gnarly cut in my right side. "I will fucking kill him!" he roared, moving toward Jared, who was still standing behind me, on the other side of the table.

"Don't!" I grabbed Henry's arm to stop him. "Don't kill him. You heard what happened to his sister," I offered as way of explanation when Henry's blazing gaze shot back to mine.

A few moments passed before the red-hot fury in his eyes cooled just a fraction. With a grunt, he braced his hand on the table, his face contorting in pain. He wasn't impervious to it, after all. He'd just wanted to make sure I was okay before he let himself feel it.

"We need to get out of here," I said, looking past Henry at the Ravager lying on the other table.

My shadows darted to her, quickly and efficiently ripping the metal bindings out like they'd done for Henry and me. They didn't touch the bolt protruding from the Ravager's chest though. I didn't want to use my powers for such a delicate task. I would do it myself. Slowly, I slid off the table. When I swayed on my bare feet, Henry gently clasped my shoulder to steady me.

"What are you doing?" he rasped in between the shallow breaths he was taking to manage his pain.

"I'm going to take the bolt out," I replied, giving a small nod toward the Ravager.

Henry glanced at her, then at the other three vampires, before his gaze returned to mine. "Getting all of us out of here may prove too difficult given the condition we are in. We may have to come back for them later," he told me.

"No," I said calmly. "We all leave together. I'll glimmer us out."

Shock splashed across Henry's features as his brows shot up. "All six of us? I thought you couldn't glimmer so many at once?"

"Not with my light magic" was all I said. I didn't need to add the rest.

Apprehension replaced the shock on Henry's face as he glanced at my shadows, which were still churning by the Ravager's table, awaiting my next command. "Sophie—" he started.

"I'm getting us out of here," I interrupted, my tone determined. "*All* of us."

Before Henry could say anything else, I left his side and stumbled on weak legs to the Ravager's table. Standing before it, I motioned toward the other three tables, sending my shadows in their direction. They would free Nova and her daughters while I freed the Ravager. Turning my attention back to the girl, I took a shuddering breath and reached for the bolt. My hand trembled as my fingers wrapped around the metal. For a split second, I considered driving that bolt through Jared's chest to repay him for his cruelty, but doing so would have made me no better than him. So I took another breath to steel myself before I pulled on the bolt. It left the Ravager's chest with a sickening sound. Once it was out, I immediately dropped it to the ground, afraid that I might change my mind and follow through on my earlier thought of driving it through Jared's heart.

"How is she?" Henry asked, coming to stand beside me.

We both stared at the Ravager for a few seconds, waiting for her to stir.

When she didn't, I looked at Henry and said, "She needs blood."

"We all do," a voice uttered from the other side of the room.

I looked past Henry at Julia, who had rasped the words. She

was struggling to sit up on the table she was lying on, but her frail body kept giving out on her.

"We're leaving," I declared loud enough for everyone in the room to hear.

Julia's delicate face scrunched up in confusion. "We are too weak," she argued.

My shadows that were still churning by her table reached for her, but she recoiled from them.

"My magic will take us to a safe place," I explained.

"Last time, your magic almost killed us," she said low, not taking her eyes off the shadows.

Understanding dawned on me then. Of course she would have been terrified of my powers. I swallowed thickly and looked at Henry. He gave a small nod and faced the other three vampires.

"As difficult as it may be, you need to trust us. She is not the same Sophie who buried you under the mountain." He gestured at me. My eyes burned at his words, and I clenched my jaw to stop the tears from falling. He was right—I was not the same Sophie. Jared's still being alive was proof of that. "Let her magic take you to safety."

Julia looked at her mother, who was still lying on the table, too weak to get up, and her sister, who had made it to a seated position.

"We have no choice," the latter said.

Julia turned back to me. Her eyes were glistening with tears, and her fear was so potent, I could smell it even past the scent of blood that hung heavy in the air. When she nodded, I nodded back, willing my shadows to gently wrap around her. Their tendrils also enveloped Nova and Monique.

"I will carry her," Henry said, reaching for the Ravager. After he'd scooped her up into his arms, I placed my hands on both of them. "Are you going to be okay if you do this?" he asked.

I wasn't sure whether he meant the toll glimmering so many

at once would take on my body or the toll the black magic might take on my soul. Either way, it had to be done, regardless of the price I might have to pay.

"I'll be okay," I told him, hoping my words were true.

I couldn't fool him though.

"You don't have to do this. We can figure out another way—"

His eyes widened, and he sucked in a sharp breath when my magic poured out of me, molding to him and the Ravager. After I'd made sure that my shadows still had a hold on the other three vampires, I glanced at Jared, meeting his unseeing gaze for a second, before I glimmered everyone out.

15

When we appeared in Stern's lair, Henry swayed on his feet but didn't let go of the Ravager, who was still unconscious in his arms. While I steadied him, my shadows gently placed the other three vampires on the rough floor in the middle of the cave.

"I think I'm going to be sick," Monique rasped. She was sitting up but toppled over, bracing her hands on the ground for support. Her mother and sister groaned in response.

"It's just the effects of glimmering. They'll wear off soon," I explained, briefly glancing at them past Henry's large frame. "Are you okay?" I asked him next.

When he nodded, my gaze dropped to the Ravager. I didn't want to utter the next words, but as much as it pained me, they had to be said. "We need to chain her before she comes to."

A feeling of shame rose and spread, but I tamped it down. Henry bristled and took a step back from me, a look of betrayal on his face. He cradled the Ravager protectively to his chest, where the wound from the bolt was slowly healing since he was no longer being drained of blood. I could hear his pulse ratchet up in his veins. Reluctantly, he tore his gaze away from me and looked at the chains attached to the wall. The same chains that had bound him once before.

"I'm sorry," I whispered, "but you know it has to be done."

He looked back at me then, and his features crumpled. "Everything in me is screaming not to do it," he said hoarsely. His throat worked on a swallow before he continued, "But I know you're right."

"I'll do it," I offered softly, stepping closer to him.

He looked down at the Ravager, and his hold on her tightened as if he didn't want to let go. Slowly, I reached for the girl.

"It's only temporary," I said in what I hoped was a soothing voice. "Until we can bring her out of bloodlust."

Another swallow and a rough exhale followed before Henry surrendered the Ravager to me.

"Blood," came Nova's gravelly voice, dragging my attention to her. She was still lying on the ground, but her arm was outstretched, and she was pointing at the crate Henry and I had brought to the cave earlier.

"Give them some blood," I instructed Henry, trying to take his mind off what I was about to do.

He didn't move for a few seconds, his gaze fastened on the girl in my arms.

"Please," Nova begged, and that seemed to snap Henry out of his stupor.

As he stepped toward the crate, I walked to the wall with the chains. After laying the Ravager on the ground as gently as I could, I stayed on my haunches and reached for the metal cuffs attached to the chains. I quickly fastened them around the girl's wrists and ankles. My hands trembled slightly as I picked up the metal collar and brought it to her neck. I knew Henry was watching me—I could feel his gaze boring into my back.

It has to be done, I repeated the words in my head before quickly snapping the collar around the Ravager's neck. Swiftly rising to my full height, I backed away from her and turned around.

Henry was standing a few feet away, watching me warily. His lips were tinged with red, and he was holding an empty blood bag in one hand. He must have drained it in the short time I'd been binding the Ravager. My gaze flicked to the other three vampires. They were still working on their bags, but the blood was already helping. Monique and Julia were both sitting up. Nova still wasn't, but her heartbeat was stronger than before, and her breathing was less labored.

I suddenly remembered the wound in my own chest, and fiery pain pierced it at the thought, making me curl into myself with a low grunt.

"Here," Henry said, at my side in an instant. He offered me a blood bag, which I gladly accepted, quickly draining its contents. When it was empty, I let it drop to the ground with a soft thud and buried my head against his chest. He immediately wrapped his arms around me, gently rubbing my back. "Are you okay?" he asked in my ear.

"I am," I told him, taking a moment to catch my breath after everything we'd been through.

"Are you…you?" he whispered next.

I lifted my head and looked into his eyes. His gaze searched mine, as if he were trying to find the darkness there.

"I am," I assured him.

I felt like myself, and the shadows were gone by then. I wondered whether they would readily come back if I summoned them, but I was too exhausted to find out. My eyelids grew heavy, and I wanted to fall into a deep sleep in Henry's arms and sleep for hours while my body healed, but I couldn't rest just yet.

"I'm going to check on Waylon and the others," I told him, stepping out of his embrace.

"What?" His forehead creased. "Now?"

"Yes," I replied without hesitation. Something was pulling me to New Haven.

Hurry, a voice whispered in my head.

Henry must have read something on my face. "Is it the threads?" he asked, paling slightly.

"I'm not sure," I admitted. "I just know I need to check on them."

"I will go with you," he said with determination.

"No." I shook my head. "Bringing everyone here took a lot out of me. I'll just glimmer myself to New Haven. I'll be back before you know it. Besides, you need to stay and take care of them." I jerked my chin toward Nova and her daughters. "And her." I nodded toward the Ravager.

Henry seemed conflicted. His gaze stretched to the Ravager for a second before returning to me. If I knew the man I'd fallen in love with, he wouldn't leave the girl. His love for me blinded him sometimes, but I didn't think that, in that instance, it would overpower his innate sense of duty to help those who couldn't help themselves. His jaw flexed, and his features tautened, but a moment later, he confirmed I was right in my assumption.

"Don't take too long," he said before he leaned in and pressed his lips to mine.

"I'll return as soon as I can," I told him as I pulled away.

Hurry! The warning blared in my head.

I scowled, summoning my magic. Henry's features pinched, mirroring my expression, but then smoothed out when light poured out of me instead of the shadows. I felt relief too, though a tiny part of me missed the black magic—or rather, the potent power that came with it. Forcing a smile to put Henry at ease, I glimmered out, leaving Stern's lair.

16

HENRY

I hated being separated from Sophie, but the look on her face had told me that whatever she had sensed through the threads was urgent. Her gift of premonition was a blessing and a curse. On the one hand, I was grateful for it because we had known something had happened to Ezra. On the other hand, a part of me wished we were still blissfully unaware. I cursed under my breath at the thought. I was not a selfish person, but when it came to Sophie, I wanted to be. I wanted to forget the world around us. It could burn down for all I cared as long as I had her in my arms. It had taken everything in me not to abandon the Ravager and go to New Haven with her. But then I wouldn't have been the person she had fallen in love with. I wouldn't have been myself.

Dragging a hand down my face with a heavy sigh, I looked at the Ravager, who was still unconscious on the floor. When I'd first laid eyes on her in the cellar on the Laurent Estate, for a split second, I'd thought I was looking at my sister, Marcy. The girl wasn't her, of course, but she could have been with her golden curls. Right then, the Ravager's hair was caked with blood. She was in bad shape and needed to feed, but I had to be careful. Once she got blood in her and started healing, I had no doubt she would try to escape. I needed to regain my strength first so I could take her on when she came to.

Bone-deep exhaustion washed over me at the thought. I remembered how hard bringing Sophie out of bloodlust had been. The process had taken an immense physical and emotional toll. I feared it would be even worse trying to help the Ravager. When I had guided Sophie out of bloodlust, she had been a newly turned vampire. That poor girl had been lost in the bloodlust for weeks. I hoped some humanity still remained inside her. A mere drop would do. I just needed something to latch on to. If I could find the ember of who the Ravager used to be, I could try to make that fragment of humanity grow and eventually flourish. It wasn't going to be easy. I wished I had known the girl before she'd been turned because then I could have drawn from those memories, but since I couldn't... There was a chance I might not succeed, and then...

And then what? My heart dropped at the thought. *No.* I shook my head. Failure was not an option.

I reached inside the crate and retrieved four blood bags. When I went to toss three of them to Nova and her daughters, I realized they wouldn't catch them. The females were sitting huddled together, weeping quietly. I couldn't fathom everything they had been through. They'd witnessed Emeric's death and gotten buried under a mountain. Then they'd been dug up and immediately subjected to torture.

"Here." I lay the blood bags on the ground next to them.

"Where are we?" Monique asked as she wiped away her tears.

"We are on the Stern Estate, in the cave deep under the mansion. The clan doesn't reside here anymore; the human

Governess does," I explained as I ripped open my bag and drank its contents.

I wished Sophie had fed more before she'd left. As vampires, we could withstand a lot, but what Jared had put us through was one of the worst things I'd ever had to endure. And Sophie was overexerting herself by using her magic. I hoped she would be back soon to get more blood in her system. And if she wasn't, I would go to New Haven to find her.

"What happened while we were…gone?" Nova asked, pulling me from my thoughts. Tears were still streaming down her cheeks, and she didn't try to wipe them away.

"The world has changed" was all I said. "I will explain later, but right now we all need to clean up. I compelled the humans living here to leave, so the house is empty. We can shower and find some clean clothing upstairs. I'll show you the way up."

I suddenly realized that Sophie had left in tattered clothes and barefoot. I should have insisted she stay and clean up before she'd glimmered out.

"What about her?" Julia asked through her tears, casting a glance at the Ravager.

Taken aback, I stared at her for a moment. I'd always liked the female because she had a gentle spirit that reminded me of Rory. Judging by the notes of concern in her voice when she'd asked about the Ravager, what Sophie had put her through hadn't changed that.

"I will try to bring her out of bloodlust," I replied.

"I can help," Julia offered after a beat of hesitation.

Nova and Monique both whipped their heads to look at her in dismay.

"You can't stay here," Nova said, her brown eyes blazing. "Have you forgotten what Sophie did to us? We need to clean up and get as far away from this place as possible before she comes back."

I inwardly winced at her words. It pained me to hear her talk about my wife like that, but I couldn't run away from the past. I knew she wasn't a monster, and that was all that mattered.

"She is different now," Julia countered, looking at me for confirmation. When I nodded, she continued, "What she did was wrong, yes. She almost killed us, but then she saved us from the humans." Nova and Monique exchanged a glance. "You can leave whenever you're ready," she forged on. "But I will stay and help Henry with the Ravager."

"You have always been too soft for your own good," Monique remarked, shaking her head in disapproval.

"And you have always been too cruel," Julia retorted. "Perhaps if, as a species, we had behaved differently in the past, we wouldn't have ended up where we are today—hunted by the humans."

Nova shuddered at her words. "Where can we go so they can't find us?" she asked me, her voice sharp with panic. Her eyes filled with the shadows of the recent terrible events she had lived through.

I heaved a heavy sigh. "I don't know. I wouldn't return to your own region since that's where their base of operations is located. I'm not sure if there are other groups like theirs who have made it their mission to eradicate the vampires. Keeping a low profile is key to our survival now."

"We can do that," Monique said to Nova, rubbing her mother's arm to comfort her. "That was our way of life before the Red War."

"The humans didn't know about us before the Red War, so blending in was easier," Nova pointed out. "The world truly has changed, hasn't it?" She looked at me.

I nodded absentmindedly, lost in thought. Before the Red War, the humans hadn't known the vampires existed. Even when they had noticed our cold, flawless beauty or the preternatural way in which we moved, they'd had no explanation, only the eerie sense that something was off. Since they had learned about us, we were much easier to spot…to hunt, if they wanted to hunt us. My mind went back to Jared and his men. We would have to do something about them. But what, I had no idea. Because we knew they presented a threat, we couldn't let them roam free, but I didn't want to slaughter them either.

One thing at a time, I told myself before my racing thoughts consumed me.

We would help the Ravager, find the one who'd attacked Ezra, and then deal with Jared and his men. Suddenly, the two weeks Sophie and I had spent at the cottage seemed like a distant memory. With all the things pressing down on me, I could have thought I'd dreamed our honeymoon. But it had been real, and one day we would return to it. I had to believe that, if only not to succumb to the dreadful weight of the situation we were in.

"We should probably head upstairs now," Julia said, dragging my attention to her. "I don't want to leave the girl unattended for too long."

My gaze snapped to the Ravager. She looked harmless at the moment, but once she came to, she would be wild and vicious. I was wary about Julia helping me but also grateful that she had offered her assistance. Perhaps I could leave her to keep an eye on the girl while I went to check on Sophie.

"Very well," I said, turning toward the shadowy exit that led out of the cave and up to the study. "Follow me."

SOPHIE

I should have found a new pair of boots, I thought as my bare feet hit the wooden slats of the front porch at Waylon's place. *And a new tunic.* I looked down at my chest.

At least my breasts weren't visible through the tear on the front—only the pink skin where the wound had barely just closed. Despite having gotten blood in me, I still felt drained and weak, which made me wonder whether using my magic so much was depleting my resources. I would check in with Waylon, tell him about Jared, and glimmer back to Stern's lair to feed more and help Henry with the Ravager. Hopefully, Nova and the others would be gone by then so I wouldn't have to face them again. A part of me was glad the threads had called out to me when they had, giving me the excuse to leave in a hurry. Running from difficult things wasn't in my nature, but I didn't have it in me to ask Nova and her daughters for forgiveness. I hoped that my saving them from Jared would begin to make reparations for what I'd done, for the suffering I'd inflicted on them.

Pulling myself out of my thoughts, I knocked on Waylon's door. While I waited, I retrieved the Tear and my locket from my pants pocket and hung them around my neck. The amulet pulsed on my chest, bathing the space before me in a pale-blue glow. Soft footsteps sounded inside the house, and Amelie opened the door a moment later.

"Sophie? You're back!" The witch's face lit up for a second until she noticed my battered state. Her eyes widened in shock as she gasped. "What happened? Are you okay? Where is Henry?" Her frantic gaze searched the space all around me.

"I'm okay, and Henry's okay," I quickly assured her.

"Thank the gods," she breathed, sagging against the door with relief. "Please come in. You can clean up and borrow some clothes...and shoes. I have another pair in here somewhere."

Before I could reply, she turned away from the door and walked deeper into the house, expecting me to follow.

"Are you sure you're okay?" She glanced at me over her shoulder as she headed toward Waylon's bedroom. "I still have the ingredients I used to make the salve for Ezra's shoulder. Do you need me to make that for you? Are you hurt?"

"I'm not hurt, just exhausted. Where is Waylon?" I asked, trudging after her.

"He was patrolling last night with Isabelle and Wren. I expect him back at any moment."

Amelie walked into the bedroom, stopping before the dresser. She pulled open the top drawer and rummaged around until she retrieved a green tunic and black pants.

"Here, you can change into these. I think the shoes are in the living room. I'll be right back."

She swept from the room, and by the time she returned, I'd changed into the clean clothes, using my vampire speed. "Here." She handed me a pair of black flats.

"Thank you." I offered a weak smile as I slipped on the shoes. "You must stay here often if you have your own drawer."

"I do." Amelie's cheeks turned pink. "Waylon and I have been spending a lot of time together, which is exciting but kind of scary at the same time."

"I'm glad to hear that," I told her as my smile grew. "And I think it's supposed to be both scary and exciting." I nudged her with my shoulder.

Amelie giggled at my words, but then her face turned serious. "Can you tell me what happened? Or do you want to wait until Waylon gets home?"

A ragged exhale left me as I felt my exhaustion settle heavier over me. "We found the Ravager. Henry is with her now at the Stern Estate in the Southern region."

"Is that who hurt you? The Ravager?" Amelie glanced at the pile of my bloodied clothes on the floor.

"No." I shook my head. "When we found the Ravager, she was being held captive by the retired guards from the border."

"What?" Amelie's eyes widened.

"They also had three other vampires, and they captured Henry and me, but I was able to get everyone out using my magic...my black magic."

Amelie's eyes grew wider as she took a step back. Her power spilled into the air between us, as did the smell of her fear. I wasn't sure whether she was getting ready to fight me or glimmer out.

"Don't!" I nearly raised my hands to placate her but then realized she might take it as a threat, so I kept my arms at my sides. "You don't need to be afraid of me. The shadows are gone." *For now.*

Amelie swallowed and took a breath, her magic slowly receding. "I thought you overcame the darkness," she said low.

"I did. I locked it away, but it's still inside me. It's...stronger than my light magic. And easier to bring forth."

The witch seemed to think it over. "When I was first learning my powers, my mother would always say 'The path to destruction is always easier than the path to creation.' Black magic destroys; white magic creates. It's easier to access shadows than the light. Dark magic wants to be used. It hungers for your soul. It tempts and seduces. Light magic takes work and effort. Every time, it's a choice."

"Even for you?" I asked her, angling my head.

"For all of us. But for you, the choice is harder because of how close you have come to embracing the darkness. Some things… Once you let them out, you can't lock them away, not completely. Once the barrier has been shattered, you can't make it whole. Even if you put it back together, tiny cracks still remain."

My skin chilled at her words as I thought about my obsidian door. "Is there anything I can do to strengthen that barrier?" I asked in a hushed voice.

"You can keep working on your light magic. You should resume your training with Celeste."

Celeste cannot be trusted. The words skimmed my mind. I frowned, unsure whether the world or the darkness trying to corrupt me had whispered them to me.

Hurry! Another warning sounded in my head. It was loud and clear, reminding me of why I had left Henry and gone to New Haven in the first place.

"I have to go," I said urgently.

"Where? Waylon should be back shortly."

"Wren's place." The words escaped as I summoned my magic. "Something is coming."

I glimmered in just as Isabelle's scream pierced the night. She was slumped on the ground in front of the house, clutching Wren's limp body in her arms. He was badly injured—much worse than Ezra had been. Chunks of his flesh were missing as if whatever had gotten a hold of him had tried to eat him alive. The smell of blood coated the air so thickly, I could taste it on my tongue.

"What happened?!" I dropped to my knees before Isabelle.

"It was a fucking wolf!" she screamed, her wild eyes filling with tears.

A wolf?! My nostrils flared as I tried to pick up on the beast's scent. I still smelled nothing. It would make sense that it was a wolf. It hadn't dawned on me until then that I'd never been able to smell wolves in the woods.

"Did you see where it went?" I asked Isabelle urgently. The attack had just happened, so the beast couldn't have made it far.

"East, toward the Black Forest," she rasped as her tears spilled, gliding down her cheeks and landing on Wren in her arms.

"I'll be back!" I threw over my shoulder, sprinting away.

There was no time to waste if I hoped to catch up to the wolf. I could have glimmered, but I didn't want to overestimate the distance between us. My heart pounding, I flew through the streets of New Haven, quickly approaching the border. That was when I saw it. Slick black fur nearly blended in with the night as the wolf raced toward the stone wall that separated New Haven from the Black Forest. Its hulking muscles rippled and bunched, and dirt flew from where it was heaving up the earth with enormous clawed paws. I doubled my efforts, gaining on the creature. It must have sensed my approach because it cast a glance at me over one massive shoulder. Wren's blood dripped from its muzzle as it bared its teeth before turning away to face forward.

It leaped over the border wall, landing with a thud on the other side.

I followed after it, launching myself through the air. My feet hit the ground softly on the other side of the barrier as I landed in a crouch before breaking into a sprint again. My breathing became labored as I ran, and my muscles burned from overexertion—an alarming reminder that I hadn't fed enough earlier. I couldn't stop at that point though. Not when I was so close to catching the thing that had been terrorizing New Haven at night.

Why had the wolf been on the prowl in the city? Was it just a coincidence that it had attacked the people I knew?

Questions invaded my mind, one after another, but I pushed them aside. I wouldn't get answers from the mindless beast, but I still had to catch it so that I could kill it, making my city safe again.

The woods rushed by as I ran, getting closer and closer to the wolf that seemed to be slowing down. Perhaps it was getting overexerted too, which was a good sign. I hoped that would give me an advantage in the fight that was coming—the fight that was already here—I realized as the beast skidded to a halt and whirled around to meet me head-on. Panic briefly flared at the unexpected maneuver, but I quickly squelched it. Without slowing down, I bared my fangs and unsheathed my claws. The sound of our collision echoed in the heart of the forest as I barreled into the wolf. We landed on the ground and rolled as I slashed with my claws and tore with my teeth.

The wolf roared but seemed to be holding back for some reason. It wasn't fighting with the viciousness I had anticipated. It was avoiding me, jumping out of the way when I lashed out. I realized too late it was waiting for me to tire myself out. When I inevitably did, the wolf threw all its might into an attack and, with a loud growl that shook the trees, brought me down to the ground, closing its maw around my throat. I couldn't suppress the panic that time when it rose, swiftly sweeping me under. My gaze locked with the glowing red eye of the wolf. A sudden realization dawned on me then. I'd fought that creature in those woods before. I'd prevailed back then but spared its life.

Would the wolf remember the mercy I'd shown it? I doubted it would as I prepared to be torn to shreds. A vampire could survive a lot, but I knew I wouldn't come back from an assault from the beast. Choking on despair, I reached inside me for my powers, but my resources were depleted. Even my shadows didn't stir. Why did I feel so drained? In the past, when I'd used black magic, I'd felt limitless. Did I have to embrace the shadows lurking within fully to wield them without restraints? I didn't get a chance to find out, as the wolf jerked its head and a deafening crack sounded before everything went black.

17

I quickly showered and got dressed in black breeches and a white shirt I had found in the master bedroom of the estate. Thankfully, the Governess's husband was a large man, so the clothing fit me fairly well. I even found some boots that were close to my size. They were snug around my calves but would have to do until I could retrieve my clothes from the cottage in Santoria.

Julia hadn't had similar luck with finding clothing that fit. The tunic and pants hung loosely on her thin frame when I met her in the study.

"Where are the others?" I asked, strolling to the bookshelf to open the entrance to the passage that led down to the cave.

"Resting," she replied, wringing her hands nervously. "They refuse to leave until I can come with them."

"You don't have to do this," I told her as the bookshelf slid to the side. I wanted to give her a way out—she was clearly uneasy about what we were about to do.

"No, I want to help," she said with determination, dropping her hands and squaring her shoulders.

I waited another moment to make sure she wouldn't change her mind before I gestured to the shadowy entrance. "After you."

We began our descent in silence, but Julia soon broke it. "We didn't know," she said so quietly I thought I had only imagined her speaking.

"What?"

"We didn't know that they had you," she said louder.

My chest constricted, and it took everything in my power not to lose my footing on the scuffed stone steps.

"We didn't learn that they'd kept you captive until after Sophie had rescued you and set out on her quest for revenge," Julia continued.

The rough walls of the narrow passage were pressing in on me, but I pushed back, refusing to succumb to the terrible memories. I wondered whether Julia was telling me all that then because I was walking behind her and she couldn't look me in the eye.

"Emeric told us they'd kept you below the Stern Estate," she forged on. Her voice sounded strained, as if she was getting choked up. "And now you're back here...I don't know how you do it—"

"It's in the past," I cut her off.

I couldn't continue with the conversation. My resolve to bring the Ravager out of bloodlust became stronger even than before. I would help the girl and turn Stern's lair into a place of hope and humanity rather than one of anguish and despair.

"The last thing I will say is...I'm sorry," Julia uttered as we walked into the cave. She halted and faced me then, her eyes glittering with tears.

"It's in the past," I repeated, stopping before her. My tone was softer that time. "I'm working on leaving what I went through behind me. My only hope is that you will eventually be able to put what Sophie did behind you too."

Julia nodded just as the sound of metal scraping the ground came from behind her. My gaze stretched past her to the Ravager.

"She's stirring," I said low.

"Do you think the chains will hold?" Julia asked, glancing behind her shoulder.

"They should. They used to hold Stern's Ravagers...and then me."

Julia whipped her head back toward me, but I ignored the look of pity on her face. What I'd endured didn't matter anymore as I became solely focused on the Ravager.

"Hand me a bag of blood for her, please," I asked Julia as I walked closer to the wall with the chains.

Dropping down to my haunches, I examined the girl on the floor. The savage wound in her chest, visible through her tattered clothing, was still open and raw, but her heart was beating stronger than before. She was healing, only very slowly—as much as her battered body allowed without blood.

"Here," Julia said as she approached.

I grabbed the blood bag from her hand and turned back to the Ravager. My gaze darted to the metal cuffs on the girl's wrists and then her ankles. I hated seeing her chained up like that, but keeping her restrained until she regained enough humanity not to act like a wild animal was necessary. When my gaze snapped to the collar around the girl's neck, I swallowed hard, feeling as if the metal band was biting into my own throat. With a ragged exhale, I reached out and gently brushed the matted blonde hair away from the girl's face. She couldn't have been more than sixteen, and I was suddenly overcome with emotion. So young... She didn't deserve anything that had happened to her.

With another heavy sigh, I ripped open the bag with my teeth and brought it to the Ravager's lips, cradling the back of her head with my other hand. For a moment, the blood only pooled in her mouth, but then she swallowed a few gulps, and her eyes snapped open, black and unseeing. She gripped my forearm, her sharp claws piercing my flesh. I heard Julia gasp from behind me. With a low curse, I clasped the back of the girl's neck in an attempt to hold her in place as I poured more blood down her throat. She bucked and began thrashing, splattering crimson everywhere. Yanking her claws out of my forearm, she went to jam them in my neck. My arm shot out to stop her just as she jerked her head up, ripping herself out of my hold. With a snarl, she went for my throat, her mouth stretching wide.

"Henry!" Julia warned in a raised voice.

"I know!" I growled, swiftly wrapping my hands around the girl's neck. When I twisted it, a sickening crack echoed through the cave before everything went quiet.

I closed my eyes and shook my head, taking a moment to calm my nerves before I stood up to my full height.

"Are you okay?" Julia asked, eyeing my shredded forearm.

"Yes," I assured her. The lacerations were already closing.

I looked down at the Ravager, hoping I had gotten enough blood into her to kick-start the healing process. Relief washed over me when I saw that the wound in her chest was growing smaller.

"Now what?" Julia asked, her gaze also on the girl.

"Now we wait until she comes to and try again," I told her, my throat tight.

"I'd like to clean her up and get her into some fresh clothes."

"Not now. We wait until she is more lucid."

Suddenly, the air next to Julia began to shimmer. A breath of relief almost escaped me—Sophie was back. Except a few seconds later, when the distorted silhouette had fully materialized, it wasn't Sophie standing before me—it was Amelie. My heart dropped like a dead weight to the pit of my stomach.

"What's wrong?!" I demanded.

The witch looked ashen as she stared at me with wide eyes. "I need to take you back to New Haven" was all she said.

My gaze darted to Julia.

"Go!" she urged. "I will take care of the girl."

With a nod, I stepped closer to Amelie and grabbed her delicate hands. I hardly noticed the pins and needles sensation of glimmering that time. All I could focus on was the feeling of dread and terrible foreboding. I might have forgotten how to breathe as my thoughts raced, jumping all over the place. As soon as the brief darkness I'd been thrust into had receded and colors returned, I let go of Amelie's hands and whirled around. I found myself in Wren's house, in his kitchen.

"What happened?!" I spun back around to face the witch.

"Henry," came Waylon's voice from the entrance to the kitchen. "There's been another attack."

"Sophie?" I asked him, panic ringing in my voice.

"No. Wren. He's in the bedroom. Isabelle's with him."

I strode past Waylon, my heavy footsteps the only sound in the eerily silent place. The smell of Wren's blood was permeating the air. It was overwhelming but laced with the fainter scent of Isabelle's essence. When I barged into the bedroom, I found Wren unconscious on the bed with Isabelle by his side. I quickly assessed the situation. Wren's body was mutilated, his pulse barely there. Two puncture wounds were marking one side of his neck. His heart was sputtering but getting stronger with each beat…because it was pumping Isabelle's blood through his veins.

"You turned him," I breathed as disbelief surged through me.

"I had no choice. He was dying," my sister said, lifting her red-rimmed eyes to meet my gaze. "It was a wolf, Henry. A fucking wolf from the Black Forest."

My heart lurched in my chest as I rasped, "Where is my wife?"

"She went after it—Henry!"

But I was already gone, dashing through the streets of New

Haven, chasing Sophie's lush floral scent all the way to the border with the Black Forest and then past it. Somewhere in those dark and twisted woods, the other half of my heart was, and I hoped it was still beating.

18

SOPHIE

My limbs felt laden and my eyes seemed to be glued shut as I slowly came to. The sensations reminded me of what I'd experienced in the cellar on the Laurent Estate, and for a second, fear that I was back in that place, bound to the wooden table, spiked. But not everything was the same as the last time—I was lying on my side, not on my back, and my wrists and ankles were free. My body still felt broken and beaten, though, as it had back then. A few more seconds passed before memories rushed in—glowing red eyes, glistening sharp teeth, jaws around my throat…

My eyes snapped open as I bolted upright, my breaths coming in short, rapid pants. Panic flooded me as I froze in the seated position. The wolf was right in front of me. Only a short distance separated us, and I felt paralyzed by fear, trying not to make any sudden movements. I tracked the beast as it paced left to right, its claws clicking on the wooden floor.

The wooden floor?

I didn't want to take my eyes off the wolf, expecting it to attack the second I did, but I needed to take a survey of my surroundings. Clenching my teeth, I forced my gaze away from the beast and quickly looked around. Broken windows, dilapidated walls, rotted floorboards... I knew that place—it was the same structure I'd stayed at when I'd trained myself to use my powers. We were still in the Black Forest, and, judging by the light that was filtering through the gaps in the decayed wall slats, it was early morning. The wolf and I were in the most shadowed part of the house, where the sunlight didn't reach.

Had the wolf brought me there to shelter me from the sun? Perplexed, I returned my gaze to the creature. It stopped pacing and stared back. Then it began to transform. The sound of bones cracking echoed in the empty space as the wolf's body structure changed. Its torso and front and hind legs elongated, while its snout broke down and shortened. The wolf shifted from its crouch to a standing position as its fur receded, revealing pale, smooth skin. The metamorphosis lasted for only a few seconds, and when it was complete, a naked man was towering over me. He was massive, watching me warily through a curtain of long jet-black hair. His eyes were no longer crimson but silver, glowing like two moons.

"What in the actual fuck?" I whispered, forcing myself to my feet. Immediately lightheaded, I braced my hand on the wall.

"She's injured," the man whispered harshly, as if to himself. "I knew I was too rough with her."

Who is he talking to?

"I need to explain... I know!" he growled, jerking his head to the side.

I cast a glance around the house, even though I already knew it was empty. When I looked back at the man, his eerie silver eyes were focused on me.

"I can explain," he ground out. It seemed speaking was a struggle for him.

"Okay…" I dragged the word out, wanting to make sure the man was actually talking to me. "Who are you?" I paused. "*What are you?*"

"I'm a wolf…and a human," he replied, his voice guttural.

I could see fangs peeking through his lips as he talked, and his fingers still ended in pointed claws, though they were much shorter than the ones he'd had in his wolf form.

"How is this possible?" I asked. I found I didn't feel dumbfounded, not truly. After all, I was a vampire and a witch, so it wasn't that shocking to encounter another creature that had duality inside it.

The man swallowed, his throat bobbing, as he prepared to speak again. "My people…shifters…roamed these woods alongside the White Witches. We had a village, families"—he paused, his gaze growing distant for a moment before it refocused on me —"but then the Dark Witches took over the forest, and we became…stuck in our wolf form. Or at least that's what I think happened. Regaining memories has been…difficult."

They had lived alongside the White Witches? I wondered why Celeste had never mentioned them. Had she chosen not to reveal that the downfall of the White Witches had resulted in such terrible consequences as trapping shifters in their wolf form?

"You don't remember anything from after the Dark Witches took over?" I felt a pang in my chest because if that was true, that man had been lost for the past hundred years.

"I only have fragments of memories from when I was in my wolf form, and I'm not sure I want to remember…"

"Do you remember your name?"

The sheet of hair shifted as the man gave a small nod. "My name is Volker."

"What am I doing here, Volker? And why did you attack my friends?" I demanded, wincing as soon as the words had escaped.

The wolf was less terrifying in that form, but I couldn't forget the beast that prowled underneath. Besides, the look in those silver eyes made my scalp prickle with unease. There was a feverish sheen to the man's gaze one moment, but then it was gone the next. I wondered how much humanity Volker had truly regained after a century of being in the wolf skin.

"Your smell led me to them. I was trying to find you. I…am not always in control," Volker said.

So it was my fault Ezra and Wren had suffered. My heart squeezed in my chest.

"Why were you looking for me?" I asked sternly. I wanted to know more before I decided how to react to what I'd just learned.

"Tell her…tell her you need help," he muttered, looking off to the side.

He wasn't speaking to me again, and I wondered whether he was talking to the wolf within. Were there truly two personalities inside him, or had the past hundred years warped his mind, making him believe there were? Had he been trapped in his mind for so long that he'd had to invent someone in his head to talk to so he didn't go completely insane?

"I need your help," Volker said, snapping me out of my thoughts. "You…you showed me mercy before…in the woods, and the witch… Tell her about the witch…" I was losing him again.

"The witch?" I raised my voice to keep him focused.

"Yes, the old one with white hair…"

"Celeste?"

"Yes…yes…she controls me…"

"She…*controls* you?" I repeated his words back to him, angling my head.

"Yes…she's planning something—"

A roar of fury thundered through the space, silencing him. My heart soared in my chest—Henry had come for me. Volker was standing in front of me one moment but gone the next because Henry had rushed him from the side, propelling him to the opposite wall. They both crashed into it with a deafening sound.

"Henry, stop!" I shouted as he began pummeling Volker.

The man didn't stay in his human form for long. He shifted, and Henry cursed, jumping away from him, his eyes wide and his chest heaving.

"Henry, let me explain—"

The wolf's vicious snarl drowned out my words as the animal squared off against Henry, crouching low and baring its teeth. Human Volker was gone, overtaken by the beast. The next second, the creature charged Henry, and they became a blur of snapping teeth and gleaming claws. I wanted to tell Henry to stop and listen to me, but I didn't dare distract him from the battle and make him vulnerable. When it came to Volker, I doubted there was any getting through to him at that point.

My chest tight, I watched the two of them fight. I wanted to break them up, but I felt weak, swaying on my feet. My body ached, and it felt as though the blood were drying in my veins. I needed to feed. When my vision began to swim from the condition I was in, I leaned against the wall and took a deep breath, trying to bring the world back into focus. I succeeded just in time to see Henry twist the wolf in his powerful hold, breaking its ribs, before he tossed it to the side. The wolf whimpered when it landed in a heap on the floor. It quickly scrambled to all fours and darted out of the house, leaving a trail of blood behind.

Henry stood in the middle of the room, breathing heavily, his dark gaze fastened on me. His eyes were still black and wild, and I wondered whether he was having trouble with reigning in the inner beast he'd had to set free to fight Volker.

"Henry—" I started.

"Don't!" he growled.

In the blink of an eye, he closed the distance between us and braced his forearms on the wall, caging me in. "Drink from me," he ordered as he leaned in and turned his head to the side, exposing his neck.

The smell of his blood from the countless cuts and scratches he'd suffered during the fight enveloped me. It was interlaced with the fresh and woodsy scent of him, which always drove me wild.

My lips parted as I recalled the taste of his blood on my tongue. His essence wouldn't provide as much nutrition as human blood would, but to me, it was the sweetest drug. Unable to resist the urge any longer, I sank my teeth into his neck, opening up the artery close to his throat. His blood poured into my mouth, and I was gone, lost in the taste and in him.

A soft moan escaped as I melted into him, my hands fisting his shirt. Henry cursed and brought his body flush with mine, pushing me more firmly against the wall. The longer my mouth stayed sealed to his neck, the heavier his breathing became, his pulse ratcheting up. His blood didn't replenish my depleted resources, but it took the edge off. It took away the pain and replaced it with something else. Pleasure began coursing through my veins. I felt Henry's arousal pressing into me, and a rush of liquid heat pooled between my thighs. I went to hook one leg over his hip to push him even closer to me, but before I could, he tore himself out of my hold and backed away.

"Enough!" he growled, his chest rising and falling heavily. "I'm taking you back to New Haven."

His eyes were still dark, but the feral gleam in them was mixed with potent lust, and another wave of arousal rolled through me as our gazes locked and held.

"Is that really what you want to do right now?" I asked, seductively licking his blood off my lips.

His hungry gaze dropped to my mouth before he forced it back up. "What I really want to do is punish you for being so reckless," he growled.

His deep, rough voice sent a shiver across my sensitive skin. If the words were meant to intimidate me, they had a totally different effect.

"You can punish me right now, if you want," I purred, my voice low and husky.

Henry's eyes flashed, and his muscles coiled as if it were taking everything in his power to stay rooted in place instead of pouncing on me. "It's not funny, Sophie! You could have died! I should punish you by not giving you what you so desperately want right now," came another growl.

He wasn't wrong. I *was* desperate for him, and I needed to make him as desperate for me if I hoped to get what I wanted.

Leaning my head against the wall, I watched him from beneath my lashes as I lifted my hands to my neck before slowly gliding them down my body, over my tunic.

"Sophie…" Henry warned when my hands dove under my shirt.

He seemed to have stopped breathing as he watched me brush my fingers across my stomach before trailing them lower, under the band of my pants.

My other hand drifted up to my breast, and Henry's lips parted, revealing his fangs. His hands twitched as if he wanted to reach for me.

"Stop," he rasped. "We're leaving."

"Why don't you make me?" I challenged, slipping my hand between my legs.

My back arched off the wall when my fingers found the sensitive bundle of nerves. I felt high on Henry's blood, and every part of me was hyperaware, every touch sending a surge of lightning through me. If my own caress felt so good, I could only imagine what Henry's touch would do to me.

"Stop," Henry repeated, his words low and thick.

A breathy moan was my only reply as I tugged on my nipple while teasing myself between my thighs.

"Stop," Henry whispered as he stepped toward me. "Or else—"

"What?" I breathed.

"I won't be gentle," he ground out.

Good. I didn't want him to be gentle. There was a primal part of him that liked to play rough, and the rare occasions when he let himself succumb to it thrilled me more than I was willing to admit.

"Last chance," he warned as he ducked his chin and began prowling toward me.

The dark promise in his voice only spurred me on, and I held his gaze the entire time as I continued building my pleasure. When he finally reached me, he immediately grabbed my wrist and yanked my hand out of my pants. He also reached under my tunic and got a hold of that wrist.

Flipping me around, he clasped both wrists behind my back, holding them with one hand as he wrapped his fingers around my throat. "I want to deny you so badly," he growled in my ear.

But he won't, I thought. *He won't be able to resist me.*

Arching my back, I ground my ass against the rigid length that was straining through his pants. A half moan, half growl was my reward as he gave a little thrust. Arousal pounded in my core at his proximity.

"If you deny me," I rasped, "you'll be denying yourself too."

Henry whimpered against my temple as his hand on my throat slid up to my chin. When he dragged his thumb across my lips, I captured it with my teeth and bit down, drawing blood. His breathing hitched as I sucked long and hard.

"*Fuck,*" he groaned, and in that moment, I knew that I'd won.

He freed his thumb from my mouth and released my wrists before clasping the back of my neck to bend me over. With a snarl of impatience, he shoved down my pants and thrust in, as deep as he could go. My body was ready for him, and I cried out as a wave of intense pleasure rippled through me. He stretched me in the most decadent way, slamming into me with fast, powerful thrusts. The Tear and my locket thumped against my chest, the amulet painting the wall before me in a faint blue glow. Releasing the back of my neck, he gripped my thighs with both hands to hold me in place. His fingers dug into my flesh to the point of pain, but I didn't feel it, too focused on the feeling of him moving inside me. Bracing my hands on the wall, I arched my back and took each punishing thrust, moaning as the pleasure climbed higher and higher.

"Bite me," I rasped when I felt myself teetering on the edge. I knew that the pleasure-pain of his bite would tip me right over.

With a snarl, Henry fisted his hand in my hair and tugged, bringing my back flush with his chest. I gasped at the feeling of fullness, my body wound up like a bowstring. At any second, he would sink his fangs into my neck. I trembled, preparing to drown in ecstasy, but the bite never came.

"You would like that, wouldn't you?" he growled in my ear instead as his thrusts slowed.

He was still punishing me, I realized, by denying me release.

"Please. I need it," I begged, trying to move faster on him, chasing my pleasure.

"You know what I need? You," he whispered harshly as he released my hair. His hand dove between my thighs, where he began teasing me mercilessly. "You destroy me in the most beautiful way," he added low, raw emotion dripping from every word.

My eyes pricked with tears, and I wasn't sure whether it was because of what Henry had said or because of how desperately I wanted to come. Bending down, I braced my hands on the wall again as I began rocking against him, impaling myself harder on him with each plunge. Henry cursed but picked up speed as he wrapped one arm around my waist. When my inner muscles began to quiver around him, he bent over me, bracing his hand next to mine on the wall. I felt his breath on my neck a second before he struck. A throaty shout tore from my lips as pleasure crested and spilled, radiating through my entire body. Henry's thrusts became erratic, and a few seconds later, he roared his own pleasure as his body bucked against mine. My legs gave out, but he held me up and turned us around. The wall groaned when he leaned against it, and I sagged against him, letting my head fall on his chest.

"Don't ever do that to me again," Henry said after we'd caught our breaths. He grabbed my left hand and held it up. "You see these rings? They are a symbol of our union. Together for all eternity."

I stared at the golden bands, once again marveling at the fact that he was mine. "They are a symbol." I agreed. "A symbol that we are a team. We're partners, and partners trust each other."

"I do trust you," he said vehemently. "I just don't trust the world not to take you from me. You shouldn't have gone after the wolf alone."

With a soft sigh, I threaded my fingers through his and lowered our joint hands. "He's not a wolf but a man. Well, he's both—"

"A shifter," Henry interjected.

I turned my head to look up at him. "You know about them?" I asked, my brows raised.

He gave a small nod. "I had never encountered one until today, but Vincent spoke of them sometimes. No one knew what happened to them when the Dark Witches took over the Black Forest. They just…disappeared. After the White Witches revealed themselves, I had a thought that perhaps the shifters had also been in hiding."

"They weren't. They were trapped in their wolf form."

"For a century? What a terrible fate."

"Volker said he didn't remember much."

"Volker?"

I nodded. "The wolf you fought. He wasn't going to kill me—"

"He hurt our friends!" Henry exclaimed.

"First, I didn't think I'd ever hear you call Wren your friend," I attempted to joke to lighten the mood. Henry just stared at me, unamused. "Volker said he can't always control the beast within… We both know what that's like," I added in a serious tone. "He said he needs my help. He said…" My brows knitted. "He said Celeste is controlling him."

"What?" Henry's scowl matched my own.

"I don't know what he meant or if it's even true. The man might not be stuck in his wolf form anymore, but he's still very much lost."

"We will deal with it after we deal with everything else," Henry said with a rough exhale. He didn't sound angry, only tired. So, so tired.

"Everything else?" I asked, stepping away from him.

He straightened from the wall and helped me pull up my pants and smooth out my tunic. He then pulled up his breeches and ran a hand through his tousled hair. "Isabelle turned Wren," he said in a strained voice.

My heart dropped because that could have meant only one thing—Wren had come very close to dying. Fury splashed my vision red for a moment as I considered making Volker pay. But I tamped it down, reminding myself that he had not been in control.

"How do you feel about it?" I asked Henry, even though I already knew the answer.

He gave me a pained look. "You know I wouldn't wish this life on anyone, but Isabelle wasn't ready to lose him."

"She loves him," I said, trying to reconcile my own emotions.

Isabelle and Wren were in love, and while I would never condone someone wanting to become a vampire, I couldn't think of a better outcome for them because then they could be together forever. The circumstances under which she'd had to turn him were horrible, but he'd been toying with the idea anyway, so it wasn't entirely against his will. Of course, turning him had been the easy part.

"You need to help Isabelle with guiding Wren through the change," I voiced something Henry undoubtedly already knew.

"I know." He dragged a hand over his face. "And then I need to return to Stern's lair and help that Ravager."

"How is she doing? Did you leave her alone when you came after me?"

"Julia is with her. She volunteered to help."

"Julia?" My eyebrows shot up.

"Yes. She has been the most reasonable of them all. She doesn't hold what you did against you."

Just like I couldn't hold what Volker had done against him.

"So we have time to check on Wren first?"

"We do. Can you walk, or do you want me to carry you?"

"I can walk. I'd offer to glimmer us there, but I think using my magic is more taxing when I'm injured."

"I shouldn't have let you go," Henry said, shaking his head.

"No! No." I stepped up to him and cupped his face. "I'm glad that you did. At least now we know who attacked Ezra and Wren."

"We just don't know why," he pointed out.

I swallowed. "He said he was looking for me. My scent led him to them."

"Why you?" Henry frowned.

"Because I'd encountered him in his wolf form before. While you were...gone. He attacked me while I was in the Black Forest, and we fought, but I spared his life."

"So now he wants your help with what exactly?"

"I don't know, but we will find out after we help Isabelle and the Ravager."

Henry leaned in and rested his forehead on mine. "Just don't run off again, okay? Whatever we need to do, we do it together."

"Okay," I said, though I wasn't sure I would be able to keep that promise.

CELESTE

"Where have you been? Why are you injured?" My voice rang out in the clearing.

My body was standing before the rock formation my eyes had seen for the very first time a little over two weeks earlier. Volker, the wolf shifter, was lying on the ground in front of it. He was in his human form and wounded.

"What happened to you?" I heard myself ask.

I had known about shifters all my life, but they had been trapped in their wolf form the entire time, ever since the Dark Witches had established dominion in the Black Forest. After Sophie had banished the darkness, the woods had begun to restore as the influence of the black magic had subsided. Its hold on the shifters had lifted, and they had started to transform back into their human form. Volker had been the first, but what had greeted him when he'd returned to his human self was not glorious freedom from the darkness. He had barely taken a breath of his new life when Damien had swooped in and ensnared him in the web of black magic. Drawing from the abundant well of my powers, he had combined them with his, subduing the shifter and binding him to his will. I couldn't have helped Volker as he had fought against the bindings of Damien's magic; my body had been nothing more than a conduit. When two more shifters had changed back into their human forms, they, too, had become bound to the demon because Volker had turned out to be the wolves' alpha.

"I got into a fight with another wolf," Volker finally answered Damien's question. He lifted up from the ground on his elbow, breathing raggedly. "I'll heal soon."

"Another wolf?" Damien demanded.

"Yes. I left the den earlier to roam the woods."

"What?! I didn't order you to do that!" Damien seethed.

"I know, but you want more of us. I was trying to find others like me to see if I can help them shift back somehow. As you can see, I succeeded at finding another shifter but failed at getting through to him. I want to try again."

No! What is he doing?!

I felt my lips spread in a sinister smile. "Yesss," Damien hissed through me. "That's an excellent plan, and truly, I won't be able to hide you much longer. Soon, we will tell the White Witches that the wolves are shifting back. Celeste will be a helpful little witch and aid them with acclimating to their new life." Damien lifted my hand to my face, rubbing my chin in contemplation.

Volker was watching me with bleary eyes. Could he tell that not everything was as it seemed? Was he questioning why I was talking about myself in the third person? Probably not... After all, the shifter often talked to himself, or rather, someone else I couldn't see.

"You shouldn't have left the den without my permission." My voice was stern as Damien uttered the words.

"It won't happen again," Volker said weakly.

"Oh, I will make sure of it," Damien promised darkly as he tightened the harness of his black magic on the shifter.

Volker's eyes blazed with hatred as they locked with mine. The message in them was clear—"You will pay for my suffering if I'm ever free from your oppression."

He grunted in pain as the weight of Damien's powers pushed him lower to the ground. My heart bled for him because even though he didn't have a demon inside him, his body and mind were still not his own. And I found myself wishing he would somehow find a way to break free because then he would kill me, putting me out of my misery.

19

———

When I rapped my knuckles on the bedroom door and walked in, Isabelle was perched on the chair by Wren's bedside, watching him with unwavering focus.

"How is Sophie?" she asked without looking at me.

"She is doing well. She's sleeping." After we had returned from the Black Forest, Sophie had consumed some blood from Isabelle's supply, showered, and lain down on the sofa in the living room. "Thank you for letting her borrow your clothes."

"Of course. I'm sorry none of Wren's clothes fit you."

"It's okay," I replied as I approached the bed.

"And you? You don't need to rest?" Isabelle asked.

"I'm okay," I lied, looking down at Wren. The truth was I could have used some sleep, but I knew it wouldn't come even if I tried. "How is he doing?"

Wren's heartbeat was strong, his breathing even. His skin still looked sun-kissed but had a faint pale undertone, and his blond hair gleamed brighter in the light of the lamp. There was no mistaking the transformation that was taking place.

"He's…changing," Isabelle said as she rose to her feet and stepped closer to where I was standing.

She reached for Wren's face and gently pulled back his upper lip. My heart turned over when I saw that his canines had elongated into fangs.

"It won't be long now," I said, my chest tight. My gaze shot to the bedroom window hidden behind the closed curtains. The city of New Haven lay beyond. A city full of people… "There is still time to take him to Stern's lair, where he will be better contained." I looked at Isabelle. "I can wake Sophie and see if she is strong enough to glimmer him—"

"No," she cut me off. "We're not going to chain him next to the Ravager you're keeping there."

"Isabelle—"

"You didn't chain Sophie when you turned her," she pointed out.

The look on her face told me she would not be swayed. There was also vulnerability in her expression—emotions she hardly ever let others, including me, glean.

"You're right. I shouldn't have suggested it," I conceded with a heavy sigh. "How are you holding up?"

Her face crumpled as her shoulders sagged. Dejection rolled off her in waves. I hated seeing her like that.

"I'm scared," she admitted low.

"I will help you guide him out of bloodlust," I reassured her.

"I know. That's not what I mean." She met my gaze. Silence stretched for a few seconds as she chewed on her bottom lip. "Before I turned him, I was scared that I would have to watch him wither and die of old age," she finally continued. "Now I'm scared he's going to leave me once he acclimates to his new life."

"Leave you?" I didn't try to hide the shock in my voice. "Isabelle, he is desperately in love with you. Everyone can see it."

"For now, he is. We have eternity ahead of us. What if he grows tired of me?" She paused. "What if *I* grow tired of *him*?" Her voice dropped to a hushed whisper, as if she were ashamed to utter the last part.

I chuckled softly and shook my head.

"Don't laugh at me," she said indignantly, lifting her chin.

I tried to smooth out my expression, but a small smile still remained. "I just don't think that's something you need to worry about," I said simply.

"I suppose I can ask you the same thing I asked Sophie before... How do you know?" Isabelle challenged. "How do *I* know?"

Her big brown eyes were on me, and she seemed to be holding her breath, waiting for my answer. I was curious about Sophie's response to the question, but I knew that moment was not the time to ask Isabelle what she'd said. My sister was looking for reassurance from me. What I said clearly mattered greatly to her.

"I think there is no secret formula when it comes to matters of the heart," I said, my expression turning serious. "We often wait for this...grand feeling. For nothing short of a sign from the gods themselves that we have found our person. But in reality, it is much simpler than that. Sure, you want passion, love, and connection, but most importantly, I think it's about finding someone who makes you feel...safe."

Isabelle gave me a skeptical look. "Sophie makes you feel safe?" Disbelief laced every word.

"She does. Because I know that no matter what happens, no matter what the world throws at us, she will always choose me."

"She didn't choose you over the darkness," Isabelle blurted out. Her eyes widened when she realized what she'd said. "I'm sorry—that was crass."

"It's okay." I cleared my throat, absentmindedly rubbing the spot on my chest where phantom pain still lingered. "She almost killed me, yes, but that was when she realized the darkness was consuming her. Almost killing me is what brought her back. So, in the end, she still chose me. Because this is what it's all about. You find someone you love, and you choose them every day, every hour, every minute, and every second. Even on the days when doing so seems difficult or nearly impossible."

The sound of Sophie's footsteps announced her arrival a moment before she walked in. When our gazes met, her eyes were misted over, letting me know she'd overheard the conversation. She didn't say anything as she approached and wrapped her arms around me.

"I love you," she whispered against my chest.

"I love you too," I told her, holding her tight.

"How is he doing?" she asked as she pulled away.

"The transformation is almost complete. I expect he will wake soon. I would prefer that we weren't in the middle of the city"—Isabelle threw me a scathing look—"but between the three of us, we should be able to handle him when he comes to."

"Before he left, Waylon offered to gather his men and set up a perimeter around the house, but I insisted against it. Now I'm wondering if I should have taken him up on the offer," Sophie said contemplatively.

"No, I'm glad you sent him and Amelie away. I wouldn't want anything to happen to them if something went wrong."

"We just have to make sure nothing goes wrong. Do we have everything we need?" Sophie asked, reaching up to tie her hair at the nape of her neck.

She was wearing a plain cotton dress, black leggings, and flats —all courtesy of Isabelle. My sister was garbed in similar attire. I quickly looked down at myself, wishing I could have gotten out of those clothes and showered, but that would have to wait.

"All we need is the blood." I jerked my chin toward the crate by the chair Isabelle had occupied earlier.

It didn't look like my sister was going to return to her seat anytime soon. She began pacing the room, filling it with palpable unease.

"I heard you talking to Waylon earlier about what happened in the mountains. About the guard he knows."

We had told Waylon about Jared. He hadn't been entirely shocked by the news, as he'd suspected the former guards might seek vengeance. He hadn't volunteered to do anything about the men, and I didn't blame him. I didn't think there was anything Waylon could do to convince his former brothers-in-arms to give up their mission.

"We will deal with Jared and his men after we help Wren and the Ravager," I told her.

"And the wolf? You never told me what happened," Isabelle continued. "You were both quite shaken up when you arrived, so I didn't want to ask any questions, but now I want to know. Did you kill it?"

Sophie and I exchanged a glance, and I gave a barely there shake of my head. That was not the time to tell Isabelle about Volker.

"Let's get through this first. Then we'll tell you what happened," Sophie said.

My sister stopped her pacing and scowled, her gaze darting between Sophie and me. It was obvious she wanted to press for answers.

"The lamp might be too bright when he comes to," Sophie said in an attempt to bring Isabelle's attention back to Wren. She left my side to walk to the window. "Let's turn it off and open the curtains instead. It's a full moon tonight, so we should have plenty of light."

With a nod, I reached for the lamp and tugged on the chain switch at the same time Sophie pulled open the curtains. Soft silvery moonlight spilled through the window, bathing her silhouette in an ethereal glow. I was instantly captivated, watching her as she turned around and walked back to me, her face illuminated by the glow of the Tear on her chest. She grabbed my hand as soon as she reached me, threading her fingers through mine. I gave it a comforting squeeze and refocused on Wren. Sophie was watching him too, from beside me. Isabelle moved to stand on the other side of the bed, opposite us. A moment later, she leaned in and pressed a kiss on Wren's cheek.

"I choose you," she whispered. "I will always choose you. Now, just come back to me."

My chest constricted as her vow reminded me of the one I'd made to Sophie before I'd turned her. *I will not give up on you,* I had told her then.

Isabelle hadn't uttered the same words, but the promise was the same—I would carry you through the river of bloodlust and pull you out before you drowned. I knew what Wren meant to her, and for her sake, I hoped she would get to keep her promise, but the truth was Wren's future was uncertain. Isabelle would fight for him, and I would help her, but in the end, Wren would have to fight for his own humanity. All my sister could do was throw him the rope. It would be up to him to grab on to it and pull himself up out of the deep red waters.

Time seemed to grow taut as the three of us waited for Wren to wake up. Minutes ticked by as his chest rose and fell evenly, his heart beating at a steady rhythm. Still, I knew it was coming... My muscles coiled tighter and tighter with each passing moment, and I released Sophie's hand to avoid squeezing it too hard. It was as if the predator inside me sensed another wild creature in the room.

Any second now, I thought, my gaze glued to Wren as the moonlight sluiced over his features. It was a strange mix of anticipation and dread. I wasn't excited about what was coming and what we would have to do, but I was ready to get it over with and put it behind us.

Wren's condition changed in a lightning-fast second. His

heartbeat accelerated just as his breathing hitched before it resumed, the air leaving his lungs in harsh, rapid pants. He broke out in a sweat, and his nails turned into claws at his fingertips. I squared my shoulders and stepped back with my right foot, ready to tackle him when he fully came to. Though I had known that moment would come, I still felt unprepared. Sophie was the only vampire I had ever turned, so it was only my second time doing that. And the stakes were much higher because Sophie and Isabelle were in the room.

"Get ready," I ordered, not taking my eyes off Wren.

In my peripheral vision, I saw Sophie assume a stance similar to mine. Isabelle stilled where she was standing opposite me on the other side of the bed. All our attention zeroed in on Wren, and a heartbeat later, he woke up. When his eyes snapped open, they weren't pitch-black with hunger as I had expected—they were crimson and glowing. I heard Sophie's sharp inhale just as Isabelle stumbled back from the bed.

"Those eyes." Sophie's words barely registered a second before my world exploded into chaos.

Wren shot off the bed—straight up in the air—before landing back on all fours. His body began to break, a sickening sound of shattering bones filling the room. I had seen that before—earlier in the Black Forest. Wren's limbs shortened while his hands and feet lengthened, and his nose and jaw elongated into a snout. His muscle mass growing, he tripled in size as russet fur flowed from his skin, covering him from head to toe in a matter of seconds.

"He's...a wolf," Isabelle breathed.

Wren whirled on her, crouching on the bed. His hackles raised, he let out a vicious growl before he pounced. I moved then, wrapping my arms around his torso to hold him back. He was strong—much stronger than the wolf I had fought in the woods—and I wondered whether it was due to the added vampire strength. If he had our species's strength, he should have also had our healing abilities. I should have been able to break his neck to render him unconscious, but I couldn't be sure he'd come back from that. Isabelle would never forgive me if I accidentally killed him. My mind raced as Wren thrashed in my hold, his snapping maw inches away from Isabelle's face.

I had to do something, so I went to twist my arms to break his ribs, but Isabelle exclaimed, "Don't hurt him!"

I hesitated, and the momentary distraction cost me. Wren whipped his head and sank his teeth into my forearm. My hold on him loosened just a fraction, but that was enough for the beast to break free. He leaped to the window and then through it, crashing through the glass.

"I'm going after him!" Isabelle shouted as she spun around.

"Don't!" I lunged for her, but she was already gone.

"He's a shifter…like Volker," Sophie muttered under her breath. When I looked at her, her face was scrunched up in thought as she tried to piece it together. "Ezra was also attacked by Volker… What if he also transforms…" Our gazes locked, and I saw the exact moment she realized that those close to Ezra might have been in danger. "My father!"

"Wait!" I went to grab her, but my hand closed around thin air as she glimmered out.

With a curse, I whipped my head toward the window, then back to where Sophie had just been standing. Should I go after my sister or my wife? My mind made up, I darted to the door.

SOPHIE

Wren's crimson eyes were seared in my mind as I glimmered. The eyes of a beast...of a killer. It had taken too long for me to figure it out. I prayed it wasn't too late. A tiny part of me still hoped I was wrong, though I knew I wasn't. As soon as I'd seen Wren transform, I'd known in my bones I was right.

My childhood home was dark when I appeared in the small living room. I could see clearly because of my heightened senses, but I still couldn't comprehend the scene before me at first. My father was on his back on the floor, and a massive wolf was hovering over him. The moonlight drifting through the window glanced off the glossy mahogany fur as the beast lifted its head from my father's limp form. Blood dripped from its mouth, and my gaze followed the fat red droplets all the way down...to where they landed on my father's ravaged neck. My heart stuttered and stopped. All sounds ceased, and my surroundings receded into pitch-black as my vision zeroed in on my father's torn throat. I felt myself growing smaller in size, the walls of the house closing in on me, until I was a little girl. I wasn't a grown woman anymore—I was a child, and I was lost. I wasn't a powerful supernatural creature—I was weak and oh-so human.

A blood-curdling growl penetrated the strange state I was in. My sense of self-preservation screamed out a warning—the wolf was about to pounce. I couldn't bring myself to care. I couldn't force my locked muscles to move. The next thing I knew, the wolf was on me, knocking me off my feet. It buried me under its weight and clamped its mouth on my right shoulder before shaking me like a rag doll. Fiery pain erupted, and it felt like my right arm was going to get ripped off, but the anguish barely registered. My senses felt muted, as if I were submerged underwater.

Fight back! my vampire part demanded, rearing her head.

Use your magic! my witch part urged me.

What's the point? the little human girl inside me wept.

I was sinking deeper and deeper in the dark waters of despair, the world on the surface drifting farther and farther away, until a thundering roar shook me, bringing me more to my senses.

When the pain in my shoulder stopped abruptly and the weight of the wolf lifted off me, I managed to roll to my side... just in time to see Henry break the wolf's neck. The loud crack echoed through the house before an eerie silence settled over the place.

"Are you okay?" Henry asked, dropping to his knees by my side.

I managed a nod as he bit into his wrist and brought it to my lips. Clasping my left hand around it, I began drinking, not really tasting the blood. My gaze was trained on the wolf, which was lying in a heap behind Henry, directly in my line of sight. The beast wasn't breathing, and when I strained my ears, I detected no heartbeat. The residual pain in my shoulder lessened more and more the longer I drank from Henry. My eyes stayed on the wolf, and after a few minutes, the beast began to transform. Henry bristled at the sound of bones breaking and reshaping and looked behind his shoulder. The wolf was still dead—there was no doubt about it—only…when the metamorphosis was complete, it wasn't a wolf that was dead, it was Ezra. He was lying on his stomach, naked, his neck twisted at an unnatural angle.

Henry seemed to have stopped breathing as he stared at the boy who was prostrate on the floor. I stopped drinking and lowered his wrist from my lips. I'd known the wolf was Ezra all along, but somehow, having the confirmation still shocked me. Henry scrambled to the boy and pressed his bloody wrist to his parted lips. I knew he wouldn't drink. Henry knew it too, but he still held the wrist to Ezra's mouth for another moment longer. When he finally gave up, his shoulders slumped, and he buried his face in his hands. I couldn't let him bear the crushing weight of the situation alone. I wanted to go to him, so I braced my right hand on the floor and pushed myself up to a seated position.

Henry lifted his head from his hands. His panicked gaze met mine for a second before it darted to his left. I followed it to the other body in the room—my father's. A choked sound left me as I doubled over, clutching my chest. It felt like my heart was being ripped out of my rib cage. Henry rushed to my father's side and bit into his wrist again to replace the previous incisions that had already sealed. He pressed his bleeding wrist to my father's mouth. What was he doing? Surely, he knew there were no signs of life. The excruciating pain in my chest became unbearable, and I sank to the hard floor again as a ragged sob escaped. Two strong but gentle arms scooped me up a moment later.

"I've got you," Henry whispered near my temple, cradling me to his chest. His voice sounded all wrong as anguish bled from every word.

An unpleasant tingling sensation swept through me, prickling my skin. It almost felt like glimmering, only it wasn't my magic breaking my body into hundreds of pieces. It was grief, as I was falling apart in Henry's arms, his tight embrace the only thing holding me together.

HENRY

My world was in shambles. Sophie was crumbling in my arms, and I felt my stoic facade shudder as the gravity of our situation crashed into me.

When she had disappeared from Wren's house, I'd known exactly where she'd gone. I'd figured she had reached the same conclusion I had—that her father, Thomas, was in grave danger. Wren, who had been attacked by the wolf, had turned into a wolf himself, and Ezra had also suffered Volker's claws.

I should have been better prepared. I should have kept my inner monster at bay, but when I had barged into Thomas's house and found Sophie on the ground with a wolf towering over her, the beast inside me had become unhinged. My vision had turned red, and I had drowned in rage. My body had moved of its own accord as I had hauled the wolf off Sophie and thrown it to the side.

Kill the beast—protect what's mine! the monster inside me had snarled as I'd jumped on the wolf and clasped its massive head with my hands. When I'd jerked it to the side, breaking the wolf's neck, the primal part of me had let out a triumphant roar.

"Are you okay?" I'd asked Sophie, dropping to my knees by her side.

She'd been injured, so I'd bitten into my wrist to give her my blood. As she'd sealed her lips around the bite marks and begun taking long, staggering draws, the crimson tint clouding my vision had started to recede. It had dissipated completely when I'd heard the sound of breaking bones. The same sound I'd heard at Wren's place only a few minutes before. Sophie had stopped drinking and released my wrist, staring at the wolf behind me. I had turned my head toward it as well.

The more the wolf had changed, the more the pressure on my chest had intensified. By the time the transformation had completed, my lungs had felt crushed, and I hadn't been able to breathe. Ezra had been lying before me on the floor. I'd known it all along, but seeing him had been a shock to my senses. I'd scrambled to him and pressed my wrist to his lips even though I'd known it was futile. When he hadn't moved or made a sound, I'd buried my face in my hands.

What have I done?!

"What have you done?!" Rory's face appeared in my mind. I'd failed her and then her brother.

When Sophie had moved to come to me, my gaze had snapped to hers, and I'd realized there was one more body in the room—her father's. I'd rushed to his side and torn open my wrist again before pressing it to his lips. Like Ezra, Thomas hadn't moved or swallowed the blood that had pooled in his mouth. A keening noise had torn from Sophie then. A noise that had carved out my insides. I'd been by her side in an instant, holding her as she'd begun falling apart.

"Henry?" Her gentle voice pulled me back to the present.

I blinked a few times and focused on her. Her gaunt face was right in front of me, her red-rimmed eyes fastened on mine. When had she gotten out of my arms?

"We need to get moving," she said, her voice cold and detached.

What?

"Are you okay?" I asked, even though I knew she was anything but.

She swallowed hard before replying, "Far from it, but I'm choosing to process everything later. I can't break down right now like I want to…like I need to… We need to go to Waylon and tell him what happened."

I glanced at Ezra's still form to my left, then past Sophie, at Thomas's body.

"Waylon can take care of the…bodies," Sophie said.

I refocused on her. A part of me wanted to scoop her back into my arms to shelter her from what had happened. But another part of me sensed that was not what she needed at the moment. She was choosing to grieve later, and who was I to take that choice away from her?

A part of me knew that I wanted her back in my arms so that I could hold on to her too…hold on to the humanity inside me that she had fallen in love with. I shoved that selfish part of me down. She wanted me to be strong, and I would always give her what she wanted.

"Okay," I rasped past the lump in my throat. "We'll go to Waylon and then find Isabelle."

With a nod, Sophie rose to her feet, pulling me up with her. "I can glimmer us there."

"Are you sure?" I quickly scanned her from head to toe. The minor cuts and scrapes had already healed. Her shoulder, shredded by the wolf's teeth, had stitched itself together, but I knew she still needed blood—human blood—to get back to full strength.

"Yes, I'm sure. I don't want to waste any time."

I decided not to fight her on that. Truth be told, I didn't want to run to Waylon's place because that would mean spending a few minutes of silence with my thoughts. So I took her hands, ready to leave Thomas's house. I knew I wouldn't be able to leave what had transpired behind. The image of Ezra's broken body would be imprinted in my mind for years to come. The faces of my parents and my sister, whom I'd slaughtered over a hundred years before, had only recently stopped haunting me, and tonight, I had replaced them with a new ghost. I swore I felt Ezra's spirit settle over my shoulders like a dead weight. The weight I took with me when Sophie glimmered us out.

. . .

"What are you two doing here?!" Waylon exclaimed as he barged into the living room a few seconds after we had appeared there.

He must have been asleep until his well-honed fighter senses had alerted him that someone was in the house. His chest rising and falling sharply, he lowered the short sword he had brought with him from the bedroom. I could smell the adrenaline pumping through his veins.

"My father and Ezra are dead," Sophie said simply as she released my hands and faced the guard.

Her voice didn't waver when she uttered the words, but her shoulders slumped ever so slightly. I didn't doubt that she had brought her own weight from her childhood home. Knowing Sophie, she probably blamed herself for her father's death—perhaps even Ezra's too—feeling like she could have done something to prevent it. Gods, I wanted to shelter her from all of that, to carry the burden for both of us.

"What?" Waylon asked as he paled.

At that moment, the bedroom door creaked, and Amelie crept into the living room. "I'm going to turn on the light," she warned softly before she flipped the switch. She then joined Waylon's side, clasping his left arm. "What happened?" she asked in that gentle manner of hers.

"Wren turned but not into what we had expected," I said, deciding to take the brunt of what Sophie and I had to reveal. I stepped closer to her and placed my hand on her lower back. Wren and Amelie waited with bated breath for me to continue, their racing heartbeats the loudest sounds in the quiet room. "When he came to, he morphed into a wolf, much like the one that had attacked him."

"A wolf?!" Waylon exclaimed at the same time Amelie breathed, "A shifter?"

"You know about them?" Sophie asked the girl.

"I've heard legends from before my time."

"The legends are very much real," Sophie said, her voice hollow.

"Where is Wren now?! Did he…did he kill Thomas and Ezra?!" Waylon demanded, raising the short sword in the air as if preparing to fight. It seemed he wasn't aware that he had done so until Amelie gently pressed on his arm, prompting him to lower the weapon.

Sophie's back grew rigid against my hand, and I swore I could hear her teeth grinding from how hard she was clenching her jaw.

"Wren is on the loose," I said. "Isabelle went after him. He didn't kill Thomas… Ezra did, when he turned into a wolf himself." All the air seemed to have left my lungs by the time I finished rushing through the explanation.

"Gods." Waylon dropped the sword and dragged his hand down his face. "What happened to Ezra?"

I froze, my fingers spasming on Sophie's back, fisting the fabric of her dress.

"He attacked me, and Henry killed him to save my life," she replied.

But that wasn't the truth, was it? The truth was I had lost control. I should have found another way to immobilize Ezra. I hadn't had to kill him.

"Gods," Waylon repeated.

Amelie stood unmoving by his side, her wide eyes staring into the space before her until she snapped out of it. "You've both been through a lot. Do you need anything? I can make a salve for your shoulder, Sophie. Do you need a change of clothes?" the young witch started muttering, clearly not coping well with the news.

It suddenly hit me that she might have grown close to Ezra. Would she loathe me because I had killed him? Even if she did, she couldn't loathe me any more than I already loathed myself.

"The only thing I need is for you to take care of the bodies," Sophie said, looking at Waylon. "We left them in my father's home."

"Of course. I'll arrange a funeral," he replied in a strained voice.

"Thank you. We are going to find Isabelle and Wren."

Waylon nodded. "Let me know if you need anything else."

Without saying another word, Sophie turned to me and clasped my forearms. I glanced behind her at Amelie and found the girl watching me with a look of utter pity in her eyes. I barely felt the pull of Sophie's magic as my body turned cold and numb a moment before we disappeared.

21

I had to keep moving to escape the grief. I feared that if I stopped for only a moment and dipped even one toe into its viscous black waters, it would drag me under and swallow me whole. So I took Henry and myself back to Wren's house, where we drank some blood to regain our strength. I cleaned up and changed, borrowing more of Isabelle's clothes—a short maroon dress and black leggings. Henry was still wearing the same blood-covered shirt and pants. I needed to take him to our cottage soon so he could shower and get fresh clothing. Doing so would have to wait, though, because the dawn was near. We needed to find Isabelle and Wren and take them somewhere to shelter from the rising sun.

"We can't track Wren in his wolf form, but we can track Isabelle's scent," Henry said when we found ourselves back in Wren's bedroom.

I suppressed a shudder as I glanced around the room. It was that place where everything had gone terribly wrong. That moment in time had set off the chain of horrible events that had followed. I didn't often wish that my magic could turn back time, but right then, there was very little I wouldn't have given for that ability.

With a ragged exhale, I reached behind my head and quickly braided my hair, tying the ends with the black ribbon I'd found on Isabelle's vanity. Henry waited silently until I was done. Despite having just fed, he looked exhausted, his mouth wan and his eyes dull. I had the urge to reach for him, to wrap my arms around him, but I fought it. For I knew if I did, the wall I had created in my mind to keep the grief away would crumble, leaving me defenseless against the onslaught of emotions.

"Ready?" I asked instead.

When he nodded, I turned toward the window, or rather what was left of it after Wren had barreled through it in his wolf form. Inhaling deeply, I picked out Isabelle's citrusy smell. Henry did the same, and a second later, we were dashing through New Haven, tracking the scent all the way to the Black Forest. We stopped running once we'd broken through the tree line and began walking instead. The forest creatures skulked and slithered in the shadows around us but didn't approach.

"Why do you think the scent leads here?" I asked quietly. "Do you think Wren was trying to find Volker?"

"I don't know," Henry replied equally as quietly as he stepped over the gnarled roots that were protruding from the ground. "I'm just relieved he didn't make any stops before he left New Haven. At least no innocent people got hurt, or so it seems."

I also felt relief with that knowledge. Because if Wren had attacked someone else, his victim would have turned into a wolf as well. My brows knitted as something occurred to me. Ezra had been attacked two days before... Why had he not turned until tonight? What had triggered the change? I replayed the events of the night in my head as we walked, following Isabelle's scent. Wren had been asleep, going through the transformation into a vampire, until…until we had turned off the lamp and I had opened the curtains. I stopped abruptly and lifted my gaze to look at the moon.

"What is it?" Henry asked, stopping beside me.

"Wren didn't shift until I opened the curtains. Do you think the moonlight triggered the change?"

"Maybe," he replied, looking up at the night sky. "It's also a full moon tonight."

As soon as he'd uttered the words, a loud howl tore through the woods. Henry and I exchanged a quick glance and darted toward where the sound had come from. Isabelle's scent led in the same direction. It didn't take long for us to reach the clearing, where she was squared off against the giant russet wolf with glowing red eyes. The beast was crouched down, emitting a low growl, its hackles raised. Isabelle was standing a few feet away, her knees bent slightly as she leaned forward, one arm outstretched toward the wolf. Judging by her tattered clothes, they had already exchanged a few blows.

"Please," she begged. "I'm not going to hurt you."

When she took a step closer, the wolf snapped its teeth at her. Then it noticed us and snarled in our direction. Isabelle glanced over her shoulder.

"I'm bringing him home," she declared into the night. Her voice shook, and her eyes glistened with tears.

"All *I* am worried about is bringing *you* home," Henry said firmly. "It's nearly dawn. You need to find shelter."

"What about Wren?" Isabelle asked, facing the wolf again. "He's a wolf, but he's also a vampire. What will happen to him when the sun rises?"

I looked at Henry for answers I knew he didn't have. He didn't know whether Wren would survive being in the sunlight, but when it came to saving Wren or his sister, he would choose Isabelle. Henry's hard eyes were full of resolve when he met my gaze.

"Get ready to grab her and glimmer out," he said so low, I practically had to read his lips.

I gave a slight nod to let him know that I'd heard him. I didn't want to leave Wren to an uncertain fate, but I also couldn't blame Henry for wanting to ensure that his sister was safe. Softly, I stepped closer to Isabelle, lifting my hand to reach for her.

"Wren, please. Let me take you home." She broke down in tears.

When she took another step toward the wolf, Henry warned, "Isabelle…"

"I won't leave him!" she shouted over her shoulder.

My skin pricked as I felt the break of dawn in the air. I glanced at the rapidly lightening sky—we were out of time.

"You won't get a choice," Henry growled, lunging for his sister.

I went to grab her at the same time, just as the wolf launched itself at her. We all converged on Isabelle, and I summoned my magic—my black magic—to glimmer all of us out. A moment later, the four of us landed in a heap on the stone floor in Stern's lair.

"What the fuck?!" Julia exclaimed, jumping out of the way as we rolled.

Henry was the first one to get back on his feet. He tackled the wolf, and a loud crack echoed through the cave as he broke its hind legs. The beast—Wren—roared in pain.

"Help me chain him up!" Henry yelled at Julia, jarring her into action.

She grabbed the chains that were attached to the wall not far from the restrained Ravager. Of course Stern would have had more than one set of chains. I just hadn't noticed them before because I'd been focused on only the ones that had bound Henry. The wolf whimpered in Henry's hold as he dragged it to the wall, and Julia snapped the metal cuffs around all four of its legs.

Henry reached for the collar but quickly gave up on the idea, as the wolf's neck was too thick.

"Don't hurt him," Isabelle rasped as she scrambled to her feet. Her hair disheveled and her eyes wild, she rushed to the wall, dropping to her knees before the wolf. The beast thrashed in the chains, but its attempt to get out was short-lived as it collapsed on the floor, panting loudly. "Shh," Isabelle crooned, setting her hand on the ground between them. The crimson glow in the wolf's eyes dimmed just a fraction.

"Sophie, are you okay?" Henry asked, snapping my attention to him.

I realized I was still sitting on the floor, surrounded by my shadows. The shadows only I could see, it seemed, because Henry didn't recoil from me. The expression on his face was not one of alarm but one of concern as he offered his hand to help me up to my feet. Even if he couldn't see the shadows, he must have known I'd used black magic to glimmer us there. I expected him to bring it up, but he didn't. Instead, he faced the wall where the Ravager and the wolf were chained a few feet away from each other.

"How is she doing?" he asked Julia, who was standing nearby.

"I haven't been able to get through to her, but she has stopped trying to rip herself out of the chains, and it's been a couple of hours since I've had to break her neck to render her unconscious." The female shrugged. "Can someone explain why you brought a wolf with you?" she asked, looking between Henry and me.

"It isn't just any wolf" was all Henry said as he stepped closer to the Ravager. "What is your name?" he asked the girl, dropping to his haunches in front of her.

The Ravager sat catatonic, staring at him with bottomless black eyes.

"Perhaps if we suggested some names, she'd recognize one of them?" I offered, coming to stand behind Henry.

"That could work," Julia agreed. "Figuring out her name could be the first step to bringing her back." She cocked her head to the side as she studied the girl. "You look like a Chloe to me."

"Or a Gabrielle?" I prompted.

The girl hugged her knees to her chest and began rocking back and forth as we kept throwing out different names.

"Marcy?" Julia said out of nowhere.

Henry's shoulders tensed at the sound of his late sister's name. The Ravager stopped rocking and turned her head to look at Julia.

"Your name is Marcy?" Henry asked, disbelief coloring his voice.

When the girl fixed her gaze on him, a soft exhale left him.

"Hi Marcy, I'm Henry," he said. "This is Sophie"—he gestured to me, then to the other female—"and Julia."

The Ravager's gaze dropped to his mouth while he talked, and her brows pulled together as if she were trying to decipher what he was saying. Her lips began moving as if she were trying to articulate the words.

Is he getting through to her? I found myself leaning forward, eager to hear the Ravager speak.

A loud groan of pain interrupted the girl's concentration, and she hissed at the wolf who had made the noise. My gaze darted to Wren. He was changing back into his human form. *Not human,* I mentally corrected myself. *It's his vampire form.* I was relieved to find that the legs Henry had broken were already healing. So he was truly a wolf and a vampire, which meant he wouldn't be able to walk under the sun. It also meant...

22

"He needs blood," Henry said, rising to his full height. He walked over to the crate and retrieved a bag before handing it to Isabelle. "I wouldn't get too close," he cautioned, but she didn't heed his warning. After she'd accepted the blood, she scooped Wren off the floor, cradling his naked form to her chest. He moaned, and I suddenly remembered what I had gone through when I'd first turned. It wasn't just bloodlust raging in his veins.

"Maybe it's a good idea to give them some privacy," I suggested, looking at Henry.

He dragged a hand through his hair as he turned to face me. "How would we accomplish that with the Ravager chained up right next to him?" he asked.

I swallowed, knowing I needed to handle the situation delicately. "Perhaps we could remove the chains binding Wren, and Isabelle could take him to one of the bedrooms upstairs."

"No," Henry interjected. "What if he shifts again?"

I glanced at Wren in Isabelle's arms. His eyes were closed, but his hands were roaming over her body. Once he came to, things between them could get intense very quickly.

"I think the risk of that happening is low. If we believe it's moonlight that triggers the change, then we should be in the clear until sundown."

A muscle flexed in Henry's jaw as he glanced over his shoulder at Wren, whose seeking mouth was on Isabelle's neck. While he still wasn't fully awake, certain parts of him definitely were.

"Please, Henry, let me take care of him," Isabelle begged.

Henry cursed but gave in. His sculpted muscles rippled and flexed as he pulled his shirt over his head. I glanced at Julia as jealousy spiked at her seeing him shirtless.

He's mine! the territorial creature inside me growled, and I had to fight the urge to flash my fangs.

But the female wasn't looking at Henry. Her gaze was glued to Wren. "Fascinating. I would love to hear the explanation for all of this," she said as Henry used his shirt to cover Wren up and helped Isabelle to free him from the chains.

"It will have to wait," he replied, scooping Wren's limp body in his arms. "I'm going to get him upstairs, and then I need to shower and change. I'm afraid I need your help again with keeping an eye on the girl." He nodded toward the Ravager, who was watching the exchange with a wary expression. She looked like a wild animal caught in a snare.

"Of course. I will try to clean her up too now that she seems more lucid."

"Thank you," Henry said warmly before he strode past Julia toward the exit, which led to the study upstairs.

Isabelle trailed behind him, the unopened blood bag in her hand.

"Wren's going to need more than that," I pointed out, walking to the crate.

When I bent down to pick it up, I heard Julia say, "Please, leave a few for the girl."

My shoulders tensed at the sound of her voice. I suddenly

couldn't stand the female. So, without looking at her, I took a few bags out and dropped them on the floor.

Henry, who had halted by the exit, gave me a nod of appreciation when I approached with the crate. He stepped into the narrow passage, illuminated by the ascending row of torches on the wall, and began climbing the scuffed steps, having to turn almost sideways to accommodate Wren in his arms. Isabelle silently followed, her gaze never swaying from Wren's form. I stepped into the passage behind her, and a few minutes later, the three of us made it to the entrance to the study. Henry kept walking, but Isabelle stopped for a second, waiting for me to fall in step next to her.

"What happened after I went after Wren?" she asked, briefly glancing at me. My throat closed up as my chest constricted. The crate creaked as my hold on it tightened. "It took you a while to find me," she went on. "And I detect Ezra's scent on Henry, and your father's…"

"They're both dead," I forced the words out.

Isabelle drew up short at the same time Henry stopped a few feet ahead of us.

"Not now," he said over his shoulder. "We need to get Wren situated before he fully wakes."

The three of us resumed walking, taking the stairs to the second story of the mansion, where the bedrooms were located.

"Sophie and I will take the master bedroom. You and Wren will stay in the room next to ours," Henry said, stopping by one of the doors.

Isabelle nodded and reached for the handle to let us into the room. Henry deposited Wren on the bed while I set the crate on the floor beside it. Wren groaned, his back arching off the mattress as the scent of his arousal permeated the air.

"You should leave," Isabelle urged, but Henry hesitated.

"Perhaps I should stay."

Isabelle's gaze darted to me. Her eyes were pleading.

"Darling," I said gently as I placed my hand on Henry's arm. "You need to shower and get some rest." He looked conflicted when he met my gaze. "They're in the room right next to ours. We'll be able to hear if Isabelle needs help."

We'll be able to hear other things too, I thought but didn't say. I would just have to work extra hard on toning down my heightened senses for the time being.

Henry hesitated another moment longer before he let out a heavy sigh. "If things get out of control—" he started.

"I will get you," Isabelle finished his thought.

He still looked uncertain, so I slid my fingers down his arm and grabbed his hand. "Come on." I tugged him toward the door.

Just as we were about to walk out, Wren's eyes snapped open, and he flipped to all fours on the bed with a menacing growl.

"Get out!" Isabelle snarled as she grabbed a blood bag and ripped it open with her teeth.

I shoved Henry through the door, shutting it quickly behind me. He stepped up to me, trying to get back in, but I stopped him with my hands on his chest.

"She needs to do this. Alone," I told him, frowning after the words had escaped as if on their own.

He studied my features. "The threads?" he asked.

"I…I think so."

He turned his ear to the door, listening. "He's drinking from the bag," he announced a moment later, even though I could hear it for myself.

"See? It'll be okay. We should go." I gently pushed on his chest.

Reluctantly, he stepped away from me. "We should probably warn Nova and Monique that there is a newly turned vampire in this house," Henry said, looking down the long hallway.

"They're still here?" I scowled. I had hoped I wouldn't have to face them again so soon.

"They didn't want to leave without Julia," he explained. "But they appear to be asleep now. I will tell them about Wren later."

"You and Julia seem to be getting along well," I remarked as Henry and I walked a few steps to the double doors of the master bedroom.

"What?" He frowned in confusion, opening one of the doors to let me in.

"You make quite the team trying to help the Ravager. With Julia by your side, you don't even need me." I spat the words out as I walked into the room.

Henry didn't say anything as he followed me and closed the door. He leaned against it, watching me with tired eyes. "You're jealous," he stated.

I folded my arms over my chest. "And what if I am?"

He scoffed and shook his head. "Sophie, every part of me belongs to you...if you still want me after what I've done."

He threw the words over his shoulder on his way to the bathing chamber. I felt the pang of jealousy subside. I wanted to go after him, but doing so would have been dangerous because then I would have had to face what had happened to my father and Ezra. My shadows churned around me, caressing my exposed arms and wrapping around my shoulders like a blanket.

We could make the grief stay away...forever if you'd let us, they whispered in my ear, lulling me in their comforting embrace.

But I needed to go after Henry. I needed to tell him that I would always want him...no matter what. He'd thrown the words over his shoulder nonchalantly, but I'd still heard the anguish in his voice. I needed to reassure him. And then...I could take his mind off what he had done, if only for a short while.

I unfolded my arms from over my chest and followed the soft hum of running water that was drifting from the bathing chamber. Henry was already in the shower when I walked in. He didn't acknowledge me as he quickly and efficiently lathered his hair and then his body while I undressed and stepped inside. Standing behind him, I watched him rinse the soap out of his hair and then brace his hands on the shower wall before him, letting the water cascade down his powerful body. When he straightened and lifted his face into the stream, I wrapped my arms around his torso.

"I will always want you," I said, resting my cheek on his back. "Nothing you could ever do would change that."

A shuddering exhale left Henry at my words, but he didn't say anything in return. His silence felt oppressive, making me desperate to bring him out of that state. So I placed a kiss on his wet back as I glided my fingertips down his slick stomach. He stopped me before my hands could reach below his navel and turned around.

His eyes were haunted as he looked into mine. "You know I will always give you what you want…but is this truly what you need right now?" he asked low.

He sounded exhausted, as if it were taking everything from him to have that conversation.

My shadows bristled around me. What I needed was to keep moving, to act, to do something other than think about what had happened the night before. I opened my mouth to tell him that but immediately shut it as my gaze dropped to his chest, to where I had delivered the deadly blow that had almost killed him. He *would* always give me what I wanted, but I couldn't always take; I also needed to give.

"What do *you* need?" I asked quietly.

Henry swallowed thickly, his throat bobbing. "I just need you to hold me," he rasped.

The shadows hissed in warning. I had to stay strong. I couldn't let emotions overpower me. But Henry needed me, and I, too, would always give him what he wanted or needed. My heart turned over heavily in my chest as I reached up and wrapped my arms around his wide frame. He embraced me back, lowering his head to the crook of my neck. When he did, the stream of water he'd been shielding me from started pelting me, soaking my braided hair. A second later, his large body began to shake, and even though he didn't make a sound, I knew that it wasn't just shower water gliding down my back but also his tears. In that moment, I wasn't able to contain my grief anymore, and I didn't stay silent as violent sobs began to rack me. Henry's hold on me tightened, and we both slid to the shower floor, sitting in the pool of water and our tears. I felt the comforting blanket of shadows slither off my shoulders. A shroud of sorrow replaced it as the shadows mixed with the swirling water, disappearing down the drain.

23

HENRY

After Sophie and I had finally managed to pull ourselves together and finished showering, she drifted off to sleep. Lying next to her, I was trying to rest, but every time I closed my eyes, I saw Ezra's broken body. So I quickly gave up on sleeping and left the bed.

I was already wearing casual pants but threw on a shirt before I headed for the door. I halted by it, glancing at Sophie. She didn't look peaceful in her sleep. Her face was contorted as if in pain, and I wondered whether she was seeing her father's death in her dreams. I wanted to return to bed and chase away her night-mares, but something was holding me back. I couldn't bring myself to do it. Because when I looked at her, all I could see was Thomas's and Ezra's bodies, and all I could hear was the mournful wail that had torn from her throat. I knew I shouldn't have been thinking like that. She was still my wife, my love, but right then, she was a reminder…a reminder that I had failed.

With a heavy heart, I slipped out of the room. I didn't go far, turning left and trudging toward the bedroom, where I had deposited Wren earlier. When I stopped before the door and listened, all was quiet on the other side.

"Isabelle?" I said in a hushed tone, gripping the handle. I twisted it, but the door was locked. "Isabelle?!" I repeated louder as panic set in.

I was about to force my way into the room when a faint click sounded and my sister peeked through the door.

"Are you okay?" I asked, my gaze searching her face. She looked frazzled, and her features crumpled as she shook her head no. "Where is Wren?"

Scowling, I walked into the bedroom. Isabelle stepped aside to let me in. I found Wren on his stomach on the bed. He was lying unmoving…because she had broken his neck. For a split second, I saw Ezra in Wren's place, and I blinked to disperse the image.

"I had to break his neck to render him unconscious," Isabelle said with a heavy sigh. I took a sweeping look around the room, which looked like a murder scene, with blood splattered over the light bedding and gray floor. My sister swallowed audibly. "I didn't realize it would be this hard."

When I looked at her, her eyes were filled with tears. I suddenly couldn't stand being near her because I had failed her too. I should have figured out it was a wolf when we hadn't been able to pick up on a scent. Maybe then Wren's attack could have been avoided. Or maybe not. All I knew was that I should have done more, *been* more for her and Sophie.

I felt the strongest urge to flee the room to escape my lashing thoughts, but I fought it. Instead, I told Isabelle, "You will get through this. I will help you."

Her bottom lip quivered at my words before she stepped closer to me and buried her head against my chest. I held her for a few seconds, but her moment of weakness was brief. When she pulled away and looked at me, my heart dropped because I knew what was coming. I knew what she was about to ask.

"What happened to Thomas and Ezra?"

I almost cast a longing look at the door as I once again considered fleeing. Clenching my jaw, I stayed put. "Ezra turned into a wolf and killed Thomas. When I arrived, he was about to do the same to Sophie."

"So you had no choice," Isabelle started.

"There is always a choice."

"Henry—"

"Don't," I cut her off. "It is done. I can't go back and change the past."

"I know that. Just…don't let it mar your future."

"What about your future? And Wren's and Sophie's? What about Ezra? He will not get a future!" I didn't realize I had raised my voice until Isabelle's eyes widened at my outburst.

"You can't possibly blame yourself! If anything, you should blame the wolf who attacked them. You never told me what happened to it. Did you and Sophie find the beast?"

"We did."

"And?"

"Do you remember Vincent telling us about the shifters who used to live in the Black Forest?"

"Yes…" she drew the word out, clearly racking her brain for the memories. "Is that what he is now?" She glanced at Wren.

"Yes. The wolf that attacked him is a shifter. His name is Volker."

"I don't care what his name is. All I care about is why he's still alive!" Isabelle seethed.

"We fought, but he escaped. And even if he hadn't…he wasn't in control when he attacked Ezra and Wren."

"So you'd give him a break but not yourself?" She arched a brow.

"It's not the same," I said through my teeth.

"Why? Because you can't make mistakes?"

"After what I did to my family, I'd hoped I wouldn't!" The

words came out as a growl. After I had slaughtered my parents and sister in a fit of bloodlust when I'd been newly turned, I had vowed to myself that I would never let myself lose control again.

I didn't know what was worse, the look of shock on Isabelle's face or the one of pity that quickly replaced it. My stomach churned. The conversation was making me sick. Thankfully, we couldn't continue with it because Wren began to stir.

"He's waking up." Isabelle glanced at him. "You should go."

"No, I should stay and help," I told her.

Her gaze turned knowing as it roamed my face. "I think there is someone else in this house who needs your help more than I do. Go check on the girl."

I opened my mouth to argue but quickly closed it because a part of me still wanted to escape. At least the Ravager was not someone I had failed. Not yet anyway.

"Alright, I'll go. But I will be back later to check on you."

When Isabelle nodded, I left the bedroom, glad to leave the conversation we'd just had behind.

"A witch was here," Julia informed me when I walked into Stern's lair. "I don't think I'll ever get used to them being able to just appear out of nowhere."

"A witch? Celeste?" I drew up short.

"No, she said her name is Amelie. She wanted me to relay a message… The funeral is the day after tomorrow."

The roiling feeling in my stomach worsened at the news. "Okay," I said hoarsely.

"Let me guess, you don't want to talk about it?" Julia prodded carefully.

"I really don't," I told her.

"Okay, well, will you at least tell me about the creature that you brought here last night? He's a wolf *and* a vampire?"

"It appears so. He was attacked by a shifter, which is someone who can change from human to wolf. He was on the brink of death, so Isabelle turned him. Now it seems he possesses qualities of both species."

Julia took a few seconds to process what I had revealed. "When you said the world had changed, you weren't joking" was all she said.

"The shifters are not new to this world. They existed before the Red War," I explained.

"Just like the White Witches," she mused. "And Sophie is one of them. Though her magic was dark, not light, when she rescued us from the cellar."

I scowled. "She is still a White Witch, a *good* witch. She only resorted to black magic so she could save everyone and bring us here."

"But her dark powers are stronger than the light ones?" Julia cocked her head to the side.

"Yes, for the time being. To be honest, I'm not exactly sure how it works." I closed my eyes and pinched the bridge of my nose with my thumb and index finger. As a vampire, I seldom got headaches, but one was coming on right then. The truth was most days, I felt I knew Sophie better even than she knew herself, but when it came to her magic, that part of her was still a mystery to me. "How is she doing?" I opened my eyes and nodded at the Ravager by the wall, desperate to change the subject.

"She's doing okay. She let me clean her up."

The girl's hair was wet from where Julia had washed it. The bucket with dirty water was still sitting nearby. No longer covered in blood and grime, the Ravager looked even more like Marcy, and my heart squeezed as I took her in. She was asleep on the floor on the pile of plush blankets Julia must have brought down for her. I figured the conditions we were keeping her in were better than the ones Yvonne had provided, but I still felt terrible about keeping her chained up.

"You should get some rest. I will stay with her," I told Julia as I stepped closer to the sleeping girl.

"Can I be honest? You look more tired than I feel," she replied.

"I won't be able to sleep," I said with a heavy sigh as I sat down on the floor in front of the Ravager.

"In that case, I will take you up on the offer. Do I need to worry about the half wolf, half vampire upstairs?"

"I don't think so. Isabelle seems to have him under control, but if you hear something, come get me."

"I will. See you in a bit."

A breath of relief left me when Julia swept from the cave because I was finally getting a break from all the uncomfortable conversations. I soon discovered, however, I couldn't enjoy the reprieve because I was alone with my thoughts—my vicious, self-deprecating thoughts that showed me no mercy.

"Well, fuck." I let out a rough exhale. That was when the Ravager cracked open one black eye. I froze for a second before I willed my muscles to relax. "I didn't mean to wake you," I told her. She opened her other eye. "Do you still want to go by 'Marcy'?" I didn't expect her to answer, and she didn't. But she did lift off the floor and sit up, leaning her back against the wall. Tucking her knees to her chest, she wrapped her arms around them and began to rock back and forth. "You know...I had a sister named Marcy." The girl stopped rocking and pinned me with a stare. "She had blonde curls, just like you. Her eyes were blue... I wonder what color your eyes will be when you overcome the bloodlust. That's what you're going through. The gnawing, ceaseless hunger, the urges you can't control... It's your vampire nature overriding everything else. Making you forget who you used to be before you were turned. You need to fight it."

As if reminding her about the bloodlust, my words set Marcy off. She threw herself forward, getting on all fours. The chains yanked her back, keeping her a few feet away from me, where she thrashed, snarling and snapping her teeth.

"My intention wasn't to set you on edge," I said as calmly as I could. "I only wanted to explain what's happening to you."

Turning at my waist, I reached for the small pile of blood bags behind me. I grabbed one and faced the girl again.

"I'm sure you're hungry. If you settle down, I will give you this." I held up the bag, jerking my arm back when Marcy swiped at it with her clawed hand. "I will tell you more about my sister if you behave." To my surprise, that got her attention, and the girl stopped throwing herself against the chains. She froze crouched down for a few seconds before she retreated to the wall. "See? You're doing it," I encouraged. "You're learning control." She didn't say anything, of course, as her gaze zeroed in on the blood in my hand. "You know…once you overcome the bloodlust, you will be able to go days without feeding," I said as I made a hole in the bag and held it out to the girl. "You can grab it, just try not to scratch me, please." No sooner had I uttered the words than her arm shot out and she snatched the bag. I winced as her claws left gashes on my wrist. "We'll work on that," I muttered, shaking out my injured hand.

As Marcy settled against the wall, drinking the blood I had given her, I began telling her about my sister. The girl had another violent episode when the blood ran out, but after that, she sat frozen, quietly listening to me speak. I quickly lost track of time, and while talking about my sister wasn't easy, I found the experience cathartic. For a few hours, I was transported to the past, reliving happy memories with my Marcy instead of being in the present, which was anything but happy. I got to spend time with my sister instead of wallowing in my misery.

I didn't know how much time had passed until a loud disturbance to my right interrupted the flow of my story. My gaze snapped to the russet wolf that landed in a heap on the ground by the wall. It took a second for me to realize that Sophie was there too, wrapped around the beast, his massive build hiding her presence.

I jumped up to my feet. "Sophie?!"

"Help me chain him up," she grunted, struggling to keep the

wolf—Wren—in place. I swiftly followed her command, securing the thick metal bands around all four of Wren's legs. He began to fight against the bindings the moment Sophie let go of him. The chains groaned but held.

"Are you okay?!" I whirled on her, clasping her shoulders. "What happened?"

"He shifted again," came Isabelle's voice from the entrance to the cave as she and Julia strode in.

"The commotion next door woke me up," Sophie said, and I swore I saw hurt in her eyes. *You weren't there when I awakened.* "Once I realized what was happening, I glimmered Wren and myself down here."

I released her shoulders and glanced at the wolf. "Was he exposed to moonlight?" I asked Isabelle, who came to stand beside me.

"No, he wasn't," she assured me. "He changed shortly after night had fallen. I had felt the nighttime outside, but I hadn't opened the curtains when the transformation started. Do you think he will shift every night?" There were notes of trepidation in her voice.

"I'm not sure. Only time will tell."

"The wolf bit me when I tried to help," Julia said, drawing my attention to her. She held up her forearm, where a gnarly looking wound was healing. "Am I at risk of becoming a shifter?"

"No." I shook my head. "I have fought a shifter before, and Sophie has too. We both incurred injuries during the fight, but we haven't turned. It seems only humans are susceptible."

Julia exhaled with relief just as the wolf howled. That startled Marcy, who hissed in his direction. Wren growled at her, baring his teeth.

"That's enough!" My deep voice rang out in the cavernous space as I came to stand between the two, still making sure I was a safe distance away from both.

Marcy bristled at my tone before she lowered to the blanket

and closed her eyes. Wren stopped growling and began pacing, his claws clicking on the hard ground.

"Impressive," Julia said under her breath.

"You should go back upstairs and rest," I told her when I turned around. "You all should. I will watch them." *Alone.* I'd rather have been alone with my thoughts than surrounded by those I had failed.

"I am exhausted," Isabelle admitted. "I will get some sleep and be back here to check on Wren as soon as I can."

"No rush. I have it under control."

With a nod, she left the cave, and Julia followed her out.

"Are you sure?" Sophie's gaze flicked over my features.

Hurt still lingered in her eyes. Hurting her more went against my every instinct, but I had to ensure she wouldn't stay down here with me.

"Amelie was here earlier. She said the funeral will take place the day after tomorrow."

Her face fell, and she shuddered, curling into herself. My muscles twitched as I was pulled to go to her, but I stayed rooted in place.

"You don't want me to stay," she said, more of a statement than a question.

"I want to be alone," I admitted low.

Hurt changed to betrayal in her gaze, but she didn't say anything else before she headed upstairs.

Once she was gone, I sat back down on the floor, facing the wolf and the Ravager. I buried my face in my hands, feeling like that was where I belonged. In a cave with other monsters.

24

SOPHIE

Darkness surrounded me. I was standing in the middle of it, completely and utterly alone. A feeling of dread surged, threatening to suffocate me. Why had I returned to that place? The shadows had stayed away for the past three days, ever since I'd given in to my grief and accepted my sorrow. I was not supposed to be here...

"Sophieeee..." my mother's musical voice whispered through the space.

Relief flooded me because at least I wasn't alone. Releasing a long breath, I quieted my mind and opened up my senses, waiting for my mother to beckon me again.

"Sophieeee..."

I turned in the direction from which the sound had come and began walking, then running. When my name sounded again, much closer that time, I stopped in my tracks as pressure clamped down on my chest. What if it wasn't my mother calling out to me? What if the darkness was playing tricks on me? Hesitantly, I took another step on the glossy obsidian surface, then another. Trepidation slithered down my spine, but I knew I wouldn't stop until I found the source of the sound. I was willing to take the risk if there was a chance it was my mother.

I walked for what felt like hours until I saw something ahead of me in the distance. A rectangular object interrupted the never-ending sea of black. The heartbeat I'd detected earlier, when I'd first heard my name, grew louder and louder the closer I got to the object. It was a black box, I realized when only a few hundred feet separated me from it. When I finally reached it, the box was much larger than it had appeared from a distance. A person or a large animal could have fit inside.

"Sophieeee..." My name sounded again, and it was coming from the box. My mother's voice seemed different then. The musical lilt was still there, but it was stronger. The voice sounded familiar though.

"Celeste?" I said, stepping closer to the box.

When I placed my hand on it, the shiny black surface felt cool to the touch. The box appeared to be made of metal but not any metal I'd ever seen before.

"Sophie?" came Celeste's muffled reply from the box.

My brows knitted. What was she doing inside? I took my hand off the box and made a fist. Pulling my arm back, I struck the metal wall, using all my vampire might. The skin on my knuckles split open, but the box didn't budge. There was not even a slight indent in the spot I had hit. Scowling, I tried again and again.

"Stop. We don't have much time," Celeste said.

"What do you mean?" I asked, shaking out my hand, where my bleeding knuckles were already healing. "Why are you in this box?"

"I made a mistake."

"What?"

I woke up before Celeste could answer.

My eyes snapped open, and I sat up in bed, momentarily disoriented. One would have thought that after three days of staying there, I would have begun growing accustomed to the opulent master bedroom on the Stern Estate. But waking up in that place still caught me by surprise. A very unpleasant one at that. I tried extremely hard not to dwell on the fact that Henry and I were staying in the room that used to belong to the monster who'd put us through so much suffering.

With a rough exhale, I threw myself back onto the mattress—only to bolt upright a second later when the dream I'd had rushed back to the surface of my mind. What I'd seen in it was more than unsettling. Why had Celeste been in a box? She'd said she'd made a mistake... Was she trying to communicate with me through the dream? Was that even possible? Or was my grief-addled mind playing tricks on me? I couldn't dwell on my dream for long as stark reality crashed into me like an icy tidal wave. It was the day of my father and Ezra's funeral.

Shivering, I glanced to my left, even though I knew I wouldn't find Henry by my side on the bed. He was in the cave below the mansion, where he had been spending most of his time. Emotions clogged my throat, but I forced them down as I threw the covers off me and got out of bed. I trudged to the bathing chamber to get ready for the day, wincing when I saw my reflection in the large gilded mirror. With my dull eyes smudged with purple underneath and pale, hollow cheeks, I looked like grief personified. I scrubbed my gaunt face and ran a brush through my hair before leaving the bathing chamber.

Going through the motions, I walked to the spacious closet, where the black dress I'd selected the day before was waiting for me. I loathed the garment and what it symbolized and had to fight the urge to tear it to shreds with the claws that had sprouted from my fingertips. Destroying the gown would do me no good. It wouldn't erase what had happened. With that thought in mind, I took a steadying breath and sheathed my talons.

Reaching for the hem of the tunic I'd slept in the night before, I pulled it up and over my head, casting it aside. My hands trembled slightly as I reached for the modest long-sleeved gown. It hung loosely on my body when I put it on, and I had to use a belt to cinch the garment at my waist.

Though the dress was too big, I couldn't help but feel like I was suffocating in it. Ignoring the burning in my lungs, I pulled the top half of my hair up and secured it with a black ribbon. Black flats completed my mourning ensemble. I'd found the shoes in one of the servants' quarters. Henry and I still hadn't gone back to Santoria to retrieve our clothes. He hadn't wanted to leave Marcy and Wren, even for a short time. I hadn't pressed for it, either. I hadn't pressed for a lot of things, giving him space, even though it was killing me on the inside.

My expression turned longing in the full-length mirror when I thought about our cottage by the sea. Back then, he hadn't wanted any space from me. If anything, he hadn't been able to get enough of me, but that was before... Would we ever return to that life? I hoped so. Though right that moment, it was difficult to imagine we would ever leave that godsforsaken mansion for good. It felt like we would be stuck there forever, slowly withering away in our misery with no end in sight. Frowning at my morose thoughts, I tucked the Tear under the collar of my dress, leaving the necklace with the picture of my mother over it. I clutched the pendant and took another calming breath, channeling my mother's strength and wisdom. I didn't feel her presence near me like I had a few times in the past, but the mental exercise worked.

When my heartbeat had slowed and my thoughts cleared, I gave my reflection a nod of encouragement and left the closet and then the bedroom. Once on the other side of the door, I turned left and walked to Isabelle's room. Surely, Henry had already checked on her and Wren, but if he hadn't... I reached up and knocked, the sound echoing in the long, empty hallway.

"Yes?" came Isabelle's voice through the door. She didn't open it, which meant Wren was awake.

"Henry and I are leaving for a few hours to go to the funeral. Do you need anything?" I asked.

Wren had shifted again the night before. When he had

changed back and passed out in the early hours of the morning, Henry had wanted to keep him chained up, but Isabelle had insisted on bringing him upstairs for the day.

"No," she replied just as a low growl erupted close to where she was standing. It didn't sound like a growl that promised bloodshed but rather…passion. "Well, maybe more blood…" Her voice turned breathy, and it sounded like she braced her hands on the door. I promptly stepped away from it.

"We'll also bring some clothes for both of you from Wren's place," I threw over my shoulder as I fled before things on the other side of the door got intense.

When I descended the grand staircase to the first floor of the mansion, I came face to face with Nova and her daughters, who were on their way upstairs to turn in for the day. Nova was still terrified of me, and the darkness within me still rejoiced every time it smelled her fear. Fear emanated from Monique in my presence as well, but she didn't try to hide how much she loathed me for what I had put them through. Julia was the only one who didn't seem to fear or hate me. Her gaze turned empathetic as she appraised my outfit.

"I am so sorry for your loss," she said softly, halting on her way to the stairs.

Nova kept walking while Monique stopped by Julia and appraised me too. Her eyes blazed with hatred and her lip curled in a snarl as our gazes met. I wondered whether she was thinking that I deserved to mourn my father's death after taking Emeric from them.

"Thank you," I told Julia past the lump in my throat before I kept walking through the dimly lit foyer.

I entered the study and then the passage to the cave. The deeper I went down the worn steps, the more the oppressive feeling of grief wrapped around me.

"I wish I could tell you that it gets easier," I heard Henry's measured voice as I descended the last step. Bracing my hand on the rough wall, I stopped and listened. "And it does…in a way… Even now, so many years after I overcame the bloodlust, the monster inside never sleeps." He paused and swallowed thickly. "It broke free a few days ago, and I…I killed someone who was dear to me."

25

*S*peeked around the corner and found Henry sitting on the ground before Marcy. He hung his head, his elbows braced on his bent knees. The girl was tucked against the wall but shifted forward slightly as if she wanted to reach for him. Her eyes were still black, but the darkness in them seemed less bottomless than it had been the day before. Her gaze tracked me as I slowly approached and dropped to my haunches next to Henry. Hesitantly, I reached up and placed my hand on his shoulder. I was afraid he would shake it off, but, to my relief, he didn't. Some of the tension seemed to leave his body at my touch, and he lifted his head and exhaled softly.

"Morning," I murmured.

"Morning," he replied, dropping a kiss on my hand on his shoulder.

My heart thawed a little more with the gesture. Maybe he no longer needed space from me. I hoped to the gods he didn't.

Marcy angled her head, watching our exchange with curiosity.

"She seems to be doing better." I squeezed Henry's shoulder. "She hasn't lashed out in a while."

"I'm cautiously optimistic," he agreed. "Perhaps I can remove the collar around her neck."

"I think it's a great idea."

I let go of him and rose to my feet. He shifted to his knees and reached for the girl. She bristled but didn't recoil from him.

"The thing around your neck…" Henry lifted his hand to his own throat to show what he was talking about. "I'm going to take it off, okay?"

Marcy lowered her chin slightly—a barely there motion that looked like a nod. I nearly gasped at the level of understanding she was displaying. Henry froze for a split second, as shocked by her response as I was, before he reached out and unclasped the collar from around her neck. He laid it to the side while Marcy swallowed audibly, as if testing out the freedom the absence of the collar granted. Henry pulled back but didn't rise to his feet. He waited to see whether the girl would try something given that one of the restraints had been taken off. His muscles tensed when she moved, but all she did was lie down on the blanket. Henry visibly relaxed as Marcy closed her eyes and went to sleep.

"Truly, she is doing remarkably well, all things considered," Henry said as he rose to his full height. In all black, he was already dressed for the funeral. "Julia will be back here soon to watch her while we are away. When we return, she, Nova, and Monique are leaving."

My eyebrows lifted. "Don't send her away on my account. What I said the other night about being jealous…I think I was just trying to find something to be angry about to avoid facing my grief."

The words were difficult to get out, but I felt better after uttering them. When Henry turned around to face me, his eyes shone with a hint of admiration because of what I'd confessed.

"I figured as much," he said gently. "But that's not why I'm sending them away. I have asked them to find the other clans and warn them about Jared and his men."

My heart dropped as the memories from our brush with Jared surfaced. I'd forgotten about him because of everything else that had happened afterward. It had only been a few days since Henry and I had left our cottage, but it felt like ages. I felt decades older. I wished I also felt wiser, but I didn't; I felt only broken.

"Your carriage is here," Julia said as she strolled into the cave.

The time had come. I wanted to sink to the hard ground and stay there. Henry looked like he wanted to do the same. But we couldn't, so he placed his hand on my back and steered us toward the exit. I tried not to make it obvious how relieved I felt that he wanted to touch me.

"The coach driver will need to be compelled, if you want to practice," Henry said as we climbed the steps to the study.

"I don't even know how I managed to compel Jared," I admitted. "I think I was just so desperate to get out of the situation, somehow I was able to force him to follow my will."

"Don't sell yourself short. Ever since you turned, you have been advancing very quickly. Perhaps you can master compulsion early on, much sooner than any other vampire."

"I can try." I shrugged, grateful for the distraction the challenge offered.

The coach was waiting by the front door when we stepped outside.

"I heard the Governess was away on vacation in the Southern region. I didn't realize anyone else was staying on the estate," the driver said as he held open the carriage door. He eyed Henry and me with suspicion.

When Henry gently nudged me with his elbow, I caught the driver's gaze and held it. "This is none of your concern. Please take us to New Haven in the Eastern region."

The driver scowled and glanced at the mansion. "Some strangers staying on the estate while the Governess is away is actually very concerning," he grumbled.

Henry clasped his shoulder and peered into his face. "Your

only concern is how much you'll get paid for this trip. As soon as we leave the estate, you will forget that you picked us up from the Governess's place. In fact, we are so unremarkable, you will hardly remember what we look like after you've dropped us off in New Haven."

The driver's eyes turned glassy, and he nodded before walking to the front of the coach.

"It would seem I still have much to learn," I said as Henry and I settled in the cabin. I'd known it was a long shot, but I couldn't hide the disappointment in my voice.

"You do, but you have plenty of time," Henry replied, staring at me from across the coach.

"You seem relieved," I pointed out.

"Compulsion gives a vampire great power—"

"Which you don't think I should have?" I interjected.

Henry frowned. "I didn't say that—"

"But you thought it."

"You're doing it again."

"What?"

"Trying to find something to be angry about."

I opened my mouth to argue but closed it when I realized that he was right. Then I opened it again, wanting to apologize for my outburst, but the pendulum of my volatile emotions swung back again. "Better than wallowing in my misery…alone," I bit out.

Henry's frown deepened. "You're not alone," he said.

"You've been distant the last two days," I countered.

Then it was his turn to open his mouth to argue only to clamp it shut. "I'm sorry," he said with a rough exhale.

He left the bench across from me to sit by my side, as if closing the physical distance between us would help us bridge the emotional one. Strangely enough, it did. When he wrapped his arm around my waist, I curled into him, resting my head on his chest. His scent and the steady rhythm of his heart had a calming effect, and I felt a spark of hope that maybe, somehow, everything would be okay in the end.

"I'm sorry I left you alone in your grief," he said against the top of my head. His deep voice reverberated through me. "The truth is…I feel like I failed you. I failed Ezra, your father, Isabelle. I failed everyone I care about."

My heart broke into hundreds of sharp, jagged pieces. Breathing became difficult as tears rushed to the surface. Henry was my rock, always formidable, never unwavering. I often forgot that he, too, could be weak sometimes. Lifting my head from his chest, I cupped his face. His eyes were glimmering with tears.

"You didn't fail anyone. If anything, *I* failed *you*. It's because of me that Ezra is dead. You killed him to save my life."

"No!" He clasped my cheeks. "Don't do this. If I could turn back time, I would find another way, but I would always save you, save your life. You *are* my life."

I kissed him then, erasing any remaining distance between us. It melted away, and a feeling of certainty replaced it. The certainty that whatever we had yet to face, we would get through it—together. Henry kissed me back, sealing the reassurance I felt in my heart.

"I love you," I murmured against his lips before I pulled away.

"I love you too."

I settled against his chest again, and we spent the next few minutes in comfortable silence as the carriage rolled over the uneven cobblestones.

"I had a dream about Celeste last night," I finally said, looking up at him again.

"You did? What was it about?"

"She was inside a metal box…"

Henry's brows furrowed in confusion. "What was she doing there?"

"I think…she was trapped."

"Do you think it was just a dream or…"

"I think there is more to it…" I trailed off, trying to recall as many things about the dream as possible. "Celeste said she made a mistake."

"A mistake? Do you think it has anything to do with what Volker claimed? That she was trying to control him?"

"I don't know." I shook my head. "Perhaps Celeste will be at the funeral. Surely, Amelie told her about it."

"If Celeste does show up, we need to tread with caution. If she *is* trying to control Volker, there might be sinister forces at play."

Sinister. The word Henry had chosen stuck with me, nagging in the back of my mind.

"Celeste told us she'd defeated Damien, but what if she was wrong? What if he's still around?" I mused out loud.

A shudder of trepidation rolled through me, and Henry's hold on me tightened, as if he feared the demon would rip me out of his arms right that second.

"Let's get through the funeral first. If Celeste is there, we will assess the situation and decide on the best approach," he said.

I nodded in agreement. The last few days had been all about dealing with one terrible trial before facing the next, and it seemed that wouldn't change anytime soon. A feeling of foreboding threatened to suffocate me, but being next to Henry made breathing easier because I'd been reminded that we were in it together. With him by my side, I could face any challenge. I curled back into him, and he rested his cheek on top of my head. Serenity settled over us. I didn't forget where we were headed or what awaited us back at the Stern Estate, but for a short while, I let all those things fade into the background as I focused on Henry's scent and the beating of his heart.

26

HENRY

When Sophie drifted off to sleep in my arms, I leaned my head back and closed my eyes, simply enjoying the moment of quiet peace. Gods knew it wouldn't last. What Sophie had said about Celeste was more than disconcerting. I should have suspected something wasn't right when the witch had told us she'd sent Damien back to his realm. It had been too easy, and I should have known, but my eagerness to start my married life with Sophie had blinded me, making me drop my guard and hope for the best. If Damien was still around, I would make sure he didn't get to Sophie. I had almost lost her once, and I would stop at nothing to ensure that didn't happen again.

As if sensing my thoughts, Sophie stirred in my arms, and I opened my eyes to look at her. Grief had left its mark on her, hollowing her cheeks and paling her complexion. She was still breathtakingly beautiful though, and she was mine. Lifting my eyes to the ceiling, I once again thanked the gods for bringing her into my life. We had drifted apart from each other over the past two days, but we had come back together, and I swore to never let anything come between us again.

The feeling of peace I had allowed myself while we were traveling dissipated more and more the closer we got to New Haven. My heart turned over in my chest when the carriage jerked to a stop in front of the cemetery. Sophie jolted from her sleep, her hazel eyes meeting mine for a moment before she looked out the carriage window.

"We're here," she said thickly before a ragged breath escaped her.

It suddenly dawned on me then that I had been very selfish for the past two days. I had shut her out because it had been difficult for me to face her, but the grief I was feeling was multiplied tenfold for her. I had lost Ezra, but she had lost her father—the only family she'd had.

"I will be with you every step of the way," I repeated the words I had spoken to her what seemed like ages before. Back then, the promise had meant I would accompany her while she faced the consequences of her actions. At that moment, it meant that I would be by her side while she buried her father.

"We will be there for each other," she said softly, cupping my cheek. "Don't diminish your loss."

My eyes burned, so I squeezed them shut and gave her a quick kiss. Her words gave me the strength to climb out of the carriage into the dreary gray morning when the driver opened the door. Turning around, I offered Sophie my hand to help her out, and I didn't let go as she joined my side, threading her fingers through mine.

"They must have been able to secure the plot next to my mother's," she said as we walked through the cemetery to where Waylon and Amelie were standing by a freshly dug grave.

"Thomas will rest next to Eloise," Waylon confirmed when we approached.

Sophie managed to nod before she broke down in quiet tears. I held her as a short burial ensued. While it lasted, I asked Thomas for forgiveness, talking to him in my head. I also talked to Eloise, though her body wasn't in the grave. After Stern had killed her, he'd taken her body with him to add her skull to his collection. Still, I let my gaze slide to her tombstone as I thanked her for her sacrifice and for bringing the love of my life into the world. Though I wasn't sure she would approve of her daughter's selection of a mate after I hadn't been able to keep her and Thomas safe. Scowling at the thought, I asked her for forgiveness as well.

Once the burial was over, our small group, which also consisted of Thomas's neighbors and Ezra's friends, moved to another area of the cemetery. The area I could picture with my eyes closed.

"At least they will be buried next to each other," Sophie rasped through the tears streaming down her face when we stopped before another fresh grave, which was beside Rory's.

I couldn't bring myself to say anything as emotions clogged my throat. Two innocent young lives had been lost because I'd failed to keep them safe.

"I think that she, of all people, would understand it wasn't your fault. She wouldn't blame you," Sophie said, as if reading my thoughts.

She clasped my arm and leaned her head against my shoulder as Ezra's burial began. The rain that had been hanging heavy in the air finally arrived, sprinkling on our small group as the funeral progressed. When it was over, people were quick to offer their condolences before they hurried away to find shelter.

"I'm so sorry, Sophie," Waylon said, pulling her into a tight embrace when it was only the four of us left. "I'm sorry for your loss too," he told me when our gazes met.

I nodded and looked at Amelie standing next to him. To my surprise, she closed the distance between us and wrapped her arms around me as best she could, considering I was so much bigger than she.

"I am so sorry for your loss," she said gently.

I had kept my composure during the funeral, but at that moment, my vision blurred. When Amelie let go of me, I cleared my throat and looked to the side to fend off the tears.

"Celeste couldn't make it?" I heard Sophie ask.

Grateful for the distraction, I glanced at her. She had pulled out of Waylon's embrace. Her red-rimmed eyes were still glistening, but the flow of tears had slowed.

"She said she had other matters to attend to," Amelie replied. "She asked me to pass along her condolences."

Sophie glanced at me before she asked, "Did you tell her about what happened?" She leaned closer to Amelie. "Did you tell her about the wolf?"

"She knows. That's the matter she is attending to," the girl replied.

"What do you mean?" Sophie's brows pulled together.

"The wolf you encountered can't be the only shifter in the woods. If they are changing back after a century of being in their wolf form, it's quite an adjustment, which can lead to violence, as you have witnessed. Celeste wants to help them acclimate but also ensure that our village is safe."

Sophie's expression smoothed out, and I felt the pressure on my shoulders lessen. It was possible that Volker was confused. He thought Celeste was trying to control him when she was just trying to help him.

"And has everything been quiet in the village?" Sophie inquired.

"Yes…" Amelie drew the word out. "Why do you ask?"

"I had a dream about Celeste last night." Amelie's expression turned apprehensive as she waited for Sophie to continue. "In the dream, she was trapped in a big black box."

The witch scowled. "That is very unsettling, but I can assure you Celeste is well. I can warn her about what you saw in your dream though."

"Don't," Sophie said—a bit too urgently.

Amelie's frown deepened. "Why not? You're a witch. Your dream could be prophetic."

Sophie chewed on her bottom lip. "I know, it's just… What if what I saw in the dream has already happened? What if Celeste is under Damien's influence?"

"Damien?" All color drained from Amelie's face, making her freckles stark against her pale skin. "Celeste banished him back to his realm."

"What if she didn't?"

Amelie's wide-eyed gaze darted between Sophie and me. The smell of her fear spilled into the air, but she quickly reined in the emotion. Waylon shifted closer to her, placing his hand on her back in quiet support. His touch seemed to ground the young witch even more as she inhaled and lifted her chin.

"I understand. I won't tell Celeste about your dream, and I will keep a close eye on her to see if I notice anything unusual about her behavior."

"Thank you," Sophie told her. "If anything happens, you can find us at the Stern Estate. We will be staying there a while longer, trying to bring the Ravager and Wren out of bloodlust."

"How is that going?" Amelie asked with concern in her voice.

"It's going," Sophie replied. "Isabelle has been able to keep Wren under control for the most part, and Henry has been patiently working with Marcy—that's the name the Ravager seems attached to."

Amelie's gaze softened as she looked at me. "I admire you for trying to help the girl," she said. "The sorrow you feel about Ezra is written on your face, and I know that nothing will bring him back, but I hope you can find some consolation in knowing that while one life has been lost, you are actively saving another."

My eyes filled with tears again at her words. I had feared she would resent me after Ezra's death, but she had offered me compassion instead.

Would Rory have had the same reaction if she were still alive?

My blurry gaze slid to Rory's grave.

"We'll give you two some space," Amelie said softly before she and Waylon walked away.

Sophie and I stood in silence for a while as the rain intensified. I wished it would wash away the last few days. But it couldn't, so I would have to learn to live with the knowledge of what I had done. I couldn't change the past, but I could focus on the future. I couldn't bring Ezra back, but I could help Marcy find herself again. Perhaps Amelie was right that by doing so, I would find solace.

27

SOPHIE

I was standing on top of the border wall, my hand gripping the stone ledge. My other hand was in Henry's, and my gaze was trained on the Black Forest ahead, where dark shadows were churning, promising death and destruction. When they began creeping toward the border, rolling over the ground like black smoke, I quickly glanced around me. Isabelle and Camilla were crouched down to my left, their claws drawn and their fangs gleaming. Celeste and a small group of White Witches were standing several feet away, magic crackling at their fingertips.

"Surrender," an eerie voice slithered up the stone wall from below. The voice I'd last heard months before and hadn't thought I'd ever hear again.

My breath snagged in my throat as I looked down and found Antaris peering up at me.

"This is not real," I breathed as I met her fathomless gaze.

Antaris had been the head priestess worshipping the Dark god Xanthus, but she had perished when I'd destroyed the Dark Witches.

Not in this reality, *I realized as I took in the army of Dark Witches behind Antaris.*

"Our numbers are too great. You will not prevail," the head priestess hissed, darkness pulsing all around her.

But I *did* prevail, *I thought as my stomach twisted. This is not real.*

"It is now or never, Sophie," Henry urged next to me.

I reached for the Tear on my chest as my gaze dropped to Antaris once more. The priestess howled, *the sound raising the tiny hairs on my body. And then she...changed. In the blink of an eye, she transformed into a giant black wolf. The border shuddered as the creature jumped on it, its claws embedding in the stone. The beast scaled the side of the wall in three lunges, and then it was on me. My hand slipped out of Henry's when the wolf knocked me to the ground. Its mouth stretched wide and clamped around my neck. I felt the wolf's teeth sinking into the flesh and muscle a second before it ripped out my throat.*

"Sophie!" Henry's voice snapped me out of my dream.

I bolted upright in the bed, breathing raggedly. My hand shot to my neck, and the panic subsided when my fingers brushed the smooth skin there instead of a savage wound.

"You're okay," Henry said as he swept the tendrils of my sweat-slicked hair from my face. "Another nightmare?"

"Yes," I rasped, my throat raw from screaming. "They're becoming more frequent."

"Was there a wolf in this one too?" he asked, running his hand up and down my back.

"Yes."

Henry seemed to think it over. "Maybe you're just anxious about Wren shifting again. Hopefully, the nightmares will cease after we get through this full moon."

About a month had passed since Wren had changed into his wolf form. He'd last shifted on the night of my father's funeral, which was also the last time the moon had been full. Henry didn't think that was a coincidence. The more nights that had passed since then without Wren shifting, the more his theory had proven to be true. I'd scoured Stern's study and found an astronomer's guide, which stated that a full moon occurred roughly every twenty-nine days and lasted for up to three nights.

"If it is a full moon that triggers the change, he might shift tonight. What's our plan?"

Henry let out a rough exhale. "I believe Wren is close to prevailing over his bloodlust, but we know nothing about his wolf part, which makes it unpredictable. I'm afraid we will have to chain him up before sunset."

I nodded.

"How did you sleep?" I asked him, skimming my fingers over his cheek.

He'd been plagued by his own nightmares over the past month. In them, he was killing Ezra over and over again. He'd even confided in me that sometimes Rory took Ezra's place. I couldn't help Henry fight his inner demons in his sleep, but I'd made sure to do so when he was awake. And he'd made sure to do the same for me. Grief was still a very tangible presence in our lives, but we were carrying each other toward a long and winding road to healing.

"I slept okay," Henry said, turning his face into my touch. "I miss being awake during the day."

We'd switched back to a nocturnal schedule a few weeks earlier so we could be awake at night to work with Marcy and help Isabelle with Wren.

"I do too," I admitted before I kissed him.

Hopefully, we can return to our old new life soon. I wanted to say the words, but something was holding me back.

"Respite is yet to come," a voice whispered in my head.

Startled, I jerked away from Henry.

"What is it?" he asked, his brows knitting.

"Just...the threads," I replied, failing to suppress a shudder as the feeling of foreboding that had been my constant companion for the past month resurfaced.

"I wish they would tell you something useful for a change," he said with a heavy sigh.

I wished for the same thing. It felt as though we'd been in our own little world at the Stern Estate. We hadn't heard from Waylon or Amelie. Volker hadn't tried to find me either. Henry thought that perhaps the shifter had figured out Celeste was trying to help him, not harm him, so he'd stopped seeking me out.

I still didn't have a good explanation for my dreams about Celeste being trapped in a black box, but those had stopped when the nightmares about the wolves had taken over. Unease stirred in the pit of my stomach whenever I thought about the witch, and I hoped that Amelie would let us know if something was amiss. I could have gone to visit the young witch or Waylon myself, but I didn't want to use my magic. I'd used it only once in the past month to glimmer to the cottage to bring back clothes for Henry and myself. Though I hadn't admitted it to him, I feared that using my powers would open me up to the darkness. I feared that in my grief, I would be more vulnerable to its influence.

"Do you think everyone is okay? Back in New Haven and beyond?" I asked Henry.

"Sometimes, no news is good news. Waylon and Amelie know where to find us if they need us."

"What about Celeste?"

"You haven't been dreaming about her, have you?"

"I haven't, but perhaps that's because I can only handle one recurring nightmare at a time."

Henry's expression became pained. "I wish I could take away all your nightmares," he said as he gently clasped the back of my neck and placed a kiss on my forehead.

"And I yours," I told him.

"I know," he rasped, resting his forehead on mine.

But we couldn't make our nightmares disappear. We would have to live with them, hoping that one day, they would stop haunting us.

"If you're that worried about Celeste," Henry said, pulling away to look at me, "we can go check on her, but we need to get through the next few nights first."

I nodded and glanced at the window. The curtains were closed, but the subtle buzzing in my veins told me that sunset was fast approaching.

"We have to get ready," I said, leaving the bed.

Henry followed, and a few minutes later, we were on our way out, both dressed in pants and tunics.

I walked out of the bedroom first, taking a few steps down the hallway before I stopped abruptly. Henry halted beside me. We both froze, staring at Wren, who'd just emerged from the bedroom where he and Isabelle had been sequestered. The room was several doors down from us since Henry and I had changed bedrooms.

When the young man turned to face us, my eyebrows shot up. There was no mistaking what he'd become. His pale-blue eyes seemed to glow in the shadowy hallway, and his lips looked fuller. His blond hair shone brighter in the low light of the sconces. The shaggy strands had been trimmed and brushed from his face. He'd also shaved, his usual stubble gone. He looked debonair in black trousers and a blue shirt that matched his eyes and molded to his torso.

Glancing at Henry, I had to fight a smile as something occurred to me. He hadn't had a haircut in over a month, and I couldn't remember the last time he'd slicked his hair back instead of letting the thick waves frame his face. Instead of dress shirts and trousers, he preferred casual tunics and pants. It was as if he and Wren had switched places.

If Henry noticed the same thing, he didn't show it. Instead, he said cautiously, "Wren."

"Henry," the young man greeted him, his fangs peeking through as he spoke. "Sophie." He focused on me.

I glanced at Henry again, waiting to see what he would do next. To me, Wren seemed completely in control of his bloodlust, but I trusted Henry's judgment more than my own in that instance. His eyes narrowed as he stared at the young man.

"I'm in control, I swear," Wren said with a sober expression.

Shadows flickered across his face, and I wondered whether they were memories of what he'd gone through mentally and emotionally to drag his way out of bloodlust.

I felt Henry's hand on my back a second before he stepped in Wren's direction. I followed his lead, and together, we slowly approached the young man.

"How are you feeling?" Henry asked when we stopped before him.

"Great!" Wren smiled, putting his fangs on full display. I instantly remembered how crowded my mouth had felt when I'd first turned. "I'm still learning to control my heightened senses, but I'm getting there."

"It takes practice. You'll get there," Henry assured him. "This… suits you." He gestured at all of Wren with his free hand.

"Thanks! Looking more human suits *you*!" Wren replied, and I had to stifle a laugh.

"I'm still a vampire though," Henry retorted. "Older and stronger than you."

And don't you forget it was what his tone implied.

"It's good to have you back!" I chimed in, trying to diffuse the tension.

"It's good to be back," Wren said just as Isabelle walked out of the bedroom. "I couldn't have done it without her."

Wrapping his arm around her waist, he pulled her to him and kissed her temple. Isabelle let out a soft gasp. She was attired in red silk, her hair and make-up done, and I almost asked why they were both dressed up before I realized that perhaps they were just celebrating the start of their new life together. A life where Wren would no longer age and could remain by Isabelle's side for eternity. They were truly a perfect match, especially because Wren's already-handsome features had become nearly flawless and his suave demeanor had intensified.

"I'm afraid you're not out of the woods yet," Henry said, interrupting the sweet moment between the lovers.

Wren's features tautened. "I know. It's a full moon tonight. I can feel it."

"Feel it how?" I asked him.

"Similar to how my vampire side senses when night is about to descend. Only this feeling is…unpleasant." He rubbed his chest with his free hand. "It sets me on edge."

"You haven't experienced it until tonight?" Henry asked. Wren shook his head. "Do you remember anything about the last time you shifted?"

"I do." The eerie glow of Wren's pale face dulled, which made him look ashen. "I remember feeling…powerless. I couldn't control what was happening to me. My body was not my own. You know how, as vampires, we feel the call of the wild? How at dusk, there is this urge to get outside and succumb to our predatorial nature?" Excitement flashed in his eyes before they lost their luster again as shadows invaded his gaze. "Of course you do. Well, when I shifted last time, the call of the wild was impossible to ignore. I *had* to go outside. I *had* to let the wolf run free…" He paused as his fair brows knitted. "Except I wasn't truly free… There was this…pull in the pit of my stomach. Like a chain yanking me to the Black Forest."

"The Black Forest?" I scowled.

"That's where the shifters are from. Perhaps the wolf wanted to reunite with them," Henry reasoned.

"It's not just a wolf," Isabelle spoke up. "It's still Wren, even in that form. Don't forget that," she said sternly, looking at her brother.

Henry's jaw hardened. "Wren just said he's not in control when he shifts," he pointed out firmly.

"He wasn't in control last time. But last time, he had also just turned. He can control his bloodlust now. Perhaps he can control the wolf part as well," Isabelle argued.

"I'm not going to take that chance," Henry said, his tone final. "We will have to chain him up again."

"No!" Isabelle snarled.

"Unless!" I said loudly to get everyone's attention. "Unless," I repeated in a lower voice when all three gazes were on me, "we don't chain him up and let him answer the call of the wild."

"What are you thinking?" Henry asked me.

"Volker can shift at will," I started to explain.

"I still might kill him for what he did to Wren," Isabelle growled.

"He said he doesn't always have control when he's in the wolf form," I kept going. "But at least he can control when the change occurs. If Wren follows the pull to the Black Forest, maybe it will lead him to Volker or other wolves. Perhaps they can teach him how to shift at will."

"It's too risky." Henry gave a curt shake of his head. "You're suggesting we let a feral wolf roam the streets of New Haven—"

"He didn't hurt anyone last time," Isabelle interjected.

"We have no guarantee he won't this time," Henry insisted. "We will get through this full moon first and then go to the Black Forest to search for other wolves."

"How will we find them? We can't track them," I said.

"Perhaps Celeste will help us find them."

"Celeste cannot be trusted!" The words erupted out of me, and I clamped my hand over my mouth as soon as they'd escaped. My voice had sounded strange to my ears.

Henry stared at me with wide eyes. "We wanted the threads to tell us something useful, and now it seems they have," he uttered in disbelief.

"Celeste cannot be trusted?" Isabelle repeated, enunciating each word. "What does that mean?" She looked between Henry and me.

"We don't know," I said, lowering my hand from my mouth. "But tonight is our chance to find out."

When I gave Henry a pointed look, he dragged a hand down his face with a heavy sigh.

"Alright. We won't chain him up." He jerked his chin in Wren's direction. "But when he escapes, we will follow him to make sure he heads straight for the Black Forest and doesn't harm anyone on the way."

I nodded and faced Wren and Isabelle. "If that's okay with you two, of course."

They exchanged a glance. Isabelle looked uncertain. "I just got you back," she told Wren. "What if I lose you again?"

Henry ran his hand up and down my back at her words. He'd said something similar to me not so long before. While Isabelle feared losing Wren to his beastly side, Henry feared losing me to the darkness again.

"I want to say that you won't lose me, but we both know I can't promise you that," Wren said gently. "But I'm sure that whatever happens, you will bring me back."

My eyes pricked with tears from witnessing the intimate exchange.

"Okay," Isabelle conceded. "We will need to change into something more practical."

"While you do that, we will check on Marcy," Henry said. "Let's reconvene in the foyer on the first floor. We'll make it as easy as possible for Wren to leave the mansion after he shifts."

Wren swallowed hard but nodded before he and Isabelle retreated to their bedroom to change.

28

"What are we going to do about Marcy while we're away from the estate?" I asked Henry as we walked down the staircase to the first floor.

"I feel comfortable leaving her by herself for a few hours. I think we have almost brought her back."

"*You* have almost brought her back," I told him. "You're the one who has spent countless hours talking to her or just being there so she wasn't alone."

Henry didn't say anything for a few minutes as we made it to the study and began our descent into the cave. "Her choosing the name 'Marcy' for herself was quite the coincidence," he finally said. "And her curly blonde hair…it's just like my sister's… She reminds me so much of her."

"Maybe she was sent into your life to help you let go of some of the guilt you feel about what happened to your family."

"Maybe you're right," he muttered, clearly distracted. "Do you hear that?"

I strained my ears as we got closer and closer to Stern's lair. "Yes. It sounds like…crying?"

I halted on the step, and Henry stopped behind me. Marcy

hadn't made a single sound in the past month, not counting the feral growls and snarls. With that thought in mind, I rushed down the remaining steps. When I entered the cave, my gaze immediately zeroed in on the girl. She was lying on top of her bunched-up blankets, sobbing. Her back heaved as the sound of her crying filled the shadowy space that was illuminated by a few lit candles and two oil lamps. Before I could react, Henry darted to her side. He dropped to his knees by the girl and scooped her up in his arms.

"Shhh… What's wrong?" he asked gently.

"I killed them," Marcy rasped. "I killed so many people."

Her small body shook as she buried her face against Henry's chest. His gaze shot to mine, full of potent relief. Relief washed over me as well before I crossed the short distance between us and lowered to my knees. Swiftly, I removed the metal bands around Marcy's ankles—there was no need for them anymore. The girl bristled when I went to free her wrists.

"What are you doing?" she asked, lifting her head from Henry's chest. Her eyes were a pale-green hue. "You can't free me. I'm a monster!"

"You're not a monster," I told her calmly, unclasping the bands from her wrists.

When I tossed the chains to the side and they landed with a loud clank, Marcy glanced at them before her panicked gaze swung to Henry.

"But I…I killed all those people." A sob escaped her, tears streaming down her cheeks.

"You weren't yourself," he said softly. "But you're more your-self now, aren't you?" His gaze roamed her face as if looking for confirmation.

"I…think so, but how…" She swallowed. "How am I supposed to live with myself after what I've done?"

Compassion poured out of Henry as he said, "It won't be easy. Not for a long time."

The girl stared at him, waiting for him to continue. She needed to hear more to give her hope. To give her a reason to keep going despite the monstrosities she'd committed. My heartbeat quickened as I prepared to tell her about my own brush with the darkness. I didn't want to relive it, but if sharing my experience with Marcy would help her not to see herself as a lost cause, I would do it. I opened my mouth to speak, but Henry beat me to it.

"I have told you many stories over the course of the last month, but I think it's time you heard the most important one," he said before he proceeded to tell the girl about his family.

By the time he was done, Marcy was no longer the only one crying. I wiped the tears off my cheeks while Henry rubbed his eyes and cleared his throat.

"I think it's so special that your name is also Marcy." He smiled at the girl, but her face fell.

"The truth is…I don't think it is," she said low. Her bottom lip quivered as she added, "I'm sorry."

Henry didn't seem shocked by her admission. "It's okay," he assured her. "You weren't in your right mind when you reacted to the name. Perhaps you simply liked the sound of it. What is your name? Do you remember it now?"

The girl gave a small nod. "It's Charlotte. But I…I think I still want to go by 'Marcy,' if that's okay with you? I know she meant so much to you… You couldn't save your sister, but you saved me."

Silence stretched as Henry stared at her, clearly at a loss for words. The girl turned to me, and there was a question in her eyes. *Did I say something wrong?*

I smiled softly at her as I reached for Henry's hand. When I pressed it, he seemed to snap out of his shock.

"Of course," he said hoarsely. "'Marcy' it is. A new name for a new life."

A shuddering breath of relief left the girl before she threw her arms around Henry's neck. "Thank you." She pulled away to embrace me next. "Thank you both."

"Of course." I patted her back. "You'll get through this. We will help you. You won't be alone."

Henry's gaze was full of approval and appreciation when it met mine, and I knew that from that moment on, wherever we went, Marcy would come with us. After we'd helped Wren tame his inner wolf.

"Henry and I have to leave soon," I told Marcy, pulling away.

"Leave?" Her voice was high with panic as her gaze darted between Henry and me.

"We have to help my sister Isabelle and her mate," he chimed in. "But we will be back as soon as we can."

"You're leaving me? You said I'd never be alone." Marcy jumped to her feet.

"We won't be gone long," I said as I stood up off the floor. Henry rose to his full height as well. "You can pick a room upstairs and clean up and get some rest. We will be back before you know it."

"No, no, no…" Marcy began shaking her head frantically, her breaths coming in short, rapid pants.

"Hey, hey…breathe," Henry said, clasping her shoulders and peering into her eyes. "You're going to be okay. You are in control."

"You don't know that."

"Yes, I do. I believe in you. Sophie believes in you. You just need to believe in yourself."

When Marcy's gaze shot to me, I nodded. "He's right. I do believe in you," I told her, even though she didn't need my reassurance. Henry believed in her, and I knew from experience that was more than enough. "Come." I offered her my hand. "Let us show you upstairs. You can meet Isabelle and Wren before we have to leave."

Hesitantly, Marcy placed her hand in mine, and I pulled her toward the exit.

"Where are we?" the girl asked as we started climbing the steps up to the study.

"We are in the Southern region, in Santoria," I replied.

"I'm from the Midlands," Marcy shared. "My family lives in Barlow, near the Maivayan Mountains."

That was an unexpected piece of information. I'd assumed she was from Yvonne's region. I'd figured she had to have been in close proximity to the female when she'd set out to make her Ravagers.

"I was visiting my aunt in Yvonne's region when she turned me," Marcy continued, answering my questions before I could ask them. "After I'd escaped her, I had nowhere else to go…"

"So you went back to your family," I surmised, hoping that her story hadn't unfolded similarly to Henry's.

"Thankfully, before I could reach them, the vampire hunters snatched me," Marcy said, and a breath of relief almost left me. Not relief because she'd been taken, of course, but relief that she hadn't hurt the ones she loved.

"You remember Jared?" I asked as we reached the top of the stairs and walked into the study. She'd been unconscious the entire time Henry and I had been in that cellar. Surely, she didn't remember much. I hoped she didn't.

"I didn't know that was his name. I only remember being captured. My next memory after that is of seeing Henry's face when I woke up in the cave." She halted by the bookshelf that slid into place after Henry had emerged from the passage. "There was a woman there too, but it wasn't you."

"It was Julia," I supplied, letting go of her hand. "She took care of you a lot when we first brought you here. She and her family left to warn the others about Jared."

"Are all vampires being hunted now?" Marcy asked, wrapping

her arms around herself and curling inward. "Is it dangerous out there for them? I mean…us."

"We don't know," Henry's deep voice rang out, drawing her attention to him. "But you needn't worry. We won't let anything happen to you. You are part of the Duval clan now."

Marcy's face lit up at his words, and something akin to pride flickered across her features. "I can't think of a better place to be," she said with sincerity as her tense shoulders relaxed.

"Good." Henry moved closer to me and placed a hand on my lower back. "Let's meet the rest of the family."

We strolled to the foyer, where Isabelle and Wren were already waiting. Even though I knew they'd heard us talking to Marcy in the study, they still looked shocked when the three of us walked in.

"Let me make proper introductions," Henry said as we stopped before them. "Marcy, this is Isabelle and Wren. And this is Marcy, the newest member of our clan."

"Our newest member?" Isabelle's brows climbed her forehead. She didn't look upset, only surprised.

"Yes. Whenever we are ready to leave this place for good, she will be coming with us," Henry explained.

"Welcome to the family," Wren said to Marcy with a warm smile. "I'm also fairly new to the clan, but I know one thing for certain—we look after our own." Gratitude shone in his eyes as he glanced at Henry and me.

"Vincent would be proud," Isabelle said, placing a hand on Henry's arm and pressing it lightly. He covered her hand with his, and they shared a quiet moment, both lost in the memories of their father. "I can't believe we did it!" Isabelle let go of Henry's arm and clapped her hands. "I pulled Wren out of bloodlust, and you helped Marcy find her way back. Things are finally looking up!"

I scowled at her words. Why did I feel like the worst was yet to come?

"Let's not get ahead of ourselves," Henry cautioned. "We still need to help Wren find a way to control his wolf part."

"I remember!" Marcy gasped. "You were chained next to me for some time!" She looked at Wren.

"He was," Henry confirmed. "And tonight, he will shift again. We think the wolf will take off to the Black Forest to find others like him. We will follow him to make sure he doesn't harm anyone on the way there."

"And that *he*, too, is not harmed," Isabelle added, moving closer to Wren.

"About that." Wren glanced at the closed door behind him. "I think it's almost time."

29

HENRY

The elation I felt about Marcy joining the clan evaporated the moment Wren said, "I think it's almost time." An ugly feeling of foreboding crept into my chest and settled there.

"Go upstairs," Sophie urged Marcy. "Pick one of the empty bedrooms and get some rest."

"Are you going to be okay?" the girl asked, looking between Sophie and me.

If I'd had any remaining doubts about her having completely overcome the bloodlust, they disappeared that instant.

"Yes," I assured her. "We will return as soon as we can."

She gave a small nod before darting up the staircase to the second story.

As soon as she was gone, Wren took off his shirt and tossed it to the side. He began pacing before the front door, his anxiety filling the foyer. My own unease climbed as I rolled my shoulders and took a steadying breath. Sophie shook out her arms next to me, shifting from foot to foot. I glanced at her, feeling an overwhelming urge to hide her away. The dreams she'd been having about wolves resurfaced in my mind, sending a jolt of dread straight through me. I wanted to ask her to stay behind, but I knew she wouldn't, so I didn't say anything as I refocused on Wren. His heart raced in his chest as sweat slicked his body.

Isabelle stood nearby, wringing her hands. "The night is almost upon us," she announced in a strained voice.

Wren stopped pacing and faced the front door. I placed my hand on Sophie's back, and we both stepped closer to him. Isabelle moved to stand beside me. Tense silence ensued as the four of us waited for the sun to lower below the horizon. We didn't need to be able to see outside to know when the last sliver of daylight was snuffed out by the night. The silence became even heavier as Sophie, Isabelle, and I stared at Wren standing before us. The muscles on his bare back tautened, and he seemed to have stopped breathing.

"Open the door," he said hoarsely. "I will shift at any moment now. I can feel it."

Isabelle bristled at his words, then strode past him to the front door. Grabbing the handle, she turned around. "Remember, we will be right behind you," she told Wren, her eyes and voice soft.

I hadn't known my sister was capable of such softness, but she was different with Wren, more human, and I liked that side of her. A silent exchange passed between them before Isabelle's features turned sharp and she pulled open the door.

My muscles tensed as moonlight drenched Wren's figure. Nothing happened for a few more seconds, but then he hunched over with a loud grunt. His spine bowed, stretching the skin on his back as other bones began to break and shift, rearranging themselves in his body.

Isabelle stood frozen by the door, looking sickly, as if watching Wren transform physically pained her.

"Come here, Isabelle," I implored. "You don't want to be in his way."

It took a minute for my words to register, but once they had, she rushed to my side just as Wren fully shifted. I had expected the wolf to take off through the door, but it lingered in the foyer. When it whipped its huge head around, its glowing red eyes fastened on my sister. Perhaps Wren wasn't completely gone. It seemed a part of him still remembered his mate.

"Wren?" Isabelle rasped, extending her hand as if to reach for him.

The wolf snarled as its head jerked toward the door, then back to Isabelle. Wren was clearly fighting the call of the wild. The call he couldn't *not* answer. With one last look at my sister, the wolf howled and dashed through the door. Isabelle immediately took after him, and Sophie and I followed.

It was extraordinary that as soon as Wren had shifted, his scent had disappeared. I wondered whether that was a defense mechanism against the predators that roamed the Black Forest. All I knew was that we couldn't afford to lose him because we had no way of tracking him if we did. So I focused on his russet form and didn't dare to avert my gaze. Thanks to my heightened senses, I was still aware of Sophie running by my side and of Isabelle a few feet ahead of me, closer to the wolf.

Thankfully, the streets of New Haven were mostly empty. It also helped that Wren was taking the back roads in the direction of the forest. Perhaps he was more himself than I had realized and was choosing the less crowded areas of the city on purpose.

We reached the border in no time, and the wolf leaped high in the air, effortlessly clearing the tall stone wall. Isabelle, Sophie, and I rushed up the steps to the top of the border before we jumped off the ledge, landing on the other side. I cursed when I noticed that Wren had already put significant distance between us. The three of us took off after him, working extra hard to catch up. After we had succeeded, we stayed several feet behind, trailing him through the woods. If he was aware of our presence, he didn't show it as he loped, heaving up the earth with his massive paws. I couldn't help but notice that the forest had changed in the short time since I had last stepped foot in it. The dark, malevolent atmosphere had returned, as had the smell of death and decay. At least the forest creatures were staying away, scattering out of the wolf's path.

We traveled deeper and deeper into the woods, farther than I had ever gone before. Just as I was beginning to worry we would run out of time before sunrise, we came upon a rock formation. Two large angular slabs were sitting together on a small hill, forming a conical shape. The wolf skidded to a stop before it, and we did the same a few feet back, staying in the tree line that surrounded the small clearing where the formation was being bathed in the silvery glow of the moon.

The rocks must have been the entrance to a den, I realized when Volker strolled out from under them. He halted before Wren as his nostrils flared. "She's here," he muttered, cocking his head as if listening to something. "I can smell her… I know…"

Sophie looked at me, resolve etched into her features. I shook my head no—she wouldn't expose herself, not yet.

"What is she doing here? I don't know," Volker kept talking to himself.

Suddenly, his head jerked in our direction. I cursed under my breath.

"He knows we're here," Sophie said low. "We might as well talk to him," she reasoned.

"Is that Volker?" Isabelle growled. "Because if it is, then there will be no talking, only killing. I will rip out his throat."

"He might be the only one who can help Wren," Sophie pointed out as she went to take a step closer to the den.

This female will be my undoing, I thought, sighing internally. I knew she respected my opinion, but she had a strong spirit that could not be tamed. It wasn't that I *wanted* to tame her. I just wanted her to be safe. The best way to ensure her safety then was to follow her out of the tree line and into the clearing.

"Sophie." Volker's gaze immediately zeroed in on her. His silver eyes softened, and I didn't like him looking at her like that. I didn't like him looking at her at all. I didn't understand the connection he felt to my wife, nor did I care to. She was *mine*.

Sophie had to stop abruptly so she didn't run into me as I moved to stand in front of her, shielding her from Volker's view. I locked eyes with the wolf, baring my fangs with a snarl. The strangest thing happened then. Wren whirled on me, crouching low with an answering snarl. He was protecting Volker.

"You prevailed last time because I was alone, but now I have my pack. And I am their alpha." Volker smirked.

Two wolves emerged from the den, coming to stand on either side of him just as growling erupted all around us, coming from the trees that surrounded the clearing.

How many shifters dwell in these woods?

"It's okay." Sophie's hand gripped my bicep as she stepped out from behind me. "Let me talk to him."

I didn't want her talking to him. I didn't want her near him. The man was naked, for fuck's sake.

My gaze roamed her face before dropping to her neck. The irrational, primitive part of me cursed Sophie's healing abilities and wished my bite marks from any of our passionate times together would have remained to make it clear to anyone that she was mine.

Letting go of my arm, Sophie lowered her hand and threaded her fingers through mine. She ran her thumb over my wedding band, as if to remind me that, although I couldn't permanently mark her for everyone to see, the rings were a display of our commitment to each other.

My gaze snapped to hers, and I found her watching me, patiently waiting for me to get my emotions under control. I gave a small nod and turned my head to face Volker. He was still smirking, and for a split second, I considered going for his throat just to erase the cocky expression from his face. Sophie pulled me closer to where Volker was standing but not too close—Wren was still crouched in front of him, growling at us. It seemed his wolf loyalty to the alpha overrode everything else.

"We need your help." Sophie's voice rang out in the clearing. "This is Wren." She nodded at the russet wolf. "He is like you—a shifter."

Volker's gaze lowered to Wren, and a breath of relief almost left me because he was no longer staring at Sophie.

"He's different," he said, sniffing the air.

"You almost killed him!" Isabelle seethed, storming out of the woods. "So I had to turn him, you stupid son of a bitch!"

I threw my arm out to stop my sister from lunging at Volker. The alpha barely glanced at her before his gaze returned to Sophie.

"I'm sorry," he said. "I told you I'm not always in control."

"But you can control when you shift," she replied. "He can't. It seems he can't stop himself from shifting on a full moon."

Volker's gaze dropped to Wren once more. "I may be able to help him if he's susceptible to my influence. Though seeing how his wolf led him here, I reckon he is."

Volker's eyes began to glow, the silver in them churning as he ducked his chin, his focus solely on Wren. The russet wolf stopped growling and rose from his crouch, turning around to face the alpha. Their gazes locked, and the longer Volker stared at him, the lower Wren sank to the ground, whimpering, until he rolled to his side on the forest floor. I watched in astonishment as he began shifting back into his human form. A few seconds later, a naked Wren lay shaking before Volker. Isabelle went to step toward him, but I held her back.

"We will help him," the alpha said, lifting his gaze to Sophie. "But you three need to leave these woods before the witch senses you're here."

"The witch?" Sophie asked. "Do you mean Celeste?"

"Yes. She is planning an attack on New Haven. That's why she has brought so many of us back…and had us make so many others."

My heart plummeted to the pit of my stomach.

"An attack on New Haven?" Sophie asked in a hushed voice.

"Yes," Volker confirmed. "I control my pack, but she controls me… I can't fight it. I can't overcome her dark magic."

Dark magic? Sophie was right all along.

"When?" I asked low.

Reluctantly, Volker dragged his gaze to me. "I don't know for certain, but we are stronger during a full moon, so she will probably wait until the next cycle."

A month. We have a month.

"What do you mean, she had you make others?" Sophie asked, interrupting my hectic thoughts.

"We have been sneaking into New Haven and bringing people back here to join the pack," Volker replied.

"Join the pack?! You have been snatching people from New Haven and turning them into wolves?!" I seethed.

Volker didn't look the least bit remorseful as he bit out, "I'm just following her orders. I told you I'm not in control." He looked back at Sophie. "You're a witch. Is there anything you can do to free me?"

I felt a twinge of pity at his pleading tone.

"I'm sorry," Sophie replied thickly. "There is nothing I can do. My budding powers are no match for such ancient magic as Celeste's."

The silver in Volker's eyes cooled as deep, dark shadows settled there. "Then you must know that fight is coming. Your kind against mine. Celeste wants bloodshed, and bloodshed she will receive."

"Why does she want to attack?" I asked.

I thought I already knew the reason but wanted to confirm that my suspicion was correct.

"Xanthus," Volker breathed, and the forest seemed to still when he uttered the name of the Dark god.

"Celeste wants a massive human sacrifice to resurrect him," I concluded.

"Not Celeste—Damien," Sophie corrected me. "I think Celeste is being controlled by a demon," she told Volker.

"Whenever I see her, she is alone," he replied, his wolfish features pulling in a scowl.

"Damien is a master of deception. I have no doubt that he has warped her mind. Celeste would never conceive of such evil on her own."

"All I know is that the witch has her talons in me," Volker snapped. "I can't defy her wishes."

"Maybe I can talk to her…" Sophie looked at me.

"No." I shook my head. "We can't reveal that we know about her plan. We go home and prepare first."

"You're right," she agreed before her gaze fell to Wren, who was still lying curled into himself on the ground. "We can't leave him here."

"We won't," Isabelle said as she strode to Wren and helped him up. "I look forward to the fight." She glared at Volker. "I will rip out your heart and bathe in your blood, Wolf," she spat in his face.

I almost winced at her words but schooled my features. I couldn't blame her for wanting revenge after what Volker had done to Wren. After all, I wanted to gouge his eyes out just for looking at Sophie.

"If you can prevail, you can bleed me dry, Vampire," Volker spat back, his eyes blazing. "At least then I will finally be free."

I heard Sophie's sharp inhale at Volker's words as they chilled my skin. He'd rather welcome death than live in slavery to the black magic. I understood his feelings well. Until I'd met Sophie, death hadn't scared me. I would never have taken my own life, but finding my demise at the hands of others would have been a blessing because it would have granted me release from the beast within, from my monstrous nature. But not anymore. At that time, I valued every second of every day because I had Sophie in my life. And if I had to fight for my future with her yet again, I would fight with everything that I was.

Sophie's fingers tightened around mine as her heartbeat picked up. Knowing her, she probably felt responsible for Volker's tragic fate, for the fate of his pack. "I wish there was something I could do," she rasped, looking at Volker.

"I wish for the same," he replied, and I gritted my teeth as his gaze roamed her features. "I'm sorry for what I did to your friend." He glanced at Wren. "And for what I *will* do in the near future." Notes of sorrow crept into his voice before he cleared his throat. "Leave now. While the cover of the night still offers protection to you and your kind."

He seemed to genuinely care about Sophie, but knowing that only set me on edge. The territorial creature inside me clawed at my skin, demanding to be unleashed to punish Volker for encroaching on my turf. Sophie's delicate nostrils flared as her wide-eyed gaze swung to me.

"We're leaving," she announced, her voice a bit husky. She was *pleased* by my strong reaction toward Volker. Jealousy was still simmering in my blood, but another feeling stirred as well when I detected the faint notes of her arousal.

Sophie turned back to Volker.

Why is she looking at him again? I growled on the inside.

"Thank you for warning us about the impending attack," she told the wolf.

"You're welcome. I wish I could stop it, but it's out of my control. For what it's worth, a part of me hopes you will prevail."

The part that doesn't care whether he lives or dies.

"We might still find a way out of this," Sophie offered, defiantly lifting her chin. My wife was a fighter—never one to accept her fate without challenging the gods themselves.

Volker's mouth curved in a bitter smile. "For your sake, I hope you do." With those parting words, he turned around and strolled back into the shadowy entrance of the den. The two wolves followed, their hulking muscles bunching with each heavy step.

30

SOPHIE

Dread had gripped my heart with thorny, frigid fingers and didn't let go as we returned to the Stern Estate, barely making it back before sunrise. Wren swayed on his feet after we'd walked into the foyer, and Isabelle offered her shoulder for support.

"Shifting back and forth took a lot out of him," she said, her worried gaze flicking over his drawn, sweat-slicked face. "He needs some blood."

"And clothes," Wren added with a weak smile.

Henry had given him his tunic, and because of their size difference, it offered quite a bit of coverage, but I didn't doubt he wanted some of his clothes and a few minutes to catch his breath in the privacy of their bedroom.

"You should go upstairs and get some rest," I suggested, looking at Isabelle and Wren.

"So should you," Isabelle replied.

My gaze shot to Henry, who closed the front door and leaned

against it with a heavy sigh. My throat went dry as I took in his bare torso, which was covered in a fine sheen of sweat.

"We need to gather the clans," he said, dragging a hand down his face. The words instantly tamped down the spark of desire. When he looked at me, impossible sadness crawled into his eyes. "Here we are again," he rasped, holding my gaze.

"Here we are again," I repeated, the vise around my heart constricting tighter.

"How are you going to round up the clans with them scattered across the country?" Isabelle asked, drawing my attention back to her. She looked exhausted. She had been through so much—we all had—and it wasn't over yet. Far from it.

"The most efficient way would be to use the Blood Pact to summon the clan leaders," I said, turning back to Henry. "We only have a month. We can't afford to waste time blindly searching the regions."

"You're right, but how are we going to get the contract? Celeste has it," he pointed out.

"I can glimmer to her cottage to retrieve it," I suggested carefully, expecting him to shut me down. "We could ask Amelie, but I'd rather not put her in danger," I added, knowing he wouldn't be able to fight me on that.

Henry's lips pressed in a thin line, his features taut. "It's risky," he finally said. "But I don't see any other way. Will you be able to use the contract once you get it? Last time, you needed Celeste's help with the spell."

"I remember the incantation. If I can't do it by myself, maybe Amelie can help me." *Or I'll tap into my black magic*, I thought but didn't say.

Henry's eyes narrowed, as if he knew what I was thinking. He opened his mouth to say something but was interrupted by Wren's low grunt.

"Take him upstairs," I instructed Isabelle. "There is nothing either of you can help with at the moment."

"When will you leave to try and steal the contract?" she asked with an undertone of concern.

"As soon as possible," I told her, feeling Henry's gaze boring into me. I glanced at him and shrugged. "There is no reason to delay it."

A muscle flexed in his jaw before he said, "I'd rather you did it during the day anyway, seeing how Damien is stronger at night." My skin prickled at the mention of the demon. "We should update Waylon and Amelie first though," Henry continued. "Give me a minute to throw on a shirt and check on Marcy, and then we can leave."

A part of me wanted to go up with him—the part that had found his earlier territorial behavior extremely arousing—but another part couldn't think of anything other than the war that would soon be upon us.

"I'll wait here," I told him grimly.

I thought I caught a hint of disappointment in his eyes, but I couldn't be sure as he turned and rushed upstairs.

"Be careful," Isabelle said before steering Wren toward the staircase.

"I will. I'm sorry about…everything."

"It's not your fault," she threw over her shoulder as she and Wren began their ascent to the second story.

Then why did it feel like it was? I should have left the Duval Estate on my wedding night and helped Celeste deal with Damien. I should have known better than to think the witch would wait for me to aid her. But I'd felt entitled to a moment of peace. Perhaps if I hadn't been foolish enough to think Henry and I had deserved it, all that was happening could have been avoided.

"I know what you're thinking." I heard Henry's deep voice near my ear as he wrapped his arms around my waist. I didn't respond, melting into his hold with my back against his hard chest. "You're wondering if you could have done something to prevent the chain of events that has led us to this point."

"If I didn't know any better, I'd think that you can read my mind," I said with a soft smile, leaning my head back against his right shoulder.

"I don't need to read your mind. I think I know you pretty well despite us only having been together for a short time." He kissed my temple.

"You do." I tilted my face up to look at him. He stared back at me as we stood in silence for a moment. The thorny vise around my heart was squeezing so hard, it felt like the organ was punctured and bleeding. I feared that if I opened my mouth, blood would spill from my lips. Swallowing, I whispered as tears pricked my eyes, "It seems we always have to fight for our future."

Henry's gaze softened as his hold on me tightened. "I will fight for our future for all eternity if I have to," he said vehemently.

"So will I," I told him before lifting on my tiptoes to capture his mouth.

When I swept my tongue against his lips, he opened up for me, and I deepened the kiss. A low groan rumbled from his chest as he met each stroke of my tongue with his own. Liquid warmth began to spread through my entire body, pooling in my core. I knew we didn't have time to take our kissing upstairs, but I still allowed myself to get lost in him for a few more seconds. By the time I pulled away, we were both breathless, and his arousal was pressing into my lower back.

"You have no idea how much I want to fuck you right now if only to prove to myself that you're mine," Henry growled, his black eyes flashing.

"Yes, I noticed you were quite territorial earlier in the woods." I bit down on my lower lip, making sure I didn't mention Volker by name lest it fueled Henry's bout of jealousy.

"I want to lick every inch of you to erase any trace of his lingering gaze on your skin," he said, his voice low and thick.

I had to press my thighs together at the intense pulse of desire. "As much as I would love that…" I breathed.

"I know, I know, it will have to wait," Henry finished my thought. He slipped his arms from my waist and adjusted himself. "For the sake of time, I think we should glimmer to Waylon's," he said, the molten heat in his eyes gradually cooling.

"Okay." I reached for his hands, and a few moments later, we stood before Waylon's front door.

"Something tells me that you two being here does not bode well," came Waylon's voice from my right.

Henry lifted my hands to his mouth and kissed my knuckles before letting go. When I turned to face Waylon, I saw he was wearing his guard leathers.

"Actually, I'm glad you're here," he said with a heavy sigh as he climbed the low steps to where we were standing. "There has been some strange activity on the border…*wolves* sneaking into the city. And the Order has been reporting disappearances… I don't know if the two are connected—"

"They are," Henry cut him off. "Do you mind if we come in?"

"Sure," Waylon replied, retrieving a house key from his pocket. "Amelie should be up by now."

"Amelie has been staying with you a lot," I remarked with a small smile.

"She has," Waylon said, walking to the front door. He froze with his key halfway to the lock before he lowered his hand and turned back around. "About that," he added, looking between Henry and me. "You two got married fairly quickly after you started seeing each other. How did you… How do I…" He wrung the back of his neck, seemingly having trouble formulating his thoughts. "What if I'm rushing things?"

Henry and I looked at each other, and for a moment, we weren't on the porch anymore—we were playing in the waves in front of our cottage in Santoria. Oh, how I longed to return to that place, to that time.

"I never felt like we were rushing things," Henry said, pulling me back to the present. "Because even an eternity with Sophie wouldn't be enough."

"I feel the same way," I confessed as emotions swelled in my chest. "I knew he was the one when I realized I was actually... overjoyed that I'd become a vampire because that meant I'd get more time with him."

I knew the words made me sound like a terrible person. Turning into a vampire had allowed me to save countless lives, and that in and of itself should have made the choice I'd made worth it. But if I was being truthful, all that was secondary. Eternity with Henry was what made it worth it. His everlasting love was my reward. I knew he still regretted turning me—he'd often said so himself—but I never for one second regretted choosing that fate, choosing *him*.

Henry's deep-blue eyes began to shimmer at my words. I knew my own eyes also glistened as my love for him filled me to the brim. When he reached for me and pulled me to his chest, I laid my head over his heart, fending off the rush of tears.

"So..." Henry's deep voice rumbled through me. "If you can't imagine your life without her..." he trailed off, letting Waylon fill in the rest.

"That's the thing," he said quietly. "I *can* imagine my life without her. I just don't want to...because it would be a sad and miserable existence."

My lips curved into a smile as I lifted my head from Henry's chest. "Then you already have your answer," I told Waylon.

"I suppose I do." He smiled, looking almost in awe of the decision he'd just made.

He turned around to unlock the door, but before he could, it opened, revealing Amelie on the other side.

"I thought I heard a commotion..." Her eyes widened in

shock as she took us in. "Sophie! Henry! Long time no see!" She ran out of the house and gave me a tight embrace before hugging Henry.

"I wish we were here under better circumstances," Henry said as Amelie pulled away.

"Let's step inside," Waylon suggested, gesturing for Amelie to go in first.

I followed after her, with Henry and Waylon trailing behind.

"Would you like some tea?" the witch asked, leading everyone in the direction of the kitchen.

I felt a pang in my chest, momentarily reminded of Celeste, who also always made tea for any occasion.

"I'll take a cup, please," Henry said as we stepped into the kitchen.

I felt another pang when my mind conjured an image of Ezra sitting at the kitchen table. Henry tensed next to me, and I heard his breath hitch—he must have been thinking the same thing. Reaching for his hand, I pressed it lightly to let him know I shared his pain.

Henry was the only one who had taken Amelie up on the offer of tea once the four of us settled around the kitchen table. The witch made a cup for herself as well, but it sat untouched the entire time Henry and I recounted everything that had transpired in the past month.

"So your suspicions were true. Celeste *is* being controlled by the demon," Amelie said slowly, clearly trying to process everything we'd just revealed. "I'm sorry. I wish I had seen the signs." She shook her head in disappointment.

"Don't beat yourself up. We didn't pick up on it either," I told her gently.

"And now you want to sneak into her cottage?" she asked. "I can help."

Waylon stiffened in his seat next to her. When I shook my head no, he relaxed just a fraction.

"It's better if I go alone—lower risk of being discovered," I explained.

Then it was Henry's turn to grow tense because I'd just mentioned there was a chance I might get caught. He turned to me. "Are you sure you want to do this?"

"Yes. It's the only way to gather the clans in time."

His gaze roamed my face for a few seconds, and I wondered whether he was trying to come up with an alternative.

Suddenly, Waylon cleared his throat to get our attention. "You said Celeste controls the wolves..." he said carefully, his tone measured. "I hate being the one to bring this up, but wouldn't taking her out of the equation help to avoid the battle?"

Amelie bristled next to him. "You're not suggesting—"

"I am. I'm sorry, but I am," he told her, his face contorting with regret.

"Celeste is too powerful, especially now with Damien by her side," Henry said.

I whipped my head around to look at him as it occurred to me that he, too, must have thought about killing Celeste to prevent the assault on New Haven.

"We don't have to kill her," I spoke up. "We just need to bring her back from the darkness. Perhaps there is a spell we can use?" I asked Amelie.

The girl shook her head. "Not that I know of. Xanthus and the other gods are fighting for her soul right now, and only she can determine what side will win."

I frowned, not quite believing there was nothing we could do to help Celeste. I was going to search her house. Perhaps I would find a spell Amelie was not familiar with. Maybe even the one Celeste had used the night she'd tried to defeat Damien but failed.

"I understand she's powerful," Waylon said, "but don't you think it would be easier to fight her now, when we can ambush her, than when she brings the battle to us and is surrounded by dozens of wolves?"

"Who is going to take her on?" Henry challenged, his voice rising slightly. "You want Sophie to do it with Amelie's help?"

Waylon visibly paled at the suggestion. "No, of course I don't want Amelie to do it. It's too—" He caught himself before he could finish.

"Dangerous," Henry finished for him. "That's why gathering the clans should be our first step so we are prepared for when Celeste decides to attack. If between now and then we can figure out a way to stop her, great, but our priority should be building a line of defense."

I saw my opportunity and took it. "Speaking of which, I should probably try to get the contract now." I got up from my chair and stepped away from the table.

Henry was at my side in an instant. "At any sign of trouble, you glimmer back," he said vehemently. "We'll find another way if you can't obtain the contract. It's not worth you getting caught or worse." His voice cracked on the last word. "Don't risk your life before the real battle even begins."

"I won't," I assured him as I summoned my magic, picturing the witch's cottage in my mind.

31

Henry's near-perfect features blurred before my world went dark. I blinked a few times, and when my vision adjusted, I was in the Black Forest, my back pressed against the rear side of Celeste's cottage. Whipping my head left and then right, I made sure the witch was nowhere near me before I peeled myself from the weathered wall. There was a small window to my left, which I knew led inside Celeste's bedroom. My hope was that she kept the contract there since I'd never seen anything related to magic lying around anywhere else in the house. Crouching down a bit, I stepped closer to the window and peeked in.

The faded closed curtains obscured most of the view, but through the thin gap between them, I managed to glean that the bedroom appeared empty. There was still a small chance that it wasn't, so I held my breath and listened to make sure I couldn't hear Celeste rummaging around. When all that greeted me was silence, I glimmered inside, still holding my breath. I exhaled softly once I'd confirmed I was alone. Turning around in a circle, I cast a glance around the crammed space, trying to figure out where the contract could have been stashed.

The bedroom was organized chaos. Scrolls were piled up atop the rustic desk, while potion bottles of various colors and sizes were scattered throughout. There was even a cauldron tucked away under the chair in the corner. Moving as quietly as possible, I quickly scanned the scrolls on the desk, my vampire speed allowing me to finish the task within a few minutes. When my search had rendered no results, I felt deflated. Standing in the middle of the room, I racked my brain, trying to figure out where the contract might have been hidden. My blood iced over as a thought occurred to me: What if Celeste had destroyed it so I couldn't summon the clans for reinforcements?

It's fine, even if she did. We can find the clans another way, I reasoned with myself.

Still, disappointment washed over me because I'd also hoped to find a spell that would help me banish Damien. To steady myself, I lifted my hand and wrapped my fingers around the locket with my mother's portrait. Her magical prowess must have been astounding. After all, she had finished creating the Tear. What wouldn't I have given to have learned more about my magic from her? As I squeezed the locket in my hand, my mind took me back to the day when I'd discovered the note about the amulet, hidden under the floorboards in my mother's study.

Hidden under the floorboards? My gaze dropped to the floor. *What if...*

I lowered to my knees and swept my hands over the flat wooden surface, looking for any imperfections that would reveal a secret compartment underneath. All the floorboards were worn and warped, but one stuck out slightly more than the rest. Letting the nail on my index finger elongate into a sharp claw, I used it to pry the board out. My breath caught when I discovered a shallow opening that contained several scrolls. Momentarily, I was thrust into the past again, and I had to glance up to make sure I wasn't in my mother's study. A feeling stirred inside me as it had back then—a strange sense of knowing that what I was about to discover would be of great significance. Suddenly, I felt my mother with me. It was as if she were right there in that room, sitting beside me. Her phantom touch guided my hand to the scroll buried beneath all the others, and when I pulled it out and unrolled it, my eyes widened in disbelief.

I heard Celeste's approaching steps a second before her herbal scent reached me. Panicking, I rolled up the scroll and shoved it in my pocket. I quickly reached for another scroll—the one that didn't look as ancient as the rest and had blood stains seeping through the parchment. With both scrolls safely in my pockets, I put the floorboard back in place and glimmered from the room but not before yanking the curtains open a bit wider. I didn't go far, crouching right on the other side of the window.

Peeking in while trying to stay undetected, I watched Celeste walk into the room. She halted when she'd stepped inside, taking a sweeping look around. My heart stuttered in my chest, but I reminded myself that the witch didn't have heightened senses, so she wouldn't be able to pick up my scent, which was still lingering in the air. A moment later, Celeste closed the bedroom door and strode to the vanity, her movements jerky and unnatural. It looked as if she weren't entirely in control of her body, and my eyes narrowed as I tracked her. The scene unfolding before me became even more bizarre when Celeste reached the vanity. Throwing her hands up, she planted them on the wooden surface, hunching over it with a loud grunt. What I was looking at reminded me of a rag doll being controlled by a puppeteer. A cry of pain left Celeste as her head jerked left and then right before her gaze fixed on the vanity mirror.

"Don't fight me, Witch," Celeste hissed in a voice that wasn't hers.

The eerie sound raised the tiny hairs on my arms and prickled my scalp. I'd heard that voice before. It was full of slithering shadows and oily blackness that oozed from the bottomless, dark void…

"Damien," I breathed, clamping my hand over my mouth in shock.

My body began to shake, and I knew I couldn't remain there any longer. I couldn't be anywhere near the vile creature inside the house, inside…Celeste. With my hand still over my mouth, I glimmered back to Waylon's place.

"Sophie?" Henry's eyes widened as he rushed to my side. "Are you okay? What happened?" He ran his hands over me to make sure I was in one piece.

I was speechless for a few seconds, tears filling my eyes.

"Just…talk to me." He pried my hand from my mouth as gently as he could.

"It's Celeste," I croaked, not seeing him before me. I was still seeing Celeste, or rather, her body, which had become the host for something insidious. "She's not just being controlled by Damien," I managed to go on. "She *is* Damien."

"What?" Henry asked in confusion.

"The entrapment spell," Amelie said somewhere on my right.

Her words jolted me out of my stupor, and I turned to the girl. "The entrapment spell?" I asked her.

Amelie's green eyes were full of terror, as if she'd gone to the cottage with me and seen Celeste for herself. Swallowing thickly, she said, "A very ancient and dangerous spell, which is forbidden because it allows a witch to trap a demon inside her."

My mind raced, the thoughts in my head toppling over each other. "When the White Witches turned Dark…it wasn't just the black magic poisoning them, was it?" I asked, trying to piece it all together, to finally learn the truth.

"Not at first," Amelie admitted. "Most of them turned Dark after they had performed the entrapment spell, trying to save the village from the demons."

"Why would Celeste perform the spell if she knew the risks?" Henry chimed in, the look on his face telling me he was trying to unravel the mystery like I was.

"I don't know. Maybe she thought she was strong enough to contain the demon inside her." Amelie looked like she was about to be sick, her face pallid and her lips white. "I can't believe she did it," she said in a trembling voice. "And I have no idea how to undo it."

"Has there ever been a witch who was successful at trapping a demon inside without succumbing to the darkness?" I asked and held my breath. Because if there had been such a witch, perhaps we could figure out what she'd done differently or what had been different about her.

"Only one." Amelie blinked back the gathering tears. "Your great-grandmother Josephine."

The world stopped at her words. Everything around me was suspended as I slowly lifted my hand to my chest and wrapped my fingers around the Tear.

"The Tear!" Waylon exclaimed, his voice speeding the time around me back up to normal. "I can't believe we haven't thought of this before! The amulet can eradicate the supernatural. What if you used it to destroy the wolves before the attack?" Waylon's eyes lit up with excitement because he'd just found a possible solution. Except...

"Wren is now one of them," Henry pointed out gravely.

Waylon's expression dimmed, but he squared his jaw and opened his mouth. I knew what he was going to say even before he uttered the words. "We might have to lose one for the benefit of many—"

"No!" my voice rang out, silencing him. "No one will be sacrificed." *Except me.*

"I'm not sure we can prevent that entirely," Henry said low, looking at me. "If Celeste is turning into a Dark Witch and there is no way to stop it...it's in our best interest to eliminate her before she fully succumbs, becoming even more powerful."

I hated that. I hated that conversation, that situation, and that world, where we had to "lose one for the benefit of many."

"Amelie said my great-grandmother was able to carry a demon inside her without turning Dark, so there must be a way," I told Henry.

I knew my gaze was pleading with him to let me find another solution. His eyes softened, but his features remained stoic, which let me know he was prepared to make the hard call, to add yet another life to the unbearable weight on his tired shoulders.

"Your great-grandmother died when she was young," he said. "Perhaps the only reason the demon inside her didn't prevail is because her life was cut short."

I had a feeling there was another reason. There had to be. Sensing I wouldn't be able to convince him, I decided to buy some time instead. "I have the Blood Pact," I told him, pulling the scroll out of my pocket. "We should still gather the clans first. Damien is powerful, so it shouldn't be just the two of us taking him on. Besides, even if we are able to ambush him, he might still be able to sic the wolves on us."

It felt easier to plan an attack on Damien than on Celeste, whose body he was possessing, so I hadn't mentioned the witch's name.

"I think you're right," Henry told me, eyeing me with a hint of suspicion. Did he think I had given up on searching for another way too easily?

"I assume you don't want the clan leaders summoned to your house?" I looked at Waylon.

"You already know the answer to that," he replied.

I turned to Amelie, whose gaze was cast down to the floor. "Can you glimmer to the Stern Estate and help me with the summoning spell?" I asked her gently.

It was obvious she was shaken up, for which I couldn't blame her. I had a feeling that if I stopped for a second, I would be back to falling apart—a condition I'd clawed my way out of in the past month. Or perhaps I hadn't. Perhaps I only thought I had.

Amelie lifted her red-rimmed eyes to me. The sparkling green hue in them seemed fractured, undoubtedly a reflection of her heart. I had the urge to gather the girl in my arms, but I fought it as it would probably only make the feeling of hopelessness worse. For both of us.

"Are you truly going to do it?" Amelie asked weakly.

The thorny torque around my heart squelched the organ completely as I repeated the words that Celeste had spoken to me in the not-so-distant past, "Sometimes the ones you care about the most are beyond saving."

32

HENRY

We had to wait until sundown to attempt to summon the clan leaders since they couldn't begin their travel during the day. I was glad for it, too, because that meant Sophie and I had a few hours to spend alone.

"I need to be inside you," I growled, hauling her to me as soon as we appeared in our bedroom on the Stern Estate.

"I need you inside me," she breathed before she kissed me deeply and hungrily.

I kissed her back with equal fervor as we began tearing at each other's clothes. A few seconds later, we were both naked, our hands roaming wildly over each other. We both groaned when her hand wrapped around my hardness while mine dove between her thighs. Her arousal coated my fingers, and I worked two of them inside her tight heat. She whimpered as her hand began gliding up and down my cock with quick, skillful strokes. My fingers moved in and out of her, matching her rhythm. When she dragged her other hand down my chest, her nails breaking the skin, the brief bite of pain only spurred my desire.

Withdrawing my fingers, I stopped her hand moving on me and lifted her up. She followed my lead, wrapping her legs around my back, which made my arousal press into her navel. Our mouths kept crashing into each other, the strokes of our tongues a violent dance, as I walked backward until the back of my legs hit the edge of the bed. When I lowered myself down, Sophie's knees fell on either side of my hips, and she lifted up, positioning herself over my throbbing length. I still wanted to lick every inch of her as I'd promised earlier, but the urgency of her movements told me that was not what she needed. She wanted to drown in our passion. I wanted to drown in it, too, so I impaled her on me with one hard, rough plunge. Sophie gasped as I groaned with pleasure. She felt exquisite, and fuck if I didn't feel unworthy of her. But she was mine, and I would do anything in my power to keep her. I was even prepared to go to such lengths as killing Celeste, and perhaps that made me a monster. What had happened to her was terrible, but a part of me was glad that Damien was trapped inside her because while I didn't know how to fight a demon, I knew how to fight a Dark Witch.

Sophie sat unmoving on me, her body molding perfectly to mine. Her kisses slowed, and she explored my mouth for a few more seconds before pulling away. Her eyes glistened with tears when she looked at me. Suddenly, I realized that our position—with me sitting on the edge of the bed and her straddling me—was how we'd made love for the very first time. Back then, we had been preparing to fight the Dark Witches. At that moment, we were about to face another threat.

"I love you. Never forget that," she rasped.

My brows knitted as I opened my mouth to tell her she shouldn't have said it like she was saying goodbye. I wanted to tell her that we would get through the fight together, but before I could, she began moving on me, and every thought left my head as all I could focus on was the feel of her body on mine.

"So, you're also a witch?" Marcy asked Sophie a few hours later when the night had descended. We were in Stern's study, gathered around the stately mahogany desk.

"I am," Sophie confirmed.

"And he's also a…shifter?" Marcy nodded at Wren.

"That's right," he replied quietly.

He looked better after getting some blood and a few hours of sleep, but unease still marked his features. I couldn't blame him for being on edge. Since he was also a shifter, there was a part of him that belonged to the pack, to Volker. My blood boiled every time I thought about the male. Sophie had assured me that my jealousy was misplaced, but while she didn't harbor any feelings for the alpha, I wasn't sure he wasn't interested in her. Though I wanted to avoid a clash with the wolves, a twisted part of me wished the battle would unfold just so that I had an excuse to fight Volker and kill him. A low growl escaped me at the thought.

Wren's eyes widened at my outburst, and I realized a little too late I was still staring at him. "Sorry, that wasn't directed at you," I said low. "I was just thinking about…" I glanced at Marcy. She didn't need to see me like that. "Never mind."

"Let me guess. Volker?" Isabelle chimed in. "He's mine to kill," she snarled, red-hot fury flashing in her eyes.

"I'm a witch, and Wren is a shifter," Sophie said in an attempt to change the subject. "But it doesn't matter what we are as long as we keep our humanity." She gave Isabelle and me a pointed look.

"So, I will see you use your magic tonight?" Marcy asked excitedly, seemingly unaffected by the slight tension in the room.

"Yes." Sophie smiled at her. "Though I'm afraid it won't be

very exciting. I'll feel the power flowing through my veins, but you probably won't be able to see it."

"And your friend is coming to help you? I can't wait to meet her!" The girl beamed. Her personality was like sunshine in a bottle, brightening the world around her.

"Speaking of which," Sophie said a moment later when a knock on the door announced Amelie's arrival. She swept from the room but was back shortly with the young witch and Waylon in tow.

After the introductions had been made, Amelie immediately took a shine to Marcy, just like I'd known she would. Their idle chatter filled the study for a few minutes until Sophie unrolled the Blood Pact contract on the desk. The atmosphere instantly changed as everyone tensed, reminded of why we were all gathered there.

"What's your plan?" Waylon asked, eyeing the bloodstained parchment.

"I'll summon the clan leaders using the contract. Hopefully, they'll all have enough time to travel here before sunrise," Sophie replied.

"They should, unless they are somewhere truly remote," Isabelle pointed out.

"We will tell them about Damien and the wolves and ask for their help," Sophie continued. "It's in their best interest to aid us, unless they want another battle like the Red War."

"Sophie and I will take on the witch," I clarified. "The clans will mostly be there in case Celeste summons the wolves to protect her."

"It's not Celeste we're going to fight; it's the demon," Sophie said sternly as she scowled.

"I know, but the demon is inside Celeste, so for all intents and purposes, they are one and the same." My tone was just as stern.

I hated challenging her in front of everyone, but I needed to make it clear to her that Celeste was gone. Sophie still seeing the witch as her friend and not the sinister creature she was could cost us when the time came to confront her. We couldn't afford to hesitate even for a moment.

"I know you're right," Sophie conceded, her shoulders drooping.

I instantly regretted being stern with her. With a heavy sigh, I came closer and pulled her to my chest. "I'm sorry. I know you don't want to do it, but it's the only way."

"What if it doesn't have to be?" Amelie said suddenly.

Sophie and I turned to the witch.

"What do you mean?" Sophie asked her.

"Maybe we can remove the demon from her? I can tell the other witches in the village about what happened to Celeste. With our powers combined, we might be able to extract the demon."

"Has that ever been done?" I asked skeptically. If it were that easy, the White Witches would have used that technique to bring those who had turned Dark back to the light.

"It hasn't…" Amelie admitted.

Just like I thought.

"But it doesn't mean we can't try?" Her eyes were pleading. I could feel Sophie's gaze on me, and I knew the look in her eyes matched Amelie's.

"If we are going to ambush Celeste at her cabin in the woods, close to the village, we have to warn the witches about our plan anyway. We might as well ask for their help. If there is even a small possibility that we can bring her back instead of killing her, I want to try," Sophie said.

I turned to her then. My jaw was hurting from how hard I was clenching my teeth. I didn't like that plan. We would be involving more people—potential casualties—and giving Damien a chance to escape. But I had sworn to always give Sophie what she wanted.

"Okay. We will do it your way, but I want to gather the clans first. We will still go to the Black Forest to ambush Celeste, but instead of killing her, we will trap her, and the White Witches can try to exorcise the demon."

Sighs of relief whooshed out of Amelie and Sophie at the same time. I hoped to the gods we weren't making a mistake.

"It's decided, then. Let's summon the clan leaders." Sophie pulled away from me and placed her hand on the contract. She began chanting words I didn't understand, her eyes closed and her features pinched in concentration. The melody of her voice rang out in the study for a few seconds until she stopped chanting and looked down at the parchment. "It's not working," she said with a rough exhale.

"Maybe I can help." Amelie stepped closer to her. "We will say the spell together. I'll supplement your magic with mine."

She clasped Sophie's forearm, and they began reciting the incantation again. Everyone in the study seemed to be holding their breath, watching them work. At first, nothing happened, but then the contract lit up with a faint blue glow. The parchment appeared to be on fire, the dancing flames licking up the entire document.

I heard Marcy gasp next to me. "Is this supposed to be happening?" she asked under her breath.

"Yes," I assured her.

The only reason I wasn't panicking about the parchment burning was because I remembered that something similar had happened when the Blood Pact had first been forged.

The blue glow rippled on the surface of the contract as Sophie's and Amelie's voices grew louder in the hushed silence. Until they abruptly stopped.

"It's done," Sophie announced, lifting her hand from the parchment and flexing her fingers. "Now, we wait."

"If you don't need my help with anything else, I'd like to go to the village and tell the others about Celeste," Amelie said, starting for the door.

"No!" I interjected, my urgent tone stopping her in her tracks. "Let us gather all the clans first. If you tell the witches about our plan too early, one of them might decide to take matters into their own hands or warn Celeste. You will tell them once we know exactly when we're going to the Black Forest to ambush her."

Amelie nodded in understanding.

"What about the Order of Light?" Waylon asked. "We can also help."

"Not a good idea." Sophie gave a curt shake of her head. "If the wolves attack and any of your men suffer injuries from their claws or teeth, they will become shifters themselves. You and the Order should remain on the border to protect New Haven if we fail."

When I glanced in her direction, her jaw flexed as she met my gaze because we both knew that if we failed, there would be very little the human guards could do against the wolves.

We can't fail, her eyes seemed to say.

We won't, I tried to convey with my look.

"I will have all my men stationed on the border on the night when you're ready to execute the plan, but I will not be among them," Waylon said with determination. "I will be by Amelie's side."

He approached the witch and took her hand. She glanced at him with love and affection in her sparkling gaze. I hoped the two would get married once our ordeal was over. They clearly belonged together.

"Okay," Sophie said, watching them with a warm smile. I wondered whether she was thinking the same thing as I was. "We'll be in touch. You should leave now before the clan leaders start to arrive."

Waylon nodded before he and Amelie walked out of the study and left the estate.

"Anyone care for a drink?" I strolled to the bar cart tucked away in the corner of the study.

"I'll take one," Marcy said eagerly, prompting a low chuckle from Sophie.

"Nice try." I smirked as I poured myself a glass of whiskey. Marcy had turned out to be older than she looked. She was close to Sophie's age, but I didn't see her as a woman but rather a girl in need of my care and protection. "Anyone except you."

"But I'm almost nineteen!" she grumbled.

"I'll take a drink," Wren said, and I poured him one. When I handed it to him, he quickly threw it back, looking as if he were nervous about something. "When we do carry out the plan," he proceeded to say, "I want to come with you all to the Black Forest."

I scowled. "You are part wolf. If Celeste ends up weaponizing the pack, you might find yourself fighting against us."

"Henry is right," Sophie chimed in as she picked up the contract off the desk and rolled it up. "I was thinking you could stay here with Marcy."

"Am I not going?!" the girl exclaimed.

"It's for your own protection," I told her, looking into her wide pale-green eyes.

"But what if I lose you? I don't want to be alone. You're my new family. I don't want to lose you right after I've found you."

"You won't lose us. And you won't be alone. Wren will be with you."

"No, I won't," Wren interjected. "I know there is a risk if I come with you, but I won't leave Isabelle's side." He lifted his chin and squared his shoulders as he faced me.

I glanced at Sophie, silently asking for backup.

"You would be doing the same thing if you were in his shoes," she said quietly, looking at me. "We can't force him to stay behind."

I gritted my teeth but gave in, throwing back the contents of my glass. The plan was getting worse and worse by the minute.

"I'll be right back," Sophie said a second before she glimmered from the study with the rolled-up Blood Pact in her hand. She was back a moment later, empty-handed. "I figured it's better to hide the contract for when the clan leaders show up," she explained.

"Are you even sure they will answer your summons?" Isabelle arched a brow.

That was when a knock sounded on the door.

"I think they already have."

Sophie came to my side and grabbed my hand. Taking the gesture as a cue, I led us out of the study and into the foyer, where I opened the front door, revealing Remy on the other side.

"I came as fast as I could," he said, his chest heaving. There was a fine sheen of sweat on his brown skin. "I felt a tug...a pull driving me here...Is everything alright?"

I wasn't at all shocked that the young leader of the Stern clan had arrived first. After all, he had been the most receptive to the new way of life Sophie and I had imposed on the vampires. His short black hair shimmered in the glow of the porch light with the drops from the rain that had just started sprinkling outside.

"Thank you for coming so quickly, Remy," Sophie welcomed him warmly. "Please, step inside. We'll explain the reason for your being here."

The vampire's brown eyes flicked between her and me, but he didn't ask any more questions before walking in and following us to the study.

"Isabelle," he greeted my sister before turning to Wren. "Wren." He nodded. "I see you've joined our ranks."

"I have," the male replied, infusing his voice with authority.

He possessively wrapped his arm around Isabelle's waist and pulled her closer to his side. I felt the display was unnecessary, as I doubted Remy was any threat to him when it came to my sister. He was much too young for Isabelle. In fact, I'd never realized just how young he looked until that moment. He must have been eighteen or nineteen when he'd turned. My eyes narrowed as I watched his attention switch to Marcy.

"I see we have another new vampire in our midst." He extended his hand with a dazzling smile. "Hi. I'm Remy. What's your name?"

Marcy smiled back as she placed her hand in his and introduced herself. The connection between them was instant and obvious. It was difficult to ignore, but I resolved to do just that for the time being. As a Duval, Marcy would live under my roof and have to follow my rules, which would involve not seeing Remy.

Sophie pressed my hand, and when I looked at her, there was a twinkle of amusement in her eyes, as if she knew what I was thinking.

"So, the reason behind your being here..." I said loudly to snap Remy's attention from Marcy.

He reluctantly tore his gaze away from her and faced Sophie and me. "Uh, yes, of course," he murmured, clearly distracted.

Son of a bitch, I cursed inwardly before I carried on, telling Remy about Damien, the wolves, and our plan. He looked shocked but quickly regained his composure.

"Most of my clan remained in the Southern region," he admitted. "I know you wanted us to spread out, but I felt it was important for us to stay close as a family. Now more so than ever. We will be ready to aid you when you need us."

"Thank you," Sophie told him sincerely.

I couldn't force the same words out of my mouth as Remy's gaze returned to Marcy.

"Until next time." He smiled at her. "Henry, a word, please?"

Letting go of Sophie's hand, I strolled with him to the foyer, feeling my wife's curious gaze on my back.

"Seeing how your plan could prove to be quite dangerous… you're not going to bring Marcy with you, are you?" Remy asked when the two of us stopped by the front door. The genuine concern in his voice was disarming.

Son of a bitch, I cursed inwardly once more. Out loud, I said, "No, she will not be coming with us. Her safety is my number one priority, *trust me*." A low growl accompanied the last two words as I let my eyes flash with a warning for him to stay away from her.

Remy swallowed but held his ground. "That's good. I understand she is quite young. I was also young when I was turned."

"Then you understand she's been through a lot and has much to learn about herself and her new life."

A hint of disappointment flickered across his features before he smoothed them out. "You're absolutely right. I understand."

I felt a smidge of pity for him, but if he longed for companionship, he wouldn't find it with my…with Marcy. At least not yet.

"This is fucking ridiculous!" A string of curses sounded from my right. When I turned, I saw Dion Bouvier making his way to the front porch through the pelting rain.

"I better go," Remy said, watching Dion warily. "Something tells me that convincing *him* to help you will require all of your focus." With those parting words, he was gone.

I dragged my hand down my face with a heavy sigh because I knew he was right.

"Dion," I greeted the vampire when he'd climbed the steps and joined me on the covered porch. "Thank you for coming," I added, attempting to be civil.

"I didn't have a choice, now, did I?" he seethed, brushing the raindrops from his short brown hair with one sharp motion of annoyance.

"You didn't, but you have a choice about how you want to behave now. And I suggest you choose to be respectful to my wife when we step inside."

"Your wife?!" He sneered. "For fuck's sake. What do you think you're doing? Building your own little empire with you as the king and her as the queen ruling beside you?"

"The only world I am trying to build is the one where everyone is safe."

"You're just like Vincent with this idealistic bullshit. Such a world does not exist! There will always be hunters and prey. We vampires used to be at the top, but now I hear we have become the hunted."

His last few words caught my attention. "What have you heard?"

"That some humans have started hunting us. Is that why I'm here?"

"No, it's not. There is a bigger predator at play," I told him as I opened the front door and walked in.

With another string of curses, he trudged inside behind me.

Dion's raspy laugh rolled through the study when we had finished telling him about the reason behind his being there. "So, you want me to gather my clan and aid you in fighting the demon and the wolves?" he drawled. "Why would I help you? I already have to live by your new rules. The condition of the Blood Pact is that you can summon me, not bend me to your will!"

He spat the last few words at Sophie, and I wanted to shove them back into his throat until he fucking choked on them. Since I couldn't do that, I settled for the next best thing. "Show respect!" I snarled, snatching him by the neck and shoving him against the wall. "She's not your queen, but I can still break your bones and make you bow before her."

I heard Isabelle say "Nice" under her breath.

I glanced at Sophie, half expecting her to stop me, but her darkening gaze told me she was enjoying me defending her honor. It wasn't like she needed me to do it. If we were to rule, she would be the queen and I her consort. When my gaze shot to Marcy, though, my rage simmered down. The girl looked frightened as she wrapped her arms around herself and curled inward, as if attempting to occupy less space. I promptly released Dion but didn't step away from him.

"Do I make myself clear?" I bit out. When he gave an indignant nod, I continued, "As for why you would want to help us, I don't think you want demons and wolves taking over the country, do you? They will kill you, but if you don't care, I'd be more than happy to do it for them."

"Enough with the threats!" He raised his hands in surrender. "I will get my clan together."

"Thank you for that," Sophie said to him in a mocking tone.

He opened his mouth but clamped it shut when I shot him a glare.

"Someone else is here," Isabelle announced before she left the room. She returned with Yvonne, Nova, and her daughters.

"Yvonne, thank you for coming," Sophie told her. "And bringing Nova, Monique and Julia with you?" She gave the three females a questioning look. Since they had been buried under the mountain when the Blood Pact had been forged, they hadn't signed it and therefore could not be summoned.

"We have been staying with Yvonne," Julia started to explain. "When she felt the pull of your magic, we knew you must have a reason for summoning her and decided to return to the estate." The glower on Nova's and Monique's faces told me it hadn't been their idea. Julia must have been the voice of reason and convinced them to come.

"Julia?" Marcy asked meekly. "I don't know if you remember me..."

"Marcy!" Julia exclaimed. "You have overcome the bloodlust! Let me look at you!" She stepped to the girl and ran her hands over her head, hair, and face. "You did it." She looked at me.

"*We* did it." I pulled Sophie closer to me to indicate I couldn't have done it without her. "Thank you for all your help," I told Julia.

"I was happy to help." She looked back at Marcy. "If you want, you can come live with me and my mother and sister."

Marcy paused, glancing at Sophie and me before she said, "I'm part of the Duval clan now."

Her hesitation was fleeting, but I noticed it nonetheless. I felt extremely protective of the girl, but protecting also meant doing things that were in her best interest. I suddenly realized she might not have the best life with us since Sophie and I could go out in the sun while she would be forced to stay nocturnal. Perhaps in the future, Sophie could forge a magical object for Marcy to grant her the ability to walk in sunlight, but until then...

"If you want to stay with Julia and her family, you can. It's your choice. You will still be a member of the Duval clan," I assured her. "Nothing will ever change that."

Marcy's eyes filled with tears as she sniffled. "Maybe I can stay with them for a little while and then with you and Sophie?"

"You don't need our permission," Sophie said softly. "Our doors are always open when you decide to visit or stay for a while."

"In fact, Julia"—I looked at the female—"you and Marcy should leave and hide away for a while. Until we've dealt with the threat in the Black Forest."

"Threat? What threat?" Yvonne demanded, her golden gaze gliding over everyone in the room.

"Wait, so Julia wouldn't have to fight?!" Dion exclaimed. "I thought you needed all the vampires' help?!"

"We do, but Julia will be helping by keeping Marcy safe," I growled, hoping my tone would shut him up.

"Safe from what?!" Yvonne exclaimed. "If it's about Jared and his men, Julia told us about them, and we took care of them. What new threat is there now?"

"You took care of them?" Sophie's brows shot up in shock. "Did you kill them?"

"We did," Yvonne replied with proud satisfaction. Dion laughed darkly, clearly pleased with the news. "Hopefully, that will deter any other human from thinking about hunting us."

Sophie closed her eyes and pinched the bridge of her nose with her thumb and index finger. Yvonne having killed Jared and his crew wasn't ideal, but at least that was one less thing we had to worry about. I hoped Yvonne was right and no other human would think about crossing the vampires, at least for the time being.

With a rough exhale, Sophie opened her eyes and proceeded to tell Yvonne, Nova, Monique, and Julia about our plan.

"Alright. I will round up my clan, but Adelaide and Delphine will most likely not make it here before sunrise. I've heard they are up north," Yvonne said.

"That's fine," Sophie told her. "We figured it would take a few days to gather everyone. Just return here as soon as you can."

We had decided to open the Stern Estate up for everyone to stay there until we were ready to move out to the Black Forest to carry out our plan. I wasn't looking forward to having all the clan vampires staying with us, but at least it wasn't Sophie's and my home.

"You're the one who turned me," Marcy's voice rang out in the study. Her accusing gaze was on Yvonne.

"Yes, I am," the female confirmed coldly. "If you're expecting an apology, you won't get one. I was desperate. I only did it because she was trying to kill me." She nodded at Sophie, who cringed at her words. "Look at it this way"—Yvonne looked back at Marcy—"I gave you a new life."

"You made me a vampire. You didn't give me new life—he did." The girl pointed at me. "And Sophie and Julia." She turned to the latter. "If we're going to live with her, I'd rather stay here."

"We won't be living with her," Julia assured her. "We'll find our own place, my family and you. I promise."

"You should probably leave now," I said. "Take some of the clothes you've found here that fit you."

"Come on. I'll help you pack." Sophie motioned for Marcy to follow her out of the study.

Dion's pale, nearly translucent eyes tracked them as they walked out. "I take it I'm free to go?" he asked.

"I take it I don't need to reinforce my words from earlier?" I gave him a pointed look.

He rolled his eyes but grumbled, "I will be back with my clan as soon as I can," before he left the estate.

"Shall we go ahead and stay here?" Nova asked me when Dion was gone.

"Sure. There is no reason for you to leave. We're just going to wait for everyone to gather here at the mansion," I told her.

"We will take the rooms we stayed in before, then," she informed me before she and Monique left the study.

Yvonne departed next, and I used the moment of quiet to take a steadying breath and pour myself another glass of whiskey. "Thank you for taking Marcy in. Please take good care of her," I told Julia, who had remained in the study with me.

"I will," the female replied. "I can see you care about her greatly. You remind me of Vincent when you look at her. That was how he always looked at you and Isabelle." A small, reminiscent smile touched her lips.

An overwhelming feeling of sadness and loss washed over me at her words. I missed Vincent terribly and wished he were here with us. He would have known exactly what to do and found the best solution to the seemingly impossible situation we were in. But he was dead and couldn't help me shoulder the pressure of my decisions. The best I could do was try to honor his legacy and hope I was doing the right thing.

SOPHIE

As we'd expected, it had taken a few days to gather everyone and finalize the plan. But tonight, the wait was finally over.

"Are you ready?" Henry asked from my right.

I nodded and quickly looked around me. The clans were flanking us on either side, their pale features stark against the dark clothing that had been purposely selected to blend in with the night. Most expressions were a mix of annoyance at being forced to help us and apprehension about potentially fighting a powerful enemy they couldn't smell. All seven clans, which equated to forty-four vampires, were standing facing the tree line of the Black Forest. I wasn't sure how many shifters were roaming inside. There had to be at least a couple dozen, judging by what I'd heard the other night when we'd found Volker's den. Still, I hoped we would be able to avoid bloodshed and that having the clans with us would prove to be just a precaution.

"Let's move out," Henry ordered, his deep voice carrying down the line of our small vampire army.

He and I stepped into the woods first, and everyone else followed. Henry glanced at me and nodded, and as soon as I gave a small nod back, the two of us broke into a sprint. Our pace started off slow, but once we'd made sure everyone was following in our tracks, our speed increased as we traveled deeper into the heart of the forest.

Several minutes later, the clearing with Celeste's cottage came into view, and I skidded to a halt just as I was about to break through the tree line and come out on the other side. Henry stopped next to me with the stealth of a predator. The moonlight that was drifting through the twisted branches bathed his formidable and unyielding form in a silver glow as I reached for his arm, getting ready to glimmer us inside Celeste's home. As planned, the clans were standing quietly behind us, scattered through the trees, where they would wait for us to carry out our mission or call for their help.

Taking a deep breath, I drew on the resources of the light magic inside me. My power hummed in my veins as it traveled to my chest and concentrated there. Closing my eyes, I imagined a bridge between the spot where we were standing and the dated living room in the witch's cottage. Just when I was about to glimmer Henry and myself out, a strangled cry of pain broke my concentration. My eyes snapped open as I jerked my head toward the sound. Before I could figure out where the noise had come from, another scream tore through the woods.

"Wolves!" someone shouted, and my heart dropped to the pit of my stomach.

We'd come here to ambush the witch, but now we were the ones being ambushed. The wolves converged on us so quickly, it seemed like I blinked and the woods had turned into a battlefield. Henry and I were surrounded by supernatural creatures clashing and colliding, their vicious growls and snarls filling the air.

"Don't leave my side!" Henry shouted as he unsheathed his claws and bared his fangs, getting ready to join the fight.

White lightning crackled at my fingertips as I nodded. I'd never used my light magic in battle before, but I hoped it would come naturally to me.

"Watch out!" Henry's warning registered a second too late.

A wolf barreled into me from my right, knocking me off my feet. I quickly rolled to my back and thrust my arm out to stop the beast's snapping jaws from reaching my throat. Digging my other hand into the wolf's torso, I sent a surge of my power through its massive body. Doing so only seemed to enrage the creature more as it thrashed in my hold, getting closer and closer to my face.

With a roar, Henry dragged the wolf off me and tossed it to the side. He grabbed my hand and hauled me to my feet. "Are you okay?" he demanded, scanning me from head to toe. When I nodded, he urged, "Use your vampire strength and agility; forget your magic! Come on!"

We jumped into the thick of the battle. I fought with my teeth and claws but didn't want to give up on my magic completely. I attempted to use it again…only to quickly realize it was futile. Wielding light instead of shadows didn't come as naturally as I'd hoped, and the charge of my powers proved to be too weak. I didn't want to kill the shifters who were attacking us only because they were following the demon's command, but I wished I could have immobilized them. There were a lot more of them than I'd originally thought. With easily three wolves to one vampire, the odds were not in our favor.

One of Delphine's clan members got torn to shreds first. Another vampire—a male from Dion's clan—went down next. His blood-curdling scream snapped my attention to him at the exact moment the wolf he'd been fighting tore out his throat. When his body dropped to the ground, two more wolves rushed to it, and the three shifters ripped him apart limb by limb. I locked gazes with Dion, who had watched what had happened to his clan member with terror in his eyes.

"Retreat!" he suddenly bellowed.

"What?!" I shouted. "You can't!"

Dion didn't respond as he turned around and fled the woods with the three remaining members of his clan. With them gone, we became even more outnumbered.

"We'll hold them off!" Isabelle shouted from a few feet away. "Get to Celeste! She controls the wolves! You need to kill the witch!"

She and Wren had their backs to each other, nearly touching, as they were spinning in a circle, fending off a ring of wolves that were rapidly closing in on them. My panicked gaze searched the blurring shadows around me, looking for Volker. I knew he was being controlled by Celeste, but perhaps there was still a chance I could appeal to his human side to stop the madness. When I'd found him in the mass of snapping teeth and slashing claws, he was in the middle of mangling one of Adelaide's clan members. Cursing, I gave up on the idea of getting through to him.

"Henry!" I yelled to get his attention.

He was instantly at my side, his wild black eyes flicking over me, looking for injuries. When he found none, his feverish gaze cooled just a fraction. He was covered in blood that wasn't his, which I knew from the lack of scent since I couldn't smell the shifters.

"Go! Now!" Isabelle yelled, jarring me into action.

I went to reach for Henry, but that was when one of the wolves rushed Isabelle, knocking her to the forest floor. With a deafening roar, Wren pulled the beast off her and slammed it into the ground. His claws gleaming, he bent down to finish the wolf, but before he could, his body spasmed, and his eyes, black with fury, changed to glowing red.

"Wren?" Isabelle asked in a trembling voice as she scrambled to her feet. Her chest heaved as blood dripped from her mouth.

Wren couldn't hear her past the sound of his breaking bones. Faster than he'd ever done before, he shifted into a russet wolf, then whirled on Isabelle. He crouched low, pawing at the ground as he bared his teeth and growled.

"Wren?" Isabelle tried again.

"Wren is no longer on our side," Henry said gravely next to me.

I looked around us. "We're losing." My voice broke as I uttered the words because my heart was breaking too.

"I know what you're thinking." Henry stopped in front of me in an attempt to block the carnage that was unfolding before me from my view.

"You always do," I told him, looking into his eyes, which turned gradually bluer as he stared back at me. "Don't try to stop me."

"I won't. I will never hold you back. I'm sorry I tried to do so in the past."

"Don't be sorry, just…help me find myself again." I might have whispered the last part; I wasn't sure, as my chest was feeling crushed by the weight of the decision I'd made.

"I will," Henry swore vehemently, his eyes glistening with tears.

I closed the short distance between us and captured his mouth, hoping that the feel of his lips on mine would anchor me to that moment, to who I was and what he meant to me. I was still kissing him when I reached inside myself and unlocked the vast obsidian door that kept the darkness contained. It seemed the shadows had been waiting because they rushed out like a tidal wave of black water, demolishing the door on the way out. Right then, I knew that there would be no putting them back or locking them away again. Strangely enough, the realization didn't frighten me. It was as if a tiny voice whispered in my ear, *It's time.*

My eyes snapped open as I sensed imminent danger. Jerking slightly back from Henry, I glanced behind him—at the giant black wolf that was flying through the air toward his exposed back. Volker was coming for him. I summoned my shadows, and my powers poured out of me, boundless and untapped. They snaked out from my body, wreathing and pulsing all around. I thrust my arm out to Henry's left and unleashed my magic onto the fast-approaching wolf. The black vines wrapped around Volker, stopping him in midair. The beast hung suspended as an inner battle raged inside me. The darkness urged me to kill him, to feed the bloodthirsty shadows, but I pushed back.

"You are not in control! I am your master. You obey me!" I shouted—or maybe whispered. I wasn't sure whether the words had made it past my lips or existed only in my head.

The darkness shrieked but obeyed, flinging Volker to the side. He collided with a tree, the impact breaking some of his bones and rendering him unconscious as his limp form crumpled to the ground. He would be out for a while, but at least he wasn't dead.

Henry was watching me with wide eyes, waiting to see what I would do next. I squared my shoulders and raised my arms, turning my palms up as I lifted my gaze to the sky. I was one with the night. I was darkness incarnate as black magic seeped out of my pores before spears of it shot out in all directions. Henry cursed and ducked out of the way, but he didn't need to be concerned. My shadows wouldn't hurt him. They had a very specific task—to neutralize the wolves.

Neutralize, not kill, I reiterated to the vines of my magic.

They followed my will, easily finding their targets in the woods around me. One black tendril wrapped around Wren, jerking him back just as he was about to pounce on Isabelle.

"Don't hurt him!" she shouted, her curled hands grasping air before her as the vine of my magic dragged Wren away from her. The russet wolf howled in pain as my powers broke his ribs. More howls carried through the woods as my shadows worked on taking out the wolves, making sure they were no longer a threat.

"Tsk, tsk, tsk," came Celeste's voice from behind me. "Not very nice of you to disable my army."

Closing my open palms into fists, I lowered my arms to my sides and was about to whirl on the witch when she latched on to me from behind. Wrapping her arms around me like a vise, she snarled, "Let's take this somewhere else, shall we?"

Before I could move a muscle, the world around me plunged into darkness as Celeste glimmered us out of the woods. We didn't go far, reappearing in the clearing between the tree line and the witch's cottage. Close enough for me to still hear the sounds of the fighting that had resumed as soon as my shadows had released their hold on the wolves.

Celeste spun me around and hissed in my face, "Look at you! Embracing your darkness..."

Her features mottled and contorted, as if the demon inside were trying to break free. Disturbed, I thrust my hand into her chest, firing a blast of magic powerful enough to launch her in the opposite direction from me. The witch landed a few feet away, on all fours like an animal—a twisted and macabre one. She scuttled over to me in a grotesque, disjointed manner that made my stomach churn with revulsion.

"See..." the creature that barely looked like Celeste hissed, the sound slithering over my skin, provoking an involuntary shudder. "See how powerful you are with black magic at your disposal? Don't you taste it? The freedom it offers?"

The creature was almost upon me, and I took a few steps back to put more distance between us before I dug my heels in and stood my ground.

"Damien," I called out the demon's name, my voice ringing out in the cool night air. Celeste's body rose to her full height and cocked her head. "Let. Her. Go," I bit out, enunciating each word.

"Or. What?" the demon enunciated back. His eyes were entirely black, and I could see my own reflection in the glossy, bottomless pools of darkness.

I'll have to fight fire with fire. The thought flashed through my mind a second before I unleashed my dark magic.

It erupted out of me, black spikes lashing out at the witch before me. Celeste screeched and jumped out of the way, crossing her arms in front of her to fend off the attack. Her own black magic flooded the space around her, the thorny whips of it darting in my direction. They reached me before I could throw up a shield, and I cried out as the thorns flayed my skin, tore my clothes, and ripped out my hair. Hooking into me, they yanked me closer to Celeste. I resisted the pull, sending a blast of magic at the witch.

The vines around me dissipated, and I dropped to the ground as Celeste deflected my attack. Scrambling to my feet, I thrust my arms out, sending my shadows toward the witch. She met them with her own churning shadows, and the ropes of our magic twisted and intertwined, wreathing around each other. I pushed with all my might, trying to overpower Celeste, until I remembered that it wasn't the witch I was fighting; it was Damien. I'd been desperate to get away from him when what I needed to do was get closer.

Gritting my teeth, I slung the threads of my shadows around Celeste and pulled her toward me. Damien thrashed in the hold of my powers as I began chanting a spell. When the words reached him and registered, he stopped resisting, a deranged smile spreading across Celeste's face.

"Clever witch… I see what you're doing… I will let you. Are you ready, Sophie? Are you ready to welcome me inside you?"

Tears began streaming down my cheeks as I pulled the demon closer and closer. I wasn't ready, but I would do it. I hoped that I stood a chance. My great-grandmother had been able to contain a demon inside her. Perhaps I could too. There was only one way to find out. I knew it was just my imagination, but the wedding band on my finger started to burn red-hot as if in warning.

Don't do this! I thought I heard Henry's voice.

Only it wasn't Henry shouting the words; it was Celeste.

"Foolish girl!" she seethed, and it was her voice, not the demon's. She cried out when a mass of oily blackness separated from her, bowing her back, stretching too far, like a tether, before it let go. Celeste fell to her hands and knees as the pulsating darkness intertwined with my shadows, eager to be united with me.

My voice grew louder as I chanted the words of the spell I'd snatched from Celeste's cottage the other day—the same day I'd retrieved the Blood Pact contract. I'd hidden the scroll from Henry, secretly memorizing the incantation any time I'd been alone.

"No!" Celeste shouted, rising to her feet. Her eyes were back to cerulean blue as her gaze fastened on the ball of coagulating blackness. She flung her arms out and began chanting her own spell, the words similar to the ones leaving my mouth.

What was she doing? Was she calling the demon back?

The churning shadows ebbed and flowed, forming a silhouette of a person. It seemed trapped in one spot, at the midpoint between Celeste and me. The demon pushed against the invisible restraints, trying to reach for me, but Celeste's magic was holding it back. I took a step closer to it, still weaving my spell. Celeste stepped closer as well, her chanting increasing in volume. Desperation laced her every word.

I was desperate too. Desperate to end the demon's reign. The decision had been made. My fate was sealed, and it was time to end the torturous descent into madness before I could change my mind. My brows knitted with effort but then shot up when the Tear on my chest floated up in front of my face. The demon roared, and the sound thundered through the clearing, shaking the ground under my feet. The wind rapidly picked up, and Celeste and I were caught in a vortex with the demon thrashing between us.

I stopped reciting my spell as I watched the amulet glow, burning brighter and brighter. The churning shadows solidified even more as the demon struggled to break free from the restraints that were holding him in place. Damien roared in fury once more, throwing himself against the bindings with such force that they snapped. He lurched toward me, his inky fingers reaching for me, but that was when Celeste's chanting reached its crescendo. Intense white light blasted from the Tear, knocking the air out of my lungs and launching me several feet back. I landed on my back, blinded and disoriented.

When the world came into focus, I was staring at the night sky, feeling the weight of the Tear on my chest. I thought it had exploded, but when I reached for it and wrapped my fingers around it, the amulet was still perfectly intact. It was hot to the touch but gradually cooled as Celeste's weathered face came into my line of vision, blocking the twinkling stars.

"Are you alright?" she demanded, her shrewd eyes roaming my features. Her long white hair was disheveled, hanging around her drawn face.

I took a few seconds to search her expression to ensure I couldn't see the demon still prowling underneath, but nothing seemed to be hiding beneath the witch's stern facade. "I...I think so," I finally rasped.

When I went to lift off the ground, my shadows helped me to my feet. They were still wreathing around me in wispy black tendrils.

"Are *you* alright?" I asked Celeste, clasping her bony shoulders.

"I am. Thanks to you." The witch gave me a small smile. "Though your plan was incredibly reckless," she remarked.

"My plan didn't work," I pointed out. "What did you do?"

I let go of the witch and lifted the Tear off my chest to look at it. The heart of the amulet was no longer pale blue. It pulsed with a dark cobalt glow.

"We trapped the demon inside." There was little triumph in Celeste's tone. She sounded tired, as if all her resources had been depleted.

"Are you sure you're okay?" I asked her.

"I am," she assured me. "My body has not been my own for a while. What I endured—" Her voice broke. "We shall not speak of it. I need to rest."

"You will," I told her.

I wasn't sure how long the reprieve would last, but maybe the next time, I could take the brunt of the work, sparing the witch.

"How long will the amulet hold him?" I asked, studying the Tear in my hand.

"Forever...I hope." Celeste sighed raggedly.

Hope. I wasn't sure I liked the word.

I waited for relief to flood my chest because we had defeated Damien, but elation wouldn't come.

There is only one way to ensure nothing can harm you in the future, the darkness whispered in my head.

My brows pulled together, and I turned my head toward the woods. Henry stepped out of them a moment later. The rest of the vampires walked out of the tree line next. Then the wolves.

You know you want to kill them all, the darkness taunted, skimming treacherously against my mind. *Destroy the clans and the wolves...leave only your family...it is the only way...*

I bristled where I stood. Henry moved then, and my gaze locked with his. He began walking toward me, and the closer he got, the more urgent the voice in my head grew.

The only way to ensure his safety...protect him...protect what's yours...

"Sophie?" Henry was in front of me then.

I looked into his deep-blue eyes and saw the most beautiful future. A future where the clans and the wolves were no more. A future where we were safe and no longer had to worry about scheming vampires and shifters who couldn't control their natures. We could just…live. Except…Henry wouldn't be able to live with me after what I would have to do to attain that future. Worse yet…I wouldn't be able to live with myself.

35

HENRY

on't be sorry, just…help me find myself again," Sophie whispered.

"I will," I vowed before she sealed her lips to mine.

I hated that she had to resort to dark magic, but I didn't see any other option. We had severely underestimated how many shifters Celeste had at her disposal. The witch must have known we were coming for her. Perhaps she had sensed Sophie at her cottage the other day because she had been prepared that night. The wolves had been waiting for us, and without being able to smell them, we had been caught unawares. We could retreat like Dion had done—*fucking coward*—but I wanted to put an end to that fight. Besides, even if we fled the forest, I didn't doubt the wolves would give chase. They would drive us to the border and then past it, carrying out Damien's diabolical plan. No, our fight had to end tonight. I just hoped it didn't end with Sophie turning Dark.

287

"Don't try to stop me," she had pleaded with me.

I had sworn then and there that I would never allow my fear of losing her to hold her back ever again. She was the strongest creature I knew. Her heart was fierce and true, and it had chosen me. *She* had chosen me. The least I could do was believe in her. And if she faltered and succumbed to the darkness again, I would bring her back. I would keep bringing her back countless times if I had to. Until my dying breath.

I kissed her back, trying to pour my unbounded love for her into the kiss. To show the darkness that it had no claim on her. She was mine. The darkness was a part of her, but she didn't belong to the shadows. *They* belonged to *her* to wield and command. And command she did.

The back of my neck prickled, alerting me to the impending attack. Before I could react, Sophie jerked back, breaking our kiss, and thrust her arm out past my left side. She became wreathed in shadows, and some of them snaked out of her outstretched hand. I spun around just in time to see the wispy vines wrap around the black wolf—Volker—who was leaping through the air toward my exposed back. The tendrils of Sophie's magic held the alpha suspended, and my gaze darted to her to see what she would do next. A part of me wished she would kill the wolf. The part that sought to eliminate another male interested in my mate. But I knew that doing so would only push Sophie closer to the dark abyss.

She must have known it too because she ground out, "You are not in control! I am your master. You obey me!"

Shadows swirled in her eyes as a triumphant smile graced her lips. She moved her hand, and the ropes of her magic tossed Volker to the side, into a nearby tree. I tried not to dwell on the feeling of satisfaction I experienced upon hearing the sound of his shattering bones. I tried to focus on another thing instead— the fact that he was still alive, which meant that Sophie was in control of the darkness. At least, I hoped she was in control as she squared her shoulders and raised her arms in the air, as if she were hugging the sky. Her gaze lifted to the stars, and for a moment, she looked divine and very in her element. My inner beast growled in appreciation. The monster inside me was drawn to her power, to her darkness, and for a heartbeat, an alternative future flashed before my eyes. A future where we let our darkness roam free. Where we ruled the world, feared and unhinged. I didn't want that future, though, not truly. I just wanted Sophie, not the world. Because *she* was my world, and she was enough.

More than enough, I thought in awe as I watched my queen of darkness.

"Shit!" I had to duck out of the way as obsidian spears of magic shot out of her. They seemed to dart in each and every direction, targeting the wolves, I realized as I followed their trajectories. Though the ropes of magic ended in spikes, they didn't pierce the shifters. Instead, they broke their bones or knocked them out. They delivered pain but not death.

That's my girl. My gaze swung back to Sophie.

She was still standing with her arms wide open and her face turned up to the sky. With moonlight sluicing over her features, she looked otherworldly and beautiful, stealing my breath away. Suddenly, my breath hitched for a different reason as two arms shot out from behind her and wrapped around her waist.

Celeste.

I stepped toward Sophie, but in the blink of an eye, she was gone. She took the ropes of magic with her, releasing the wolves, and as soon as they were free, the fighting resumed, more savage than before. Wren attacked Isabelle, and they rolled until my sister jumped to her feet, trying to get away. The russet wolf swiped at her ankles, bringing her down again. She was holding back because she didn't want to hurt him. With a growl of frustration, I rushed to her aid, heaving Wren off her. I swiftly broke his hind legs before dropping him in a heap by her side.

"I know you love him, but right now, he's trying to kill you," I snapped, hauling her to her feet.

"I could use some help!" Yvonne shouted from my left.

Glancing in her direction, I found her fighting three wolves at once. I wanted to help, but my priority was Sophie, whom I could hear in the clearing a few feet away.

"I'll help her. Go!" Isabelle urged me a second before she took off toward Yvonne.

Stepping back with my right foot, I set off to go to my wife but was immediately jerked back by two wolves that came at me from opposite sides. They clamped their jaws around my forearms and slammed me to the ground with such force, I grunted in pain as a few of my ribs broke from the impact. A third wolf jumped on top of me, burying me under its weight.

Being pinned down like that reminded me of when I'd been in the same position, restrained by Emeric and Beatrice, with Moreau towering over me. Instantly, my vision turned red as uncontrollable rage flooded my senses. With a violent roar, I hiked my knees to my chest and kicked out, throwing the wolf off me. I ripped my arms out of the other wolves' jaws at the same time, barely noticing the sting where their teeth left deep, jagged cuts. My blood poured from the wounds, splashing to the forest floor, when I jumped to my feet.

The wolf I'd kicked off me was back on all fours and coming toward me. My fangs and claws at the ready, I crouched as I prepared to meet my attacker head-on. The rational part of me realized that the shifter was not in control of his actions, but I needed to get to Sophie, and nothing and no one would stand in my way. When the wolf leaped in the air, flying toward me, I launched myself in the air as well, slashing my talons across its midsection when we collided. At that point, not only my blood marked the ground underneath. The wolf dropped down behind me as I landed with a faint thud. I spun around to finish the beast but halted when I found a man lying before me.

"Please," he begged weakly, blood spilling from his mouth.

I blinked at him as my pulse beat in my ears. Slowly, I lifted my head and looked around. The crimson-tinted haze that was painting my vision began to dissipate when I saw that the other wolves had stopped fighting and were retreating into the darkness of the forest.

"It's over," I heard Volker's voice.

When my gaze darted to him, he was trying to stand up, using the tree Sophie had thrown him against for support. "The witch no longer controls us," he added hoarsely.

"What does that mean?" Remy asked as he bent down to help one of his clan members up. "Did we win?"

I glanced at Isabelle to make sure she was okay before I turned and walked toward the clearing. We might have won, but I refused to declare victory until I knew that Sophie was okay. That she was still *my* Sophie. When I stepped out of the tree line, my gaze immediately locked on hers. She watched me, her brows knitted, as I approached. Celeste was there too, and fear spiked when I wondered whether it was all a ploy by the demon. A cunning plan to have us drop our defenses and lure us out of the woods.

"Celeste," I said sternly, looking at the witch to gauge her reaction. She didn't look possessed, only worn out. Of course, I had missed the signs before. "Are you okay?" I asked her.

"I am. I'm back to being myself."

That was a relief, but my main concern was Sophie and whether *she* was herself.

"Sophie?" I turned to her. Shadows were still churning in her eyes, and that made me uneasy. "Darling?" I lifted my hand to her cheek.

Her scowl intensified as her gaze grew distant. My muscles tensed as I watched her, wondering whether she was slipping through my fingers again as she had done in the past.

Was the darkness whispering things to her at that very

moment? Was Sophie fighting a battle that no one else, including me, could see?

I was about to beg her to let me in so I could help her, to tell her she didn't have to fight alone, when her scowl smoothed out and she said the three words that always had the power to bring me to my knees.

"I love you."

They weren't spoken with heaviness or desperation. They weren't spoken with the finality of a goodbye. No, they sounded like hope, a promise of a future. They shone with the brightness of the rising sun.

At first, I thought I might have dreamed it, but then Sophie turned her face into my touch and all my doubts disappeared. I released them with a loud sigh of relief before I pulled her to my chest. My wife. My everything. Back where she belonged. In my arms. She hugged me back with an eagerness that only reinforced my belief that she was herself and in control.

"I love you," I murmured against the top of her head.

SOPHIE

"Darling?" Henry lifted his hand and gently cupped my cheek. He looked concerned, and I wondered whether he could see the inner turmoil in my eyes.

No, I told the darkness. *I'm not a monster. I will not commit such a monstrous act. But I will no longer fight you either. You are a part of me. My ally, not my enemy.*

I wouldn't try to lock the darkness away. We would coexist in harmony. And if it ever tried to overpower me, Henry would be by my side to help me find myself again.

"I love you," I told him, turning my face into his touch.

A sigh of relief whooshed out of him as he pulled me into his embrace. As soon as he hauled me to his chest, I felt the darkness recede. The longer I stayed in his arms, holding on tightly, the more its whispers lost their allure until they dissipated, falling silent.

"I love you," Henry murmured against the top of my head before he pulled away.

Celeste watched our exchange in silence until she said, "Your magic—"

"Is wreathed in shadows…I know," I interrupted. "But I am no longer afraid."

Her knowing gaze flicked to Henry before returning to me. "With him by your side, you shouldn't be."

I hadn't realized I needed her approval until she gave it to me. Her words solidified my belief that I was doing the right thing by embracing my inner darkness.

Suddenly, Celeste's gaze shot past us, and her eyes widened as Volker approached our little group.

"Hello, Witch," the shifter growled. He glared at her from beneath his brows.

Henry's hold on me tightened.

"Wolf," Celeste replied, her trembling voice betraying her nervousness. "You must understand, I wasn't myself. You thought you were being controlled by me, but the truth is I was being controlled by a demon. Much like yours, my body and mind were not my own. I know that doesn't change anything about the past, but I want to atone for my crimes…if you'll let me. Let me help you and your people build a new life for yourselves in these woods."

"We will help too," came Amelie's voice from the other end of the clearing. Waylon was by her side, and they and a handful of witches were all walking toward us. "We waited and waited for you, according to plan, but then we felt a surge of magic… We weren't sure if it was a good or bad thing; we just knew something big had happened. I'm so glad you're okay!" Amelie hugged Celeste. "You are okay, right?"

"I am. Sophie saved me."

"No! No." I shook my head. "You trapped the demon in the amulet. *You* saved *me*."

"So Damien is trapped in the Tear?" Henry asked, his gaze dropping to the amulet on my chest. When I nodded, a smile pulled at his lips. "It's fascinating. The magic of your ancestors has saved us twice now."

I smiled too as I wrapped my fingers around the Tear. The witches of my bloodline had sacrificed so much to create the amulet, but their lives had not been lost in vain. I hoped they felt immensely proud of the legacy they'd left behind and had found peace in the void after their deaths. Whether *I* would ever find peace remained to be seen, but I decided to allow myself that moment to celebrate our victory over the darkness. We'd won the battle, not the war, but the war between light and dark would rage for as long as there were creatures capable of both good and evil. And perhaps that was how it should be. One should have to fight for the light in their life because that was what made it worth living.

"I'm sorry about your men," Volker said, pulling me out of my thoughts. He was talking to Henry.

"And I yours," the latter replied.

I looked at the vampires and shifters standing behind Volker. Several more lives had been lost after the demon had snatched me from the woods.

"If this is over, we need to head back to New Haven before sunrise," Yvonne said, raising her golden eyes to the sky.

"You're free to go. Thank you for your help," Henry replied, his gaze stopping on each of the remaining vampires to convey his gratitude.

One by one, they left the clearing, disappearing into the woods. They'd been our allies that night, but only time would tell whether they would remain on our side. As immortals, they had ages ahead of them to scheme against us, against the new world order.

"I'm sorry I fought against you," Wren said thickly, drawing my attention to him. He was talking to Isabelle, who was standing before him, blocking some of his naked form from view. "I hurt you." His voice broke as he uttered the words.

"You weren't yourself," she told him, placing her hands on his bare chest.

"Speaking of which," he said with a heavy sigh. "I still need to learn to control my wolf nature so I don't shift on every full moon." He looked past Isabelle at Volker.

The alpha nodded. "If you want to stick around, I'll teach you," he offered.

Isabelle glanced over her shoulder at him. Her eyes were still blazing with residual loathing for the alpha, but I thought I also saw understanding in them. Understanding that just like she couldn't blame Wren for attacking her during the battle, she couldn't blame Volker for having nearly killed Wren.

"Thank you," she said, the words a visible effort for her. "We will remain in New Haven and come to the woods every night so Wren can learn to tame his inner wolf."

"You're not coming to Santoria with us?" Henry asked her.

She shook her head. "Not yet. I won't leave Wren here. Where he goes, I go. We will join you there later."

"Maybe we should stay in the area too," I suggested. "We could help the shifters with building a new home in the woods—"

"No," Waylon interrupted me. "You've already done more than enough. We can take care of the rest. You two should return to your honeymoon." He smiled at me, but I couldn't bring myself to smile back.

Was our trial truly over? It felt surreal, and I wanted to pinch myself to make sure I wasn't dreaming. I looked at Henry, waiting for him to confirm that we'd won.

A moment later, he did just that when he kissed my temple and said, "Let's go home."

ONE MONTH LATER

month had passed since the events in the Black Forest. A month Henry and I had spent at our coastal cottage but not entirely cut off from the rest of the world. Not wanting my magic to sit idle, I'd glimmered us to New Haven a few times to check on our loved ones. With Volker's help, Wren had been making great progress in taming his inner wolf. He and Isabelle were waiting until the next full moon to make sure he would be able to control the shift before they moved to Santoria. As for the rest of the shifters, they had begun building a settlement in the Black Forest not far from the White Witches' village. Though Volker still harbored some animosity toward Celeste, he and the witch had been working together, laying the foundation for peaceful coexistence between their two peoples.

During our visits with Celeste, Henry and I had made sure to check the Blood Pact to ensure that the clan leaders were abiding by the rules. I'd been tempted to use the power I held over them to hunt down Dion and make him pay for fleeing the battle, but Henry had cautioned against feeding my inner darkness. I had to be especially careful not to give in to my vicious tendencies since my shadows were no longer contained. To better manage them,

I'd persuaded Celeste to resume my training to help me find and keep the balance between the black and the white magic that was flowing through my veins. I had committed to glimmering to her at least once every fortnight.

As for Waylon and Amelie, they'd announced their engagement shortly after the ordeal with the wolves had ended. The ceremony was set to take place in New Haven the following night, which would allow Isabelle and Wren to attend. I hoped Celeste would soon help me forge magical rings for them so they would no longer be bound by that law of vampire nature. Eventually, I wanted to make a ring for Marcy too, but I had to be careful. We didn't want all the vampires to learn there was a way to walk in daylight. Some of them still belonged only in the shadows.

At that time, Marcy was living in the Northern region with Julia, Nova, and Monique. I'd glimmered Henry and myself to visit her a couple of times in the past few weeks, and she was also coming to the wedding.

"Why aren't you asleep?" Henry's deep voice drifted from the entrance to the library, pulling me out of my thoughts.

I dragged my gaze away from the book I was reading and looked at him. Leaning against the doorframe, he folded his arms over his bare chest, and my breath caught as I took my time drinking him in. The loose black pants he was wearing hung low on his hips, and my mouth watered as my gaze traced the delectable V-shaped muscles of his abdomen. I followed the dusting of hair on his navel down to where it disappeared into the waistband.

"Enjoying the view?" One side of his mouth kicked up as he arched a brow.

"I am," I replied, my voice low and husky. "Why don't you come closer so I can take a better look?"

Smirking, he swaggered over to me. "Couldn't sleep?" he asked, lifting the book from my lap. He glanced at the cover before he set it aside on the nearby end table. Little did he know that the innocent cover was misleading about the novel's not-so-innocent content.

I shook my head in response to his question. "I have a lot on my mind," I confessed.

Henry's smirk disappeared for a few seconds as his deep-blue gaze roamed my face. The longer he stared at me, the hotter I felt as his eyes gradually turned darker. A moment later, his arrogant smile returned as he lowered to the chaise I was lying on.

"Let me take your mind off things," he drawled, reaching for me. He clasped the back of my neck and pulled me to him before he sealed his mouth to mine. The strokes of his tongue were languid but firm and oh-so perfect as he devoured me.

When he pulled away, I was breathless but tried to hide it as I teased, "Actually, the novel was doing a pretty good job of distracting me."

"Is that so?" He glanced at the book lying on top of the end table. "What's it about?" His eyes were nearly black as they refocused on me.

I swallowed to relieve the dryness in my throat. "Well, it's about this couple," I started, my lips stretching in a small smile.

"Yes?" Henry prompted, his gaze traveling over the short, flimsy nightgown I was wearing.

"They fall in love, but then something happens and tears them apart." Breathing was becoming difficult under his intense perusal, and I felt my nipples tighten against the silky fabric of the nightgown.

My body's reaction didn't go unnoticed by Henry, whose lazy smile grew, revealing the tips of his fangs. I dragged my own fangs over my bottom lip when his gaze returned to my face.

"And then what happens?" he asked low as he glided his fingers up my bare leg, eliciting a pleasant shiver.

"I just got to the part where they're reunited after spending years apart."

Henry's eyes were on me as he caressed my thigh. I opened my mouth to tell him more about the book, but it was hard to concentrate as his hand slid under my nightgown. Reclining back against the rolled arm of the chaise, I parted my legs slightly to give him better access, but he didn't take advantage. Not at first. He kept brushing his fingertips on the inner side of my thigh, close to where a throbbing ache was beginning to build.

"Tell me more," he said as he leaned in.

His lips skimmed the delicate skin of my throat and the thin chain attached to my locket. The Tear wasn't around my neck, hidden on one of the bookshelves instead. I didn't want to wear it anymore since a demon was trapped inside it, so I'd found a storage box masked as a book and hidden it among other titles.

A soft gasp left me when Henry's fangs pierced my throat. My eyes fluttered closed as I tilted my head back, the pleasure-pain of the bite rippling through me. He brushed his lips over my jaw while a thin trail of blood glided down the side of my neck. He caught it with his tongue before it reached the hem of my night-gown and licked it all the way back to the bite marks. Sealing his mouth over them, he sucked long and deep at the same time his fingers finally touched the aching spot between my legs. I moaned as arousal flooded me.

"What happens when they're reunited?" Henry asked, lifting his head from my neck.

"What?" I managed to get out as his fingers kept teasing the sensitive bundle of nerves.

"What happens when they're reunited?" he repeated, and I opened my eyes to look at him.

"They fuck," I said with a low laugh.

Henry chuckled. "'They fuck'? Surely, you can do better than that?"

When he went to pull his hand away, I grabbed his wrist to keep it in place. "Well, they kiss at first." Satisfied with my playing along, Henry continued his ministrations between my thighs. "Then he touches her."

"Touches her how? How I'm touching you?" he demanded as he reached up with his other hand to pull down the top of my nightgown to expose my breasts.

"Yes, at first. Then he begins using his fingers."

Henry closed his mouth around my nipple at the same time he slid one finger inside me. "So wet already," he growled against my breast.

"I told you it's a good book," came my breathy reply. A low curse followed it as Henry inserted another finger, rubbing the spot where the pressure was curling tighter and tighter.

"What does he do next?" he asked before he swirled his tongue around the other nipple.

"He…feasts on her."

At that point, I wasn't sure how I was still forming words when all my attention was zeroed in on Henry's mouth and his fingers moving inside me.

"Mmm" was my only warning before he withdrew his fingers and prowled down my body. He slid off the other end of the chaise, his knees hitting the floor, before he reached for me and grabbed my thighs, pulling me down until my back hit the padded seat.

"He feasts on her?" he purred as he slid my undergarment off me and cast it aside. "Like this?" He dove down between my legs.

A throaty moan was my only reply as he dragged his tongue through my drenched sex. Wrapping his forearms around my thighs, he held me in place while he licked and sucked, bringing me closer and closer to the edge. Grabbing the arm of the chair over my head, I clawed at the cushion as Henry increased the speed and intensity of the pleasure he was bestowing on me. My breathless pants became harsher and louder as I writhed on the seat, the ache between my thighs growing so intense I wasn't sure whether I was trying to get away from Henry's skillful mouth or push myself on him harder. He must have decided I'd had enough because he bit me, right where my arousal was pounding, wild and overwhelming.

My cry of ecstasy tore through the library as the brimming pleasure crested, arching me off the chair. I was still holding onto the arm when Henry pounced on me, his pants gone, revealing his proud, rigid length. With a loud groan, he plunged into me as deep as he could go, and I welcomed the feeling of fullness, of being stretched almost to the point of pain.

"So fucking perfect," he growled in my ear before he retreated, slowly pulling out of me. Just when I thought he was about to withdraw completely, he began thrusting back in, inch by decadent inch. The muscles on his neck stood out as he closed his eyes and kicked his head back, enjoying every second until he was fully seated in me once more.

"I love you," I rasped, staring up at his flawless features, which were taut with raw, uninhibited pleasure.

He opened his eyes and looked down at me, his raven hair tumbling over his forehead. "I love you," he breathed as the heat in his eyes intensified. "Hold on," he added with a roguish smile.

Wrapping my legs around his lower back, I grabbed the arm of the chair tighter as he began moving in and out of me with quick, rough thrusts. Pleasure began rapidly building again as he slammed into me for several minutes until he stopped and switched positions. He laid me on my left side facing the glass door that led onto the back porch. Weaving one arm under me, he grabbed my right breast as his other arm came under my right knee. He lifted my leg up to grant himself better access before he thrust in and up. I gasped at the sensation at the same time he moaned against my neck. Promptly picking up speed, he plunged in and out, going deeper with each thrust.

Our rough, loud pants filled the quiet space as he pounded into me, taking us closer to the edge until we were both trembling on the brink of release. Letting go of my leg, he toppled over me, driving me into the cushion. Bracing on the velvet surface, I lifted my upper body and twisted at the waist. I reached up and fisted my hand in his hair before I pulled him to me, sinking my fangs in his throat. If I'd been swimming in pleasure before, I was drowning in it then as his blood, smoky and sweet, coated my tongue. Henry roared as his thrusts became wild and erratic, and a few seconds later, his body bucked against mine. I found my release at the same time, boundless pleasure crashing into me, wave after powerful wave.

With a rough exhale, Henry dropped onto the chaise behind me, immediately tucking me against him. His arm draped over my side, and I relaxed into him, utterly satiated and spent. A few blissful minutes later, I felt him shift behind me as he lifted up on his elbow and propped his head on his fist. "Was that better than the book?" he asked smugly.

I laughed softly as I also lifted up on my elbow and reached up to brush my lips over his. "Life with you is better than the most beautiful fairytale," I murmured against his mouth.

"Then what's troubling you, darling?" His knowing gaze searched mine when I pulled away.

My chest tight, I unwrapped myself from his hold and left the chair. Without saying a word, I walked to the glass door and stepped outside, the breeze washing over my naked body. I knew he would follow. He would follow me anywhere for the rest of our eternal days. My husband, my best friend, my everything.

"I live in constant fear," I said low when Henry joined me on the porch.

He didn't say anything as he came to stand behind me, wrapping both arms around my waist. I leaned my head against his chest.

"What is it that you fear?" I heard his measured voice in my ear.

I almost laughed at the question. The better question was what *didn't* I fear.

"I fear what our next trial will be because you know there will be one. It's only a matter of time. Damien wasn't the first demon to prowl this realm, nor will he be the last. Just like Jared won't be the last human with a vendetta against the vampires. But most of all, I fear losing you…or myself." The last word was a whisper as I took a ragged breath.

We stood in silence for a moment.

"I won't tell you that your fears are not valid—they are. But you can't live like this. If you constantly worry about what might be, you won't be able to enjoy what is. Don't rob yourself of the joys of the present by fearing the future."

I swallowed the lump that had formed in my throat. Henry was right. I felt that even an eternity with him wouldn't be enough, and I was wasting our precious time together instead of enjoying it to the fullest.

"Let go," he whispered in my ear.

I took a deep breath and exhaled, letting the balmy sea air carry my worries away. As the gentle breeze scattered my fears across the glistening water, I filled the space in my heart where they used to dwell with hopes and dreams until I felt it. Peace.

ACKNOWLEDGMENTS

Just like that, the Crimson and Shadows series is complete. I honestly can't believe it. It seems like only yesterday I received the life-changing news that I was going to be a published author. Thank you, Oliver Heber Books, for taking a chance on me. Thank you, Tanya, for believing in my story; Kim for helping me make it the best it can be; and the rest of the staff, who worked hard behind the scenes to make my dream a reality.

Writing these books has been one of the most challenging but also rewarding experiences, and I couldn't have done it without having an incredible support system. I want to thank my husband for being my rock and the most amazing partner I could have ever wished for. Without you, Henry wouldn't exist. The only reason I know how to write such a devoted man is because I have one in my life. Thank you, Laura, for being there when the impostor syndrome struck and for not letting me give up. Thank you, Claire, for being the first one to read my books. You were the first one to fall in love with Henry, so for all intents and purposes, he's yours. Thank you, Alicia, for cheering me on and being invested in Sophie and Henry's relationship.

One of the best parts of this journey has been meeting other authors and readers, and I've encountered many wonderful people along the way. My dear friend Sarah, I'm so glad that our paths have crossed. I love your relentless optimism. Thank you for your unwavering support. Thank you, Qilanna, for being such a lovely and genuine person. Thank you, Devan, for being the ultimate hype girl. My dear Nichole, I'm beyond grateful to have you in my corner. Thank you for being a trusted friend and my sounding board. This journey wouldn't be the same without you. Thank you, Kathryn, for beta reading for me. I loved your unhinged comments. Truly, the list can go on and on. If you're reading this and you've extended a kind word to this self-doubt-riddled author, just know I thank you from the bottom of my heart.

And thank YOU, the reader, for choosing to spend some of your precious time in the company of my characters. I'm forever grateful.

ABOUT THE AUTHOR

V.I. writes romance with a touch of fantasy and magic. She's currently in her vampire era. When she's not weaving tales filled with fierce heroines and devoted heroes, you'll find her curled up on the sofa, lost in a book, with a blanket and delicious treats by her side. If you want to follow along on her author journey, you can sign up for her newsletter (www.vidavisauthor.com) or find her on Instagram (@vidavis.author).